Water Pressure

David Fabio

Hope you enjoy the mystery.

David Fabio

2013

Avid Readers Publishing Group
Lakewood, California

Contents

Chapter		**page**

Author's Notes:

I hope you enjoy reading "Water Pressure." As you read this book, you need to realize it takes place in the future. Setting a mystery in the future allows a writer to write around many current events and project several "what if" scenarios into the future.

There is no reason to believe that the events in this book will happen. Then again, there is no reason to believe they might not. As you read the book, use your imagination. What do you think is possible?

The main characters in the book are fictional. The places and facts are as close to real as one might believe they might be 10+ years or so from our actual knowledge. Any similarities of the fictitious characters to real people are totally by coincidence.

In writing "Water Pressure," I found it required considerable time to research many "what if" situations. When you are writing about the future, you need to be able to tie it to the present with enough credibility that one can wonder – could this happen?

I have included a list of characters to assist those that read a couple chapters each day and may forget who's who.

I hope you enjoy the book and allow the story to take you where your mind wants to go. See how soon you can solve the mystery.

List of Characters

Martin Berman – news reporter

John Berman – father of Martin Berman

Hank – friend of John Berman's

Shawn Peterson – news cinematographer

Tracy Saunders – Duluth news reporter

Linnea Hastings – Tracy's aunt

Jake Schwartz – news reporter

Tim Baker – news cinematographer

Skip Largent – pilot

Lester Johnson – Governor of Minnesota

Francis LaCrea – Minister of Natural Resources - Ontario Canada

Lester Townsen – LT – TV station office manager

Franklin Wahlbusher – Photo – intern news cinematographer

Howard Long – geologist

Luke Carpenter – man from Wyoming

Lieutenant O'Riley – homicide detective

Agent Mark Lawson – FBI

Butch Thomas – FBI field investigator

Josiah Simmons – pipeline engineer

Bill Epstein – Senator from Minnesota

Kurt Norstrom – farmer from Williston, ND.

Ken Payton – person of Interest

Jenna Iken – person of Interest

Neil Paulson – manager, Wyoming Security Firm – S&G Security

Bent Mountain, Inc. – Idaho firm

Scott Lenard – person of Interest

Peter Skiff – engineer from Denver

Mrs. Albush – Tracy's neighbor

Cal Young – person of Interest

Art Singer – police dispatcher

Arnold Marble – Howard Long's brother-in-law

Eddie Starr – person of interest

Benjamin Cahill – President of RG Holdings – land speculation firm

Victor Mann – President of Deep-Pipe Engineering

Captain George Morrissey – Royal Canadian Mounted Police - retired

Chapter 1

The Heist

Minutes before 3:00 pm, a short, stocky, masked burglar, dressed in dark clothes entered the Second State Bank on the north side of Minneapolis. He handed the teller a tan cloth sack along with a note telling her to fill it up with cash from the drawers.

The teller reluctantly handed it over to him. She did not want to find out if he really had a gun or not. Only the two tellers and the two customers in the bank knew what was happening. The other employees of the bank were in their offices. It wasn't until the silent alarm button was pushed inside the tellers drawer that anyone else knew something was wrong.

As soon as the bag was filled, the masked robber turned and made a quick exit out the front door. His accomplice was waiting in a car parked right next to the door with the engine running. As he left the bank, he had a grin on his face; the robbery went off just as planned. He had been in and out in less than five minutes. No violence and no one playing hero.

The two robbers had scouted the bank for weeks before robbing it. They had decided on just before closing time to hit the bank when it was normally almost empty of customers. Today was no exception.

As they sped away from the bank to the closest freeway entrance, one of the two customers that were inside wrote down the license number of the car. The police were already on the way to the bank thanks to a silent alarm, when they received the 911 call informing them of the make, color and license number of the getaway car and the general direction it was heading.

A police squad intercepted the reported dusty, dark blue Chevrolet getaway car just before the freeway, forcing the robbers to make a detour onto the city streets with the police in hot pursuit.

When the robbers approached a busy intersection near Lake Street, a car, swerving to avoid the fleeing robbers, collided with a Metro bus sending it into a storefront. The resulting traffic jam temporarily blocked the intersection. Due to the accident with the bus, which was left angled across the intersection, the pursuing police car was blocked off and lost sight of the get-away car. Their backup squads were too far off to pick up the direction of the speeding robber's car. It looked as though the bank robbers had made a clean get away.

Fortunately, one of the local TV stations traffic helicopters was flying in the area and had been listening to the police scanner. It only took a few minutes to spot a blue car swerving in and out of traffic. The robbers never realized that a helicopter was following them. The helicopter was flying high, at about 4,000 feet, being careful not to fly into the airspace reserved for planes coming into the airport. Since the tower had been informed of the helicopter's assistance of a police pursuit, as a safety issue, all outgoing flights were routed east of their location. The suspects thought they were free and clear as they headed back to a duplex in South Minneapolis to hide the car and count their money.

Our crew in the copter was directing the police department to the action as well as letting me, reporter Martin Berman, and Shawn Peterson, my cinematographer, know where to go to report on the capture. We sped through the city streets, arriving just behind the squad cars. As we arrived on the scene, we spotted a blue car parked in front of a duplex and the squad cars just starting to block off both ends of the block. Our copter was still circling the neighborhood, capturing the scene from the air and watching to make sure no one escaped unnoticed. The copter's onboard camera could zoom in on a dollar bill lying on the sidewalk if necessary.

"Thanks for the information," I told the crew in the copter as we arrived.

"It's all yours Martin," the pilot replied. "We need to head for the closest gas station. We hadn't planned on this little side trip."

"Didn't know you were using unleaded this week."

"Well, you know the boss; we have to save a nickel wherever we can. If gas stations sold jet fuel, you know he'd have us find the cheapest station in town to buy fuel and land in the street in front of it," the pilot replied. With that, he made a direct shot to the airport.

The police had a standoff. It appeared that the burglars were not planning to give up. As a result, a SWAT Team was brought in, and the neighbors evacuated. They had the gray, two-story duplex just off Chicago Avenue surrounded. Now, all the police could do was to simply wait them out.

Shawn and I gathered some video of the neighborhood to accompany the shots from the copter and sent in a quick story for the 6:00 pm news. There was no way of knowing how long the standoff would take. By 8:00 pm, we notified our over-night crew that they might have to finish our coverage. They sent a message to us saying they planned to relieve us about 10:00 pm unless something broke.

Just as we were writing a short revision to our 6:00 pm news report for the 10:00 pm news, the police decided it was time to end it. At 8:45 pm, they shot tear gas canisters into the upstairs windows and charged the doors. In a matter of minutes it was over, they had their two robbers in custody.

The action was much quicker than we had anticipated. I had just enough time to send in a full report along with videos for the 10:00 pm news.

By 9:40 pm, it was in the can. The editors at the station had clipped the video we shot, and edited the story line to fit the time slot. With any luck, Shawn and I would be back in our homes by 10:30 pm to watch the DVR copy of the news.

Somehow, it was just another day on the job. What started at 8:00 am, finished just after 9:15 pm. The good thing was that tomorrow I finally had the day off.

When I got home, I watched the news to see how my story looked. The news led off with the headlines: "Our lead story tonight is the daring daylight robbery of the Second State Bank. We have exclusive footage of the high-speed escape, which led to a multiple car accident with a bus, and the SWAT Team's charge to capture the robbers. Stay tuned for more information."

I grabbed a beer and started to relax back in my chair as I watched the edited version of my story about the bank heist. I figured my boss would leave me a text message in the morning saying "good job" after all the hours we spent on the story. It would be just one more "attaboy" to put on the stack.

Chapter 2

A Day Off

It was the first day in three months I had taken a day off work. I decided to spend the late afternoon with my father, since I had not seen him for several weeks. It was a good chance to show him my new car, a showroom shiny, dark-green, 2025 BMW. I figured we could go for a spin right after dinner. It was considerably more refined than his old 2010 BMW, which I had purchased from him when he got a new car a few years ago. The old one still had the standard gas engine.

My new car, equipped with a hydrogen fuel cell and four independent electric motors, made his old car feel like a dinosaur on the road. I knew that his first statements to me would be, "It just doesn't sound like a BMW to me."

My father lives in the corner apartment of a senior center, in a western suburb of Minneapolis. He calls the complex of large brick buildings, "The Castle." I think he gave it the name because of the gray stone arches used at the entrances. Its tall walls and four buildings built into a square, look like the walls of a medieval castle. However, they open up to a lovely courtyard in the center. Seasonally, there are trees and bushes that bloom, and in the fall, the colors of the leaves are spectacular. A path weaves its way through the landscaping with benches and tables for people to sit and enjoy the view by a fountain. Fortunately, the moat surrounding his Castle is missing. Underneath everything is a hidden underground garage. At least for my father, the buildings are not the prison that some of the other care centers tended to be called. The staff at his place always works hard to make sure the residents are respected and acknowledged. Even though I try to call him daily, he always asks me, "Martin, when you coming over?" Today was my first chance to spend some extra time with him.

We sat and visited for a couple hours.

My father, John Berman, has lived at the center for seven years. My mother died three years ago just before her 66th birthday, after being sick for four years. He keeps himself going with the help of several life-long friends, who live in the same building. A few of them have been friends of his since high school. Except when someone comes for a visit, the group has a standard routine of meeting for breakfast and again at dinner.

"Hey Dad, can you turn on the afternoon news, while I throw a pizza in the oven?"

"Yeah, I suppose so. I don't know why I watch the news. It's all that sensational stuff. Martin, you are the genius behind all those stories on TV, why can't you find something enjoyable to report on?" he asked trying to give me a hard time. He hit the switch that electronically converted the wall mural into a video center.

That was one feature of his apartment I liked. He could select a sunrise scene for the mornings, mountain scene for the afternoon, and a sunset scene for evenings. The images would change automatically, and fill the three-foot by six-foot mural on the wall that converts to a high definition television. It fit right in to what he joked was his "man cave." The black leather sofa and chairs were properly positioned for him and is guests to watch whatever sporting event was on the air that week. He also kept a few extra beers in the refrigerator for such events. What was missing was the warm tones in the room. Decorations that a female touch would have provided. After my mother died, he wanted it his style. If I joked about it, he would always say, "Well, if you want color in the room, just select a different scene on the wall." It was his way of

6

saying; don't mess with what I like. One thing for sure, he did not like spending hours watching the national news.

Unfortunately, my father was right. After being a journalist for the local television network for five years, I had to agree with some of his opinions. Most of the stories that make it to the news spot are usually about tragedies or significant problems affecting the public. Television stations never seem to be able to spend a lot of time on the good things that are happening in everyone's lives. As they told me, excitement sells.

My job, as a television journalist, has kept me extremely busy, because I am on call for spot news almost every day. Many days, I would travel from one end of the Twin Cities to the other; only to find out I was needed for a special story sixty miles away. Between those stories, I have a number of long-term reports I am working on. As a result, I have little extra time at the end of the day for anything other than work.

"Well, when I get to be president of the network, I'll make sure they balance out their reporting," I told him. He knew that I was reporting on issues assigned to me by my editor. He just loved to jab me with reporting on something good for a change.

I threw a frozen pepperoni, mushrooms, black-olives, and cheese pizza in the infrared pulse oven for us to eat as we watched the six o'clock news. It was my father's favorite pizza. I knew the station was going to run a story that I finished yesterday, on the netting of fish in northern Minnesota by one of the Native American tribes. They seemed to run the story every year. According to a treaty, the Native American tribes are allowed to net fish in areas where the general public cannot. With allowable fish locations and fish populations decreasing, there is a lot more pressure on the tribes to start to open general fishing in their areas.

The piece I put together showed how they were working with the Department of Natural Resources to maintain the fish population in their lakes, as well as supply the DNR with yearlings that could be stocked in other lakes and rivers once the DNR started their long awaited restocking plan. So far, the cooperation was working for everyone.

As the news started, the anchor brought up his first report. "Now, about the projected water shortages that are affecting Minnesota cities. The state is proposing to construct a water pipeline from Duluth to the Twin Cities, with branch lines heading to Rochester, Mankato, St. Cloud, and Alexandria. Discussions on the project are scheduled to begin at an international conference in Grand Marais, tomorrow."

The five-minute timer on the oven went off just as the news was going into the discussion of the pipeline. I rushed out and got the pizza out of the oven. Then, I threw a couple pieces on our plates before the sports came on.

My story was tagged to run at the end of the sports segment. I wanted to see how the final edit looked. Depending on time available, they had the option of running the piece as written, or editing it to fit the slot.

When I came back to the gathering room, my Father griped, "Did you hear that? Now they want to run a pipe from Lake Superior to the Twin Cities for drinking water. I don't want to drink any water fish swim in."

I decided not to answer him. It would just get him started on yet another long lecture. I had heard it from him more than a few times in the past.

When my feature story came up, we watched intently. They had cut it slightly to fit the slot, but most of the article was still intact by the time it ran.

"Good job," my father told me. "I still think they ought to put you on the television for the station instead of that guy. He just has no charisma. I think the pictures you shot of the fish had more expressions than he does."

"Dad, you know it takes time. You have to work your way up in the system. Give me a couple more years." I watched the sports announcer. Dad was right; the normally highly excitable sports commentator looked like he was reading the script tonight. Obviously, they had made some last minute adjustments, and his mind was on something else.

We polished off the pizza, and sat and talked.

"What's your next assignment?" he asked me.

"I think I have a report on eliminating subsidized meals for senior citizens," I answered. "Think of all the money the state could save if we insisted that your 'grey-beard gang' had to purchase your own food every night." I figured that would get a rise out of him. All of his friends had grey hair and grey beards. As a result, one day one of the staff people coined the term 'grey-beard gang,' and it stuck.

He smiled to acknowledge that I just got even with him.

"How many years have you gray-beards hung around together anyway?" I asked.

"Well, three of us went to high school together. The other two lived in the area and went to another school. We played softball and hockey together for years after that. I guess we have known each other for a long time. I keep reminding them that they are a lot older than I am."

"So, how much older are they?" I asked.

"Well, I'm almost 70, and I've got the next guy beat by two months. Hank is the oldest. He's almost 72 now, but he doesn't look it. You know, he works out two hours every day in the gym next to the lap pool. He can still lift over 200 pounds. I'll bet he could out-lift your skinny 37-year old body."

My father was six-foot and weighed 185-pounds. To stay in shape, he has worked out for an hour every day for the past twenty years. Compared to the physique of Hank and my father, I simply look like just another skinny five-foot ten person. I have my father's skinny genes;

9

however, I do not have the luxury of having an extra hour to work out as they have for years.

Just then, my cell phone rang. From the caller ID, I could tell it was my office. I told my father that I needed to check the call.

"Hello, this is Martin Berman. What's up?

Oh! I see…

Okay, I'll be there in an hour."

"That was my office, Dad. I think I just found out why your sports announcer was less than enthusiastic about the news. Apparently, one of our helicopters appears to have crashed near Two Harbors. They are trying to get the facts now. The station wants me to fly up there and cover the crash. One of our best reporters was on the flight. I need to pack a set of clothes and leave as soon as I can.

"After that, I have to go up to Grand Marais to attend the conference between the US and Canadian water resource managers that he was destined to cover. I'm sorry, but I guess we'll have to wait a few days for that evening together."

"That's too bad. You be careful that you don't have the same problem. You know I hate when you fly with them at night. They get those hotshots for pilots that think they can fly through anything. That's probably why they crashed.

"So, tell me, why <u>are</u> those bozos still talking about piping water from Lake Superior to all the major cities in the state for drinking water? Can't you tell them to stop wasting all that tax money?"

"Dad, that's what they told you on the news. Weren't you listening? You heard it before, I take it."

"They were talking about selling water to California when I was younger. I do not think this state can manage anything anymore. This is the land of 10,000 lakes. You know, the land of sky blue waters. There is water all over the state. Why do we need to pipe it all the way from Lake Superior?" he asked. "Surely someone can come up with a better idea."

As I cleared my dishes, I told him, "They say there is a water shortage. I guess you and your over-the-hill, grey-beard gang are taking too many long showers, and have finally drained all the water out of the water table."

He grumbled, "In your dreams. I just don't understand this state. In my days, we used to fish all the rivers and lakes. Then, they let those exotic fish get up the river. Next thing you know the DNR decides to poison out the rivers to kill all of the fish, and promises to restock the river like it used to be. I had a brand new fishing boat back in 2015; they didn't even offer to buy it back from me after screwing up the river. That was ten years ago, and we still can't fish in the rivers. You just can't trust the government anymore. When you get up there, you tell them I don't think they know what they are doing."

"Well, the state says it is only a matter of time before they feel the fish in the rivers are safe enough to eat," I told him. "I'm sure they know what they are doing. But, if you insist, I'll tell them they need to call you and discuss it."

"Yeah, my aching foot! Those yahoos just blunder through everything, and find someone to blame after they screw things up. You should know that. You report on enough of their programs. If they spent the money to fix the problems rather than constantly blaming the public, the problems wouldn't be this bad. Besides, in this case, they probably won't even start that pipeline until next year. With winter coming, it will be 2026 before they can do anything, especially with that cold wind coming off that rough lake in the winter time."

"Well, that's the way government works, Dad. You throw money at a problem and see if it fixes the problem. If not, you can always have a commission study the problem and find another way of throwing money at it. That's why we pay taxes."

That got a dirty look from him. He switched off the video center, and the image converted back to a sunset picture. "That's better. Enough of the bad news," he griped.

I had to quickly say good-bye to him and headed down to my car. On the way down in the elevator, I was thinking, my father was right. People were starting to get leery of many of the government programs. Usually, the problem was in the way the information was presented to the public. By the time it was broken down into sound bites for the news, most of the discussion and technical information had been left out. It was no wonder that people did not understand most of the government programs.

I had a "go-bag" stashed in the trunk of my sporty dark-green BMW for just this type of situation. However, having to attend the conference would mean I needed more than one set of clothes, especially for near Lake Superior where the temperature changes with the wind direction. I rushed home and packed for a couple extra days, remembering to turn off the automatic alarm by my bed, so it would not go off each day and irritate the people in the next apartment. Then, I dashed off to the airport to pick up my flight.

After parking my car in the stacks at the private terminal, I spotted my cinematographer – Shawn Peterson, waiting for me near the helicopter, along with the pilot. It was only then that I realized that one of our other cameramen must have been on the original flight. We had always been a close group of people that worked together on all our projects. I hated to think what might have happened to the crew if the copter crashed.

"Any news?" I asked them.

"Just that the flight went down about twenty-five miles from Two Harbors. Fortunately, they landed in the wooded hills northwest of town, and not out in the cold lake. Technically, I guess they are small mountains. No word from the chopper crew or from the ground yet. We should get some word before we get there," the pilot told me, "let's get moving."

I handed off my luggage to the ground crew as we climbed aboard the chopper, belted ourselves in, and waited for clearance from the tower to leave the hanger area. I was impressed; with the newly installed sound eliminating headphones. We could talk to each other as if we were back in the office. All the noise of the aircraft had been electronically eliminated – even from the sounds from our microphones. The old system eliminated about 75% of the noise. These new upgrades should make our trips more enjoyable. The only thing missing was our choice of music.

As fancy as the copter was, I still hated to fly. There were just too many variables out of my control, not to mention the fact that someone else was flying the machine. All I could do was watch out the window.

Nevertheless, it was the other conditions that made my stomach churn. Flying in snow or thunderstorms, in a machine that somehow defies gravity in spite of all the conditions was unnerving. On top of that, it was without the assistance of any wings. Something goes wrong, like our copter, you can't just glide onto the closest road.

Watching the calmness our pilots exhibit on such days just amazes me. What did they know about flying that gives them the confidence to fly in all kinds of conditions?

Chapter 3

The Crash

It was a brisk fall evening. The weather was partly cloudy and 65-degrees. Even though it was an almost perfect night for a Monday in the middle of September, somehow, something mechanical must have gone wrong on the helicopter that it crashed. Weather would have been an unlikely cause.

When we were about half way up there, we got a report on the chopper's radio. They had a fix on the crash site along with satellite images. They sent us the GPS coordinates, which the pilot plugged into his computer-guided autopilot. It had gone down in a heavily wooded area. As a result, they told us that it broke up on landing. The report indicated that so far everyone onboard was alive. We all breathed a sigh of relief. They were airlifting the injured from the scene to the emergency hospital in Duluth. However, to get them to an opening where they could be lifted out by an emergency chopper, the injured had to be carried almost a half a mile to a clearing, since they had crashed deep in the woods.

The pilot turned to my cinematographer and me. "I'll take us as close as I can to the crash site for you to get some pictures. The search light should light up the area fairly well as long as they let me get close to the site. Sometimes, they restrict the airspace around crashes. Since it was our chopper, I think they will let us in. Then, we can make a quick detour to Duluth. I'll let you check on the crew before I have to take you both up to Grand Marais and the water diversion meeting."

We just nodded and got our equipment ready. Even without the spotlight, the almost full moon lit up the hillsides as we traveled north.

The crash site was visible almost five miles away. There was a small fire glowing in the middle of a hill up ahead. Apparently, some of the fuel spilled from the tanks and ignited, burning a small hole in the dense forest. Now that they had the victims out of the area, a small team was attempting to put out the fire that had started from sparks of the crippled chopper as it hit the trees.

We received clearance to circle over the site to take videos. I sent off a video report to our station to assemble and edit for the 10:00 pm news.

The spotlight, shining on the trees, showed that the choppers blades had sheared off when they struck the trees. There were a few trees that were chopped off near the tops, and branches were all over the ground.

The copter was nearly intact after reaching the ground. It was obvious that the impact had cracked the carbon-fiber exterior and broken off the tail section from the rest of the fuselage, but it was a reassuring sight to see that it was not in a thousand pieces. At least the crew had some protection from the trees when it crashed. Since they had their seat belts on during the flight, they had a chance of survival.

After we finished our report, we vectored south and headed for the Duluth hospital.

The flight took us out over Lake Superior to avoid the air lanes for the Duluth airport area. On top the cliff at Palisades, we could spot the radio antenna's red lights. Then we saw the ground lights at the Split Rock Lighthouse. Unfortunately, the big warning light at the lighthouse was not shining. It is only lit on festive occasions. They say that in the old days you could see it for miles out on the lake, even in the rain. With the lighthouse built on a 130-foot cliff, the beacon would shine out into the dark lake for 22-miles.

As we approached Duluth, the skyline of the city became visible with its landmark lift-bridge all lit up with its yellow lights. We could see the landing pad on top of the hospital light up, as they were expecting our chopper. Fortunately, the winds were light and the pilot made a gentle landing. I told our pilot we would be as quick as possible. If he had to move, we would understand. He could put down temporarily at the airfield. We would contact him by cell phone when we were ready.

As we entered the hospital, we were met by one of our local sister station's reporters who had gone to the hospital to cover the condition of our crew. Tracy Saunders' news director had given her a heads up that we would probably be stopping in on our flight up to Grand Marais, and knowing that we would be concerned, she met us at the door.

I recognized her long reddish-brown hair as we stepped inside. She was dressed in casual clothes, her station logo jacket and jeans. Obviously, she got the call at home and rushed over. "Tracy, good to see you, I was wondering if you were covering the crash. Did you get a report on their condition?" I asked her.

"Yes, Martin. I heard you were flying up so I checked on them before I came up to meet you. Figured you would be worried and make a quick stop before heading on to your assignment. Nice to see you, too.

"They must have had a wild ride through the trees. Lots of bruises and jars, but nothing penetrated the cabin. They were lucky; a tree could have easily speared one of them when it went down. Sounds like the soft pine-tree limbs slowed their descent to the ground."

"Sorry I was so direct when you met us," I told her. "Did you get a chance to see them?"

"No, they are still in the emergency room. It sounds like they might have some compression problems from the landing. Sore backs, shoulders and necks. I think the pilot has a broken leg and wrist as well, from trying to guide it manually to the ground and holding on to the controls. Overall, I think they were lucky", she told us.

16

"Will the hospital staff let us see them?" I asked.

"I think you will be able to as long as they are not in x-ray or having an MRI. They will probably be there for another couple hours until they make sure there are no internal injuries. How soon do you need to leave?"

"We have time. We'll share some of our footage with you if we get some shots. We took some video of the crash scene earlier."

"Thanks! I'll let you know if I hear anything different on your crew after you leave. By the way, it is nice to see you again," Tracy said with a smile.

"Oh, I'm sorry; I don't think you have met Shawn Peterson, my cinematographer. Shawn, I want you to meet Tracy Saunders. We've met a few times at political conventions and other meetings here in Duluth."

"Nice to meet you," Shawn told her as he was trying to keep the shoulder straps of his video gear from being caught in the door.

We took the elevator down to the emergency room, and after a quick meeting with the charge nurse, we were allowed to go in and talk to our crew, as long as we kept it short. She told us that she would keep us on a very short leash.

As she led us into the room, we could hear Jake Schwartz and Tim Baker talking to each other behind the curtains. When the nurse let us in to see them, I gave them a greeting: "What a sight for sore eyes. You guys will do anything to get out of an assignment."

Jake looked up and saw us coming. "If we didn't give you something to write about, I heard they were talking about laying the two of you off. What took you so long to get here? Our make-up is probably needing a little touch-up by now."

I could see that Jake Schwartz had a neck brace on, and his cinematographer, Tim Baker, was taped up around the ribs and shoulder. They were dressed in a hospital gown. "Looks like you both got your money's worth out of that ride, how's the pilot doing?"

"He'll live. Broke an ankle and wrist when the craft hit the ground. Guess he forgot to let go of the controls before we hit. They have him in x-ray right now. Doc said they would set his breaks as soon as they were sure he did not have any other injuries," Jake told me. "He did a heck of a job setting her down. We think the tail rotor had a problem. I think both of us owe him a steak dinner for setting it down in one piece. Anyone else might have let it auger into one of those big hills."

Then Jake gave us his interpretation of the accident. "As you know, we were taking this flight up to Grand Marais, and we decided to take some pictures of some of the military jets flying out of Duluth. They were doing some low level maneuvers in the hills north of town, and we figured we could kill two birds with one stone, so to speak.

"Well, we had altitude on them so it made a perfect shot as the birds were flying low to the terrain. Then, as we banked to get a better camera angle on their flight, we heard something snap. Tim Baker shouted at me, 'You think they're shooting at us?' Well our pilot didn't take any chances, with the skills he learned in combat training, he ducked us down between two hills in a sharp valley where the fighters would not go. I doubt they even saw which way we went.

"It was a heck of a ride. The tail router was damaged, and he managed to bring us in down into a row of old growth white pines. With his skill, he used the straight planted rows of trees to eliminate the spin caused by the loss of the rotor, and flew us toward a clearing. The helicopter's blades were cutting off the tops of the trees like a barber cuts hair. I'll bet there is someone right now picking up the tops to sell for Christmas trees. However, it was the brushing of the branches on both sides of the fuselage, as we rushed down the row of trees that prevented us from spinning as we slowed our descent. When we looked up at the sky, all we could see was a sea of green. There were so many pine needles in the air that the windows started getting covered by the long green needles. I'll bet we looked like a gigantic green bug going through the woods from the view of the satellites.

"Unfortunately, there was an old oak tree mixed into the pines. When the blades hit the mighty old oak's hard limbs, we could hear them shear off as they cut the branches into firewood, and the craft sailed into the slope of the hill like a roller coaster gliding along the tracks.

"Wow, what a ride! Then, when we hit a small bump, the pilot dropped the landing gear and steered us around some rugged rocks that were on the side of an old logging trail. We'd have made it all the way to the highway, but someone left the chain across the road, with a no trespassing sign, at the gate."

I finally gave a wave to my cinematographer to shut off his video. The station was not going to give us airtime for fiction. Still, it sounded good right up to the point where they were driving down the road.

Tim Baker looked over at us and laughed. "Don't you know better than to believe a reporter? They hire you guys for your imagination not reporting the facts. That's why they send us with a camera. It makes it harder to make up stories. I just wish he'd let me know when he's going to let a good story rip. Laughing hurts my ribs."

Even the nurse got a laugh out of that one.

Jake Schwartz gave me a short summary of his goals and expectations on his assignment in Grand Marais as we videoed a few glamour pictures for the 10:00 pm news, and waited to see the pilot. I wanted to make sure we had his picture in the shot, and got his reaction to the problems with the helicopter. Tracy could handle any follow-up interviews once they were feeling better and the shock of the accident wore off.

After about 20-minutes, the pilot, Skip Largent, was wheeled back into the room. Fortunately, the only significant injuries were his ankle and wrist. He was sore from head to foot, but in a few days, most of those would heal. We spent the next 15-minutes getting as much information from him as he could remember prior to the crash. It would make timely sound bites for the news.

He told me that everything was normal until he heard a crack and started losing control immediately. Lights were flashing all over the control panel, and he figured he had lost something in the rear rotor. He knew his best chance was to try to keep it level as they spun out of control. His only hope was that they would hit the trees and not some rocky cliff. It was a miracle that they were still alive after that landing.

Before we left, we let all of them know how relieved we were to hear their voices. They thanked us for our concerns. When we had left the Twin Cities for the crash scene, we expected the worse.

We had stayed long enough for them to know we were concerned and to get footage for the news. Then, with a little extra push from the charge nurse, we excused ourselves from the emergency room and headed back to the roof, and our transportation.

Our helicopter was waiting for us. The pilot had been forced to move for a few minutes when another emergency came in. However, he was allowed to set it back down, while he awaited our imminent return. The hospital knew we would not be staying long, and let him stay on the roof as long as he stayed in the helicopter and there weren't any gusty winds to cause problems.

In just a few minutes, we were back in the air, headed for Grand Marais. It was a relief to have talked to our crew to make sure they had no serious problems from the crash.

Chapter 4

International Discussions

The flight up the vast lake did not take very long. Traveling in excess of 300 miles-per-hour, it took longer to get out of Duluth airspace and then to vector in to the new conference center, than to travel down the lake. It was fascinating to watch the line on the horizon on the way up. On one side, there were lights from resorts and houses; on the other side was the dark space of Lake Superior. We could only spot two of the "thousand footers" out on the lake as we traveled up the shoreline. The big boats were probably carrying wheat to markets along the east coast or Europe.

Approaching Grand Marais, we could make out the harbor with its lighthouse and breakwater lights shining out into the dark spaces. The new conference center, history center and hotel, was just up the hill from town. The new building was a monument to spending in an effort to attract tourism. It was the last in a string of tourist centers built by the state.

It was built so that the connecting wings of the history center and convention center arched over the road that led to the famous Boundary Waters. The road, the Gunflint Trail, was a 58-mile long road that led to the pristine lakes bordering the area between Minnesota and Canada. The area had been protected from development for years, and many of the lakes are navigable only by canoe. The water that drains from this long series of lakes provides a fair percentage of the water that feeds Lake Superior. The remainder flows in from Canada or Wisconsin.

After we set down on the helipad, we made our way into the center, to the reception desk. We had to explain to the front desk that the names they had for our rooms were for the crew that crashed. We finally got our door keys and settled our gear into our rooms. Morning would come quickly, and we would have to setup our video equipment and be ready to go, before the conference started.

The alarm went off at 5:00 am. By 6:30 am, we had gathered for breakfast and discussed the printed agenda for the day. The program showed that they were planning on speeches by the Governor of Minnesota, the Minister of Natural Resources from Ontario, Canada, the head of the US EPA, and the head of the DNR for Minnesota.

These were some of the high profile people here to discuss the plan to siphon water out of Lake Superior. It seemed that each group came with a delegation of five or six people to help manage the details. As a result, we figured that we would get plenty of opportunities for airtime with our stories, which would be shared nationwide on the network. As much as I did not wish any harm to our other crew, this story might give Shawn and me a chance to put the spotlight on our abilities. One thing for sure, for the next two days we were not going to have to worry about covering any car crashes or shootings, our time would be spent trying to get quotes from the speakers while covering the meetings.

The morning speeches went off as planned. It took a lot of time to introduce the dignitaries, and then each of them gave an introductory talk about the important part their agency was playing in the participation of the conference. It was well orchestrated to give each person time for a publicity photo and a few sound bites. You would think that each of them was running for office. By noon, sound clips from each of the main speakers were sent off to the major news organizations, and the meeting was adjourned for lunch.

The luncheon was served to about 150 people who were attending the conference. Shawn Peterson and I spread out so we could pick-up on the discussions at more than one table. The station logo on our shirts gave us the opportunity to get reactions from others at the tables. So far, we had not seen a lot of contention to the proposition. It was surprising, since it was rare that agencies ever agreed about diverting water, let alone water on an international border. Now, if the issue had been how many walleyes you could catch on a border lake, the group would have been split four ways, until someone asked if they wanted walleye or pork for lunch. Then, most would have reached one agreement – the walleye.

After lunch, Shawn and I met to discuss how we wanted to handle the coverage of the afternoon discussions. Both of us noted that there actually was very little discussion at our tables as to whether or not the project should go through as planned. Things were going ahead far too easily. There were also a few people missing from the conference. No one was representing Wisconsin or any of the other Great Lakes states. Diverting large amounts of water would surely affect the other lakes, as Lake Superior drained its clear water into the other four Great Lakes. Even the representatives from the large ore-boat industry were missing. It felt strange to both of us. These conferences rarely had such easy agreement, and usually someone would cry loudly if they were not included.

In the post luncheon presentations, the head of the Minnesota DNR discussed the proposal for the 12-foot diameter pipe, which was to be laid from about 12-miles north of Duluth to Minneapolis/St. Paul, with proposed branch lines that could eventually support Rochester, Mankato, St. Cloud, and Alexandria. The pipe would start in an area almost 150-feet deep offshore on the Minnesota side of Lake Superior.

Maps showing where the pipeline would run were presented, and they showed where the major pumping stations would be placed along the line. Huge pumps would be needed to lift the water from the lake over the high hills surrounding Lake Superior. After that, pumps

would be needed to maintain the water pressure and flow for the long distances needed. We were given the maps in our press packets so that we did not have to try to video the presentations from the screens.

The 12-foot pipe would supply enough water to supplement those water shortages expected for the next ten years of development in the Twin Cities. It was hoped that natural cycles would alleviate the problems before shortages occurred. However, if it did not, the state wanted to have a backup plan. By placing the pipe in place now, they would be prepared.

The Army Corps of Engineers showed a study they had completed, which detailed how they would need to restrict the St. Mary's River outlet that led from Lake Superior into Lake Huron, to maintain Lake Superior's water levels. Somehow, diverting a 12-foot diameter pipe of water verses the flow through this river did not seem like more than a drop in a bucket. Nevertheless, in the whole scheme of things, it was essential to maintain the water levels for shipping. Another season with low snow runoff would cause the lake to drop, and if the pipeline's effects were not addressed, people would be screaming to shut it down. After all, that 12-foot diameter pipe would be capable of over 414,700,000 gallons of water per day, although the actual pumping rate would probably be less than half of that amount to fill the demand.

Most of the afternoon's discussion related to the route of the pipeline and the construction problems, which were expected in crossing highways and underground utilities. Apparently, a set fee had been worked out for disruption of farm and industrial operations, while the construction of the line progressed. There did not seem to be terribly much concern about lawsuits or other disruptions of the line.

At the end of the afternoon's seminar, most of the dignitaries headed back to their jobs. They left their staffers to iron out any small details left over and complete the overall agreement on the project the next morning.

Shawn Peterson and I headed back to Shawn's room and ordered some room service – a sandwich and beer. We had a couple hours of work to polish off our report on the conference, along with suggesting footage that the station could use for on-the-air reports. Unless something unusual happened tomorrow morning, the information we had would provide the basis for the final story on the conference. There did not seem to be a smoking gun that would change the outcome of the meeting.

We finished reviewing the video footage and summarized the video clips, along with our summary report by 8:30 pm. In a blink of an eye, they were transmitted from my netbook back to the station in time for the 10:00 pm news. The station manager could select the images he wanted to show along with the video clips we sent earlier in the day. It had been a long day, but we both felt good that the story was finished, and the sound clips were exactly what our program manager was looking for. The clips showed the high cooperation that each organization was giving to the project to provide ample and safe drinking water.

To celebrate, we decided to head down to the bar for a quick drink before getting some well-deserved sleep. On the way down, I called my father on my cell phone.

"About time you called," he answered. "I thought you would call earlier and fill me in on the crash. I saw your story last night on the news. They got lucky."

"Sorry, I didn't get a chance to call last night, and I have been busy all day covering the conference. How about a second chance to enjoy one of your pizzas – say Friday? I think I can get an evening off after this trip. They owe me one."

"I'll write it on my calendar – in pencil."

"Thanks Dad. I'll try my best to make it."

I hated to say it, but he was right. It seemed like the majority of the times we planned to spend an evening together, I had to cover something critical that came up that day. I made one more call – to the office. I left a message that I was unavailable Friday evening. I had an important appointment.

We relaxed and enjoyed a beer in the Broken Paddle Bar at the conference center. There were a few conference attendees lingering at the bar, but we did not see a lot of bargaining or discussing of alternatives. It was almost anti-climatic. Meetings like these usually ended up in closed room agreements or discussions at the closest bar. This one looked like it was over long before the participants were scheduled to leave.

My cell phone chimed. It was an audio text message from Tracy Saunders. She was following up on our colleagues, and since she had agreed to keep us informed, was calling to let me know their condition.

Reporter Jake Schwartz's soreness apparently was diagnosed as a pinched nerve in the shoulder and a compression fracture in his neck. It looked as though he might be out of service for a month or two. Since he would not be able to do a lot of bouncing around or carrying of heavy equipment, he would probably have a few months off that included some physical therapy after they fused the vertebrae in his neck.

26

His cinematographer, Tim Baker, had a cracked rib and bruised shoulder. The rib would make carrying around a heavy camera and gear difficult for the next 3 or 4 weeks. As a result, your station will probably be leaning on the two of you to do more assignments for the near future.

I sat and wondered about that. I was not sure if I should call my father back now, or just hope they would let me have an evening off.

I sent Tracy a thank you for keeping us up to date.

To wear off the tensions of the trip, Shawn and I walked down to the harbor before retiring for the night. The lights surrounding the harbor glimmered on the still water. As we looked out from the breakwater, all we could see was the darkness. Lights from the other shoreline were too far away to be seen. It was hard to imagine how much water there was in Lake Superior. The proposal of draining up to 400 million gallons of water a day seemed immense. With an average depth of over 480-feet and the deepest spot over 1,330-feet, somehow, it was still just a drop in the bucket. However, if you take enough drips out of the leaking bucket, it eventually starts to show up.

We stood at the warning beacon at the end of the breakwater, until the cool, moist air from the immense lake started to penetrate into our bones. Then, Shawn Peterson and I headed back up to our rooms to get a hot shower and a good night's sleep. The next week might not give us very much down time.

Minnesota's DNR and EPA led the next morning's speeches. The Wednesday discussions were on making sure the source of the water was not contaminated, and making sure the construction of the pipeline did not disturb wetlands or other sensitive locations along its route. It was pretty generic, and it seemed like they were going through the motions just to say that they had addressed the issues at the conference.

By noon, the conference was over. We picked up a couple short interviews before packing up and waiting for our shuttle to pick us up and bring us back to the Cities.

While we were having lunch, I got a text message from Tracy Saunders. She said she got a call from my station manager asking if she would consider a temporary assignment replacing Jake Schwartz until he was physically able to come back to work. She wanted me to call her and discuss the offer.

As we waited for the chopper to take us back, I called Tracy to see what she had heard.

"Oh, thanks Martin for calling back. From what I heard, your station manager talked to my manager and got permission to talk to me about a temporary assignment with your station, until Jake Schwartz can return to full time. Your manager said it would be a positive experience for me and give me a lot of exposure just in case I ever wanted to change jobs. I was wondering what you thought?"

I was a little surprised, but under the circumstances, glad to see that the station was not expecting everyone to pick up all of Jake's work. "I think he is right. This would be an excellent opportunity for you. Especially, if you could do it for a few months and still have your old job held for you if you wanted to go back. Who knows, you might find an opening and want to stay on. Did they mention a salary bump?"

"Yes, they said they would give me a housing and travel stipend along with my regular salary. You think I should push for more?"

"No, I would take the experience. If it develops into something else, you will have room to bargain."

"How is your manager to work for?" she asked.

"He is pretty fair. He expects a long day out of you. However, if there is a conflict, he is willing to listen. What did he say you would be doing?"

"He said that he wanted me to tag along with you for a couple days, and then start picking up the loose ends that you were working on. I guess I would sort of be working under you for some time."

"In that case, you might want a gigantic raise. I hear that guy is terrible to work for."

28

"That's what I hear also," she snapped back. "So you think I should take the offer?"

"In a heart beat. I'll be glad to have you on board."

"Thanks. That's what I was hoping you might say. I'll let you know what I hear."

"OK, good luck." As I disconnected, I was relieved to hear that I might have someone to work with that I knew. It would make things a lot easier than working with a stranger.

The helicopter picked us up at 1:45 pm, and in a very short time, we were back in the Cities trying to figure out how we were going to cover the weekend duties. I was hoping my program manager would still remember I wanted to have Friday evening off.

Chapter 5

Orientation

The next day, Thursday, we had a short meeting at the station. Lester Townsen - LT, my office manager, informed me of his discussions with Tracy Saunders at the Duluth station, and asked me my opinion of working with her. "Well, so far all my dealings with her have been at arms length," I told him. "We have shared some facts on news, but I have not dealt directly with her in a working relationship. From what I have seen, I think she is fairly levelheaded. She's been with the station in Duluth for a number of years."

"Good. That is what I was hoping you might say. I sent a message to her to call me at 11:00 am. I was planning on taking Miss Saunders on, temporarily, and wanted your input first. We are a little too short of feet on the ground right now, and if you want an evening or day off once in a while, we need some help. I talked to her boss and worked it out with him. He owed me a few favors, and I told him I was calling one in. If she agrees, she starts Monday. Think you can get her up to speed in two or three days? It's not like she's straight out of school. From what I saw on her bio, she's 33 years old, so she ought to know the business fairly well."

Well, that answered my first question. At least he remembered I wanted an evening off. "Sounds good. Just let me know when you get the paperwork filled out," I told him. Now, we were just short a cinematographer. Knowing LT, he would probably tap the local technical college for someone near graduation, who wanted an internship. It would be excellent training for them.

LT was a short, thin man about 50 years old. He had been in the reporting business since he was in high school. One of his assignments in school was working for the local TV station, reporting on their sporting events. He always wanted to be a basketball star. However, being only five foot eight, he realized quickly, his first year in high school, he was too short for the team. Reporting on the players gave him the feel of being on the team. As soon as he defeated the jitters of being live on the air, there was no stopping him. He continued reporting on high school events while in college, and then went to work full time for the station. As a result, he was always looking to give someone their break into the business.

The assignments were reviewed, and everyone was reminded that they would probably have to put in some extra time, until we had a full crew again. Then, we split up to cover the current events in the Twin Cities.

Friday evening, I managed to spend the whole evening with my father. I picked up some lasagna from an Italian restaurant and brought it over to him.

"You don't like my pizzas," he greeted me.

"Thought you needed some changes in your diet. If you want, I can take it home and eat it tomorrow."

He took a long sniff of the aroma and answered, "I guess it will do. Just don't tell the gang that you brought in the good stuff, and we didn't invite them."

"OK! You can tell them that we ate pizza. Your secret is safe."

We spent an enjoyable evening talking about the helicopter crash and staying safe on the job. Both of us were impressed at the crash worthiness of the station's helicopter. Rumors had it that a replacement was already negotiated with the insurance company.

"I saw your story on the conference," my father told me. "Was it my feelings, or was there a lack of negotiating on the agreement."

"You felt that way too?" I answered. "Yes, it was pretty cut and dried long before anyone got involved. Knowing the history between Canada and the US on border issues, it seemed strange. They can't even agree on how many walleyes you can take from a border lake. Just stray over the invisible line in the middle of the lake, and they can grab you for having the wrong number of fish in the boat. Wonder how they agreed on diverting water so easily?"

"I'm going to stick to beer," my dad stated. "Don't want to drink water that fish swim in," he snorted at me. "At least beer gets cured."

"Good answer Dad. Suppose you will use it for brushing your teeth too. What happened to the old days when you used to drink the water straight out of the lakes? Did you forget those stories you told me?"

"That was before I knew about beaver fever. Like I said, if they swim in it, I don't drink it."

"I think you mean giardia, Dad. I think they will filter and disinfect the water before they deliver it. Although, if they want to save some money, maybe they could pump it directly to all our senior citizens. Since you are all drinking beer, it will probably disinfect everything, and you probably wouldn't know the difference."

"You know what I mean. Well water is filtered by all those layers of sand between the ground and the water layers."

"OK, I'm pulling your leg a little. I guess the Cities are pulling too much water, and they need another source to meet the demand. By the time the state gets the pipe built, we will probably be in a wet cycle and it will not even be needed. I think you can tell your gang that they are safe for at least the next couple of years. After that, I'll get you some worms and you guys can all go fishing in the bathtub. It's a lot cheaper than buying gas for that old boat of yours that you keep in storage."

"You will see. I may be old, but I know when something sounds fishy," my father told me. "Besides, how do they know they will not be picking up some of that asbestos dumped into the lake, or washed into the lake by the great flood of 2012? You know, that flood washed half the hillsides into the lake around Duluth."

"Dad, that was sand and clay that washed into the lake. I'm sure they will have filters and test the intake to make sure they are not close to either sediment area on the lake."

We sat there until 9:30, talking. Then, I had to leave to get some sleep. The weekend shifts would be long and tiring. It felt good to have taken an evening off.

The weekend seemed like it was a full week. After covering three shootings, two crashes on the freeway, a fire in a hotel room, and a senator that was giving a speech, I was exhausted. In the middle of all the hassle, I got a text message: *Meet Tracy Saunders at the station at 9:00 am Monday. She will shadow you for the next three days.*

It looked as though LT and Tracy had worked out their agreement. Whatever favors LT had to give to her manager in Duluth, they must have been good ones for him to give her up this quickly.

Monday morning, I ran into the station before hitting my list of possible stories. Tracy Saunders was there to meet me along with LT.

"Martin, I would like you to do one of your famous speed training courses for Tracy. She knows her stuff, so if you can give her the "what's for" of how we do things here and where things are sent to be edited, I think she can start to handle some of her own load later in the week."

"Ten-four LT. I'll give Tracy the cook's tour of the station here and we can talk shop, while we are out interviewing your jay-walkers."

LT turned to Tracy and joked, "Tracy, if you can put up with Martin for three days, you'll be fine. If he gets carried away, you have my permission to stuff some bubble gum in his mouth and take over."

"I think Tracy will figure it out quickly," I told both of them. We left the office. I gave her a tour of the editing area, and introduced her to the main people she would be talking to.

When we finished, I checked my text-mail and put some priority into the next few hours of investigations. I still had a couple reports left over from the weekend, which required some follow-up.

As we left the station, we picked up Shawn Peterson and headed out to cover a house fire in NE Minneapolis. "Nice to see you again Tracy," Shawn greeted her. Have you gotten an apartment, or did you get stuck with a hotel room?"

"Thanks Shawn. LT had a townhouse rented for me as part of the agreement. Not my colors, but it was better than a hotel room for the next couple months."

Arriving at the location, we could see the roof of the two-story building was still smoldering, and a few firefighters were gathered around an ambulance. Shawn was able to get a few shots of the fire, while we checked with the police, fire and ambulance people. A couple firefighters received some smoke inhalation and were sitting in the ambulance breathing oxygen, while their systems caught up. We got Shawn to get a few shots of the firefighters for news clips. Then, Tracy and I split up, talking to a few firefighters and neighbors to see if there were any surprise stories about the fire.

When we were finished and had not found anything but a possible overheated portable oven, we gathered to crank out a compelling story line. As soon as we finished, we sent a few sound clips to the station along with a general coverage note to the editor. The new sound translation software at the station made it easy to file a report. All you had to do was call in, and leave the verbal report. The report would be translated into text, and sent to the day-editor immediately after you closed the call. Then, they could compare it with the sound clips sent in, and decide if they wanted it for the news or not.

"Thanks for letting me interview the neighbors and firemen," Tracy told me.

"You're a professional. You know what to ask. It saves us time if we split the things you already know how to do. Besides, what better way do I have to see you in action," I told her with a wink in my eye.

"You know what I mean. You could have just told me to follow you for the next couple of days, and stay out of the way. I just wanted to say thanks."

"OK, you see, I honestly need your help by the end of the week. One person can only cover so much territory before they get burned out. You probably know that from Duluth. In this job, we have to be able to work together. You will be surprised to see how many times events are related. Unless we are talking, we might miss the links."

As we were heading to our next assignment, we passed over the Interstate 35W Bridge that spanned the Mississippi over the Upper St. Anthony Falls Dam. Tracy leaned over and asked, "With all that water heading over the falls, wouldn't you think there was enough water for the Twin Cities without that pipeline?"

"Probably, but there might be a few barges stuck on sandbars downstream if they diverted too much."

Actually, most of the water for the Cities was already being drawn out of the river miles above the dam. The water going over the falls was what was left, and it was an impressive sight. There did seem as though there might be enough water for both river travel and drinking water. Watching the water flow over the dammed up falls, which dropped several times in a short stretch, I wondered how many millions of gallons of water were passing over the falls per day. At the Upper St. Anthony Falls Dam, the drop is over 40 feet and stretches about a quarter mile across the river. Just down river a few miles, after another drop at the Lower St. Anthony Falls Dam, the Minnesota River joins the Mississippi River and adds more water to the flow.

The rest of the day was spent on cars crashing into buildings, a meeting on highway construction plans, and concluded with covering a bar shooting on Hennepin Avenue about 9:00 pm. It made for a long day. By the time we dropped Tracy off at her townhouse, Shawn and I were eagerly looking for some sack time. It was almost 12:30 am.

Tracy had an enjoyable day. She observed most of the methods we used for covering and transmitting our stories. Fortunately, because the stations in Duluth and the Twin Cities were affiliated with the same network, the way we did our reporting was close to the methods used in Duluth. Just the names of the editors were different.

The next morning came terribly early. It seemed like the pillow was just starting to warm up. I picked up Tracy a little before 9:00 am and drove to the station to meet Shawn. There we met with another surprise. LT had picked up an intern – Franklin Wahlbusher, and he was planning to have Shawn train him in as a cinematographer during the next week. The station's van was starting to get crowded.

Franklin Wahlbusher, or "Photo" as his friends called him, was a senior at Dunwoody College of Technology. He decided that an internship at the station was an experience he should not pass up, even though it would delay his graduation for a quarter. Besides, if he played his cards right, maybe it would lead to a permanent job – either at our station or one of our affiliates.

We all welcomed him to the group. Shawn realized that he had his work cut out for him, trying to get him up to speed in a week. Unlike Tracy, Photo did not have the direct experiences that would allow him to quickly step in. He knew how to run the equipment from the technical school. Now, he had to learn to get the kind of shots that the editors expected.

The day started with a press conference by the Governor, Lester Johnson. It gave us the usual sound bites and was an easy start to Photo's training. Fixed camera positions were easy to setup, and shoulder shots for comments, gave him the feel for the video camera. Photo's six foot three height gave him an advantage over many of the other photographers. He could hold his camera on his shoulder and see over other people.

While we were covering the after-speech comments, I noticed that Tracy was on her phone. She had slipped into the corner of the room and was looking like she had something important. I wondered who was more important than asking questions of the governor – a boy friend?

As we were packing up our gear, and Shawn and Photo had taken a load to the van, I asked her, "Something important that you missed the governor's questions?"

"Yes, it was a lead I was following up on, from Duluth."

"Hmm! You passed up the governor for a phone call from a lead? Do we need to talk about it? I'm not sure that would be LT's priority ranking."

"Well, this one might be. Besides, I knew you had it covered. Otherwise, I would have stayed with the interview. Give me a day to finish the lead, and then I'll bring you up to speed."

I decided to give her a little rope. I knew that LT would have blown a gasket if he knew she blew off Governor Johnson's comments.

Shawn had his work cut out for himself. Franklin Wahlbusher knew how to set up cameras and how to operate them, but the experience he lacked was in watching the background of the shots. It was important to make sure you were getting the sun in the right angle, watching the people in the background, and not cutting the shot too early – you had to leave some cutting space. All day long, we could hear him trying to teach him everything he needed to watch for, before he would be allowed to go on his own. This was not a "watch what I do" learning experience. It was a grab the camera and learn quickly as we go.

Shawn knew that the only way Photo was going to learn what he needed to know in a week was to be thrown headfirst into the fire, as Shawn was watching everything he was trying to do. A plug-in adaptor on his tablet allowed Shawn to see everything the camera would see. Fortunately, Photo also realized the urgency of the situation, and was grateful that Shawn was willing to talk through each photo experience. Many people would have been upset with such close reviewing of each situation. However, Photo appreciated the help.

I hated to ask Shawn how it was going. However, I knew that by next week, there would be times that Photo would be covering events with me, and his skills, or lack of them, would reflect on my coverage.

Near the end of the day, I asked Shawn. His only comment was, "He learns quickly." I took that as meaning there was at least hope.

The night crew was stretched as tight as we were. The lack of a third crew was cutting into our schedules. They were running extra long days trying to give us some overlap on events from the evening as well as early morning. Except for a few calls between us, we had not had time to let the newbies meet the other crew. We arranged for a hamburger stop the next evening, to get everyone acquainted. LT normally called one of these meetings every couple of weeks. However, since none of us knew how LT was going to swap up the crews, we felt it was essential that everyone got to know everyone else quickly. One emergency could get all of us into action at the same time. If we were called out to an event tomorrow evening, the other crew would bring the burgers to us, and we could still greet each other.

We thought we had it all figured out. Somehow, I think all of us knew that if something could come along and spoil our plans, it would.

Chapter 6

Complications

Wednesday morning started out with a bang. Well, at least it was a call for a shooting in an alley in downtown Minneapolis, just off Hennepin Avenue, about two blocks from Target Field.

When we arrived, Tracy and I tried to get the facts, while Shawn and Photo took some video clips to use for the noon news. The tall brick buildings and the cobblestone alley made for a scene that looked like it was a movie set. The officers told us they had received a call that there was a body near a dumpster in the alley. When they arrived, they found a male, about fifty years old, shot dead. His wallet and watch were missing. No one had witnessed the shooting. They were waiting for the coroner to determine the time of death.

As our crew shot some pictures of the narrow alley way located behind a couple bars, Tracy glanced over at the body and gasped while taking a step back. I noticed the arching of her back, and asked her if she had a problem. I was not sure how many shootings she had reported on in Duluth.

"Remember the person I was talking to at the governor's speech? Well, that's the guy. He was going to call me today with the information he had found, and set up a meeting with us," Tracy told me.

I looked her in the eyes and told her "You better tell the officers."

"OK, but I'm not sure we should tell them what he was working on. We need to work this one through."

While Tracy gave the officer a name to put with his John Doe, I gave LT a heads up. I told him that we may need some time to investigate whatever Tracy had been following, and LT agreed to alert the other crew if we needed assistance. So far, the day looked slow. However, things had been known to change in a moment's notice. Whatever it was that Tracy was working on, it had LT's and my interest. Any investigation that leads to a shooting is either rotten luck, or someone wanted to end the investigation.

Tracy did not give the officer very much information on the dead man. Two weeks ago, she had met him in Duluth, and had talked about some information he had on a story. That was the last time she saw him. She left out the part that he was to call her today for a meeting. When pushed for details about the story, she told them she needed to talk to her boss before she could release any more information.

I gave her a smile. Good answer. Whatever it was that she knew, she did not want to let the cat out of the bag before it was time.

When we left the crime scene, we headed back to the station to allow Shawn to show Photo how the editor would take his clips and edit them for the noon news. More important, it gave Tracy and me a chance to talk in private, in one of our meeting rooms. It was time for Tracy to let me know what was going on.

"OK, Tracy, let's start from the beginning. Who was the person in the alley, and what was he working on that was more important than the governor's speech?"

Tracy began, "I recognized the shoes and the tattoo on his arm. Just before the conference in Grand Marais, where your station's chopper went down, I had a phone call from a stranger. He said he had some information for me that would make the headlines for a week and he needed to meet with me.

"I get crank calls all the time, so I'm careful who and where I meet with people. We arranged a meeting at Grandma's Restaurant at the bridge. I had one of our copywriters sit at a table close by, to make sure the guy was on the up and up.

"When I met with him, he said he had information on the water pipeline that no one else had. He used to be a geologist and had taught geology at the turn of the century, before the big oil business in the Dakotas. Then, he went to work for the oil companies at three times what he was making while teaching. He said he retired early – rich. Apparently, he had invested his earnings in mineral rights, and as the exploration expanded, in his words – he cleaned up. I ran a check on him after the meeting – Mr. Howard Long. That part of his story stood up.

"Anyway, he told me the stories in the press about supplying water from Lake Superior to the major cities sounded phony to him. He started doing some investigating and came up with some things that would 'knock your socks off.' Those were his words.

"Howard Long told me that he lived on a lake just north of St. Cloud. He called me yesterday to say he was going to take the Link to Duluth, and wanted to meet with me and give me the information that he had. When I told him that I was working in the Cities and was not in Duluth, he said, "Great, now I don't have to transfer trains in the Cities to head up to Duluth."

"He was going to call me this afternoon and set up a meeting. Those were the last words I heard from him until we went into that alley. When I saw his shoes, I recognized them from up in Duluth. Not many guys wear blue leather shoes with red rubber soles. Then, when I saw the tattoo on his arm, I knew it must be him. That's why I gasped. I've never had a person I was supposed to meet with killed before. Do you think it was a bar fight, or did someone kill him for a reason?"

I sat back and thought for a moment. Even my father thought the story stunk. Maybe there was more to this than an idle story. "I'm glad you did not say much to the police. They will be down here looking for information soon enough. I'm sure their investigators are on the way as we speak.

"We need to work with the police to slow down this story. As of now, I think we should go with the John Doe in the alley for as long as the police will let us. They will track down the family. Then, they will have to determine where this goes."

As we were speaking, LT opened the door and said, "Mind if I join you? Looks like you're about to upset my temporary staffing solution in a heartbeat. What gives?"

We filled LT in on what Tracy had told me.

"OK, that explains the phone calls I've had from the detectives and from the other stations. Somehow, they got wind that we knew more than what the police were telling them. I stalled everyone off until I could find out myself. If there really is something brewing under the table, the less that gets out the better. Homicide Lieutenant O'Riley is coming over to talk to us. Tell him all you know, and hopefully he will put the skids on the news until they check out the rumors. I told the other stations, that as far as I knew, it was a bar fight gone bad. I think I can hold them off for a day or two."

Thirty minutes later LT showed Lieutenant O'Riley into the room. He was used to reporters saying that they could not give out information about informers and was expecting the same old story. He was surprised when we laid out everything that Tracy knew about the man.

"So, you never met him except for the one time in Duluth, where you had a co-worker sitting at a table close by? In addition, you only talked to him by phone yesterday? That does not give us much of a lead to go on. I spoke to the coroner before I came over. He told me the body was dragged into the alley. It was not a bar fight. He was shot around 10:00 pm. The bar owner said there was no body in the alley when he closed up at 2:30 am. That gives us a small window for what may have happened.

"Did you have an address for the man?" O'Riley asked.

"Yes, I can look it up for you. It is on my netbook," Tracy answered.

"And, you said he called you yesterday? What time? Is it still on your phone?"

"Yes, Lieutenant O'Riley. Here, you can see it was 10:23 am."

"Good. I can have the phone company run a scan on that number, and get a fix on where our mystery man was yesterday morning when he called. That will give us a starting point for the investigation. Did Howard Long send you any information giving you a hint as to what he had found?"

"No, that was why I was anxious to meet with him. If he did have any information that no one had leaked to the public, I thought there might be a compelling story involved. When you check his house, will you let us know what you find?"

O'Riley nodded his head. "I'll let you know if you folks let me know everything you know."

I jumped into the conversation, "Lieutenant, unfortunately you know as much as we do. If there is some cover-up on the water deal, we need to keep it quiet until we are sure all the information is in our hands."

"OK, Martin. I'll keep it as a John Doe from a bar fight, until we check out his place, notify his next of kin, and feel like we hit a stone wall. I have a feeling someone did a good job of making sure Howard Long did not talk to anyone."

He thanked us for our openness and headed back to the police station.

LT turned to us and said, "OK, looks as though I'm helping the midnight crew for the next two days. Tracy, you run with this as hard as you can. Take Shawn with you. Tell him small gear. We don't need to advertise things any more than we have to. He has a good extra set of eyes. You can probably beat O'Riley to Howard Long's house if you use the chopper. Be there when he goes in. Martin, you sniff out the state. Secrets are hard to keep; someone must want to leak something. If it is there, find it. I'll pull the night crew into regular coverage for the next few days. We'll just run night coverage on an urgency level only.

"Remember, work together. Small leads can connect to something worth checking. I'll let Photo work with the night crew for the next day or two. Jake Schwartz is obviously out for at least four more

43

weeks, but maybe I can convince his cinematographer, Tim Baker, into cutting his vacation short and helping us coordinate from the desk. His busted rib will be too sore for fieldwork, but he might be willing to help us free up an inside person if we need someone. I'll call Tim, and talk to him informally."

We were given our marching orders. Obviously, LT thought there was something in this death worth pursuing also. It was not going to take too long for the other stations to get wind of it. As soon as we switched our assignments and the stations found other teams were showing up, someone would know we were looking for something.

* * *

A chopper, landing in a rural area near homes, would be too obvious, so Tracy and Shawn flew up to St. Cloud and borrowed a car from the local affiliate station. Then, they drove the 25 miles to the home of Howard Long. When they arrived, they found the local sheriff's deputy was already stationed at the end of the long blacktopped driveway. The house was just visible through the trees that lined the long driveway all the way to the three-car garage and rambler style house. Looking at the house, you could see that the owner was financially well off. The stone front of the exterior gave the appearance of a well-designed house on a lake in the middle of nowhere.

After introducing themselves to the officer, he told Tracy and Shawn, "You beat O'Riley by about two hours. You might as well make yourselves comfortable. O'Riley told me that he might have company and asked that no one be allowed to go in until he arrived. Heck, why didn't you just give him a ride up here with you?"

Shawn answered, "Thought about it. Unfortunately, except for certain circumstances, we are not allowed to get too close – you know, conflict of interest policies."

"Yeah! Think of all the time and money we waste making sure we follow policies."

"Did you check the house out?" Tracy asked.

"No one was home. Owner lives by himself. Didn't see a dog or anyone. Back door was open though. It looks like someone has been in there. Do I need to call the crime lab? O'Riley didn't give me a lot of clues on this one. He just told me to cover the house and he would be on the Link – have someone pick him up."

"If someone broke in, you might want to give O'Riley a hand and call the crime lab," Tracy told him. "The owner was shot last night."

"Thanks, now I can see why O'Riley wanted to check it out personally."

The three of them sat out on the end of a quiet dirt road for about an hour and a half before they saw a deputy's car coming down the road. While they were sitting listening to the radio, the news reported on a death of an unidentified man in Minneapolis overnight. It was reported as a probable bar confrontation taken out back. Tracy nodded to the sheriff's deputy indicating – "that's your man."

So far, Tracy had gotten a little information about Howard Long from the deputy. He had met Howard Long on a couple occasions when he was called that hunters were on Howard Long's land, and Howard had requested assistance asking them to leave. From what he remembered, Howard was a quiet man who did not seem to like confrontation. At least when it came to hunters, he preferred the sheriff's department handle it, rather than confronting the hunters himself.

When O'Riley got out of the car, he put a big smile on his face, "Figured you would get here before me. Where's your partner?"

"Left him in the Cities to help direct traffic since you weren't on the corner," Tracy answered.

O'Riley laughed. "OK, I earned that one. What do we have here?" he asked.

The deputy told him that he made a cursory check. "No one home. No dog. Back door is ajar. Tracy told me Howard Long was found dead in the Cities this morning, so I called the crime lab to see if we could find any prints."

"Good. Let's have a look around. Put gloves on. No sense making it harder for the lab than necessary. As soon as the lab arrives and gives us the go ahead, we can see if there are any clues left to explain why he was killed."

A regional crime lab truck arrived about an hour later. It was a good thing it was a lovely day. Sitting around outside waiting for the truck, we found an enjoyable distraction by watching the wildlife in the lake and in the trees. The ducks were flying in and out of the shallow areas. You could sense that they were getting ready for the fall migration. Even the squirrels were loading up their favorite hiding places with all the acorns they could find on the ground. The signs of fall were all over.

It took a couple hours for the lab to go through, checking for signs of blood, fingerprints, or footprints. Then, O'Riley was given the go ahead to enter without touching things. If a full search was needed, it would take several more hours.

The inside of the house was a mess. The person who broke in was obviously looking for something. The long built-in bookshelves were emptied, drawers opened, and everything was disturbed or trashed. Not the way to treat a beautiful house. It was what everyone had expected. No pages left open to point to a reason for the break-in. It was a thorough job.

"Be nice if we knew what to look for," O'Riley told Tracy.

"Yeah, he didn't make it easy to know if there is anything here or not. Did you pull a trace on the phone number?" Tracy asked.

"Yes. He called you from Minneapolis. Therefore, I don't think we are looking at his house as the crime scene, except for the break-in. It does tell me that whoever murdered him was searching for something extremely valuable as well. We'll let the lab do the full house. Doubt our intruders left us a print, but maybe we'll get lucky. If there is something left here, hopefully they can find it."

"Thanks for letting us look see," Tracy told him. "Give me a call if you find anything."

"Likewise," O'Riley told her.

Tracy and Shawn got into their car and headed back to return the borrowed car. They called Martin and told him what they had found.

"Well Tracy, what do you think? Dead end?" Shawn asked.

"Unfortunately, unless Martin can shake out some cobwebs in his searching, we probably will never know what Long discovered."

They picked up their flight to the Cities and arrived back at the station about 8:00 pm. LT met them when they arrived. "Looks like we called out the cavalry for a dead end," he told them.

"Sometimes the best fires get put out by one bucket of water," Tracy replied. "I take it Martin had the same results."

"So far. We'll keep snooping, but we need a lead to know which way to go. Looks like the compass is just spinning. Tomorrow, I think we will scale back. We can check out leads, but we'll have to go back to regular coverage," LT told them.

LT knew there was a story out there. However, without someone tipping them off, it would be too hard to find it on their own. At least for now, the killers probably thought everyone was buying the bar fight story.

Thursday morning, just as Tim Baker was planning to head back to work, at least office work, he got a phone call from LT. "Tim, good news. Your vacation plans are back on. Our leads hit a roadblock. This will give your ribs an even chance to get better, and probably make the insurance company happy that we did not interfere with your couple weeks off."

It was not what Tim was expecting. However, he had seen it before, where they scaled up for something important only to have it fizzle out right in front of their eyes. At least this time, LT told him before he got to the station.

Tracy spent the rest of the day with Shawn and Photo covering the news scene. LT had Martin spend one more day trying to find someone in the state buildings that did not like their job, and was willing to loosen a few tales. So far, no luck, just a few rumors about office romances in the government.

At supper, Tracy finally had a chance to meet the night crew. The previous attempt was aborted after the killing of Howard Long and the trip to Howard's house. They had burgers at a bar downtown. It gave them all a chance to ask: What was it that Howard Long was trying to tell them? The guesses were all over the map. To LT, it looked as though his patchwork quilt of crews had blended well, and until he got his regulars back, it would be business as usual for the station.

By Friday, it looked as though it was time to give up the ship. Lieutenant O'Riley had called LT and told him that the place had been wiped clean. The crime lab had not come up with a single clue from their all day search. He was not sure how long he could keep the story out of the papers, but for now, his Captain was willing to let it ride a few more days.

In the middle of the afternoon, Tracy, Photo and Shawn were following up on a bank robbery in one of the suburbs, Edina, when Shawn whispered in Tracy's ear, "Don't turn too quickly, but you see that guy over by the light pole. He was at the last location we were at also. I just checked the photo clips, and I have him in both locations. Think he is following us?"

Tracy gestured as if she was telling Shawn to get a better angle down the street and looked over by the pole. There, she saw a muscular man, about 40 years old, standing and observing all the police activity from the bank robbery. She turned back to Shawn, "You sure?"

"Yup! Same guy, both places."

Tracy turned to Photo, "You think you can drop your station gear and blend in with the crowd for an hour? How would you like to watch the guy by the pole from about 50-feet behind him? See if he gets in a car with a valid license number, or where he goes."

"No problem," Photo replied. Blending into the crowd is my specialty. I have done it all my life. He went back to the truck, took off his hat and news shirt, put on his everyday shirt and blended into the crowd, with only his small digital camera on his cell phone. So far, the man in the crowd had not noticed him. He was concentrating on watching Tracy and Shawn.

After about an hour, Tracy noticed that the man was gone. She saw Photo heading back from the truck with his regular gear on.

"What did you see?" she asked him.

"He was unquestionably watching you. I don't think he saw me at all. His eyes were glued on you wherever you went. I did get a few quality pictures, if that helps, a good side profile, even a front shot when he turned and went to his car. It was a black Chevy, license ARM-1139. Wonder what that was all about."

"I'm sure we will find out," Tracy told him. Keep an eye out for him, or anyone else that seems curious. I think a crowd shot at each place today might be in order.

The rest of the day, nothing seemed out of the ordinary. That is except for the events of the day. It felt as though it must have been Friday the 13th.

When they were done with the shift for the day, each of them was glad it was over. It had been a long day, and they were even happier to be heading home. That is until Tracy got home.

As she reached her townhome, she noticed that the door inside her garage to the townhouse was open slightly. She knew she had shut it when she left, because she caught her purse strap on the inside door knob and had to reach around to get it loose, before shutting the door. She decided to play it safe and back out of the garage, lock the doors and wait a few doors away, until someone could check out the place with her. She did not want any surprises inside.

"Martin, this is Tracy. Are you free?" she asked.

I was still on my way home and had just stopped at a stop sign. I was surprised by the call. Women usually did not call me at night, asking if I was free, especially good looking women I worked with. On top of that, with the new law, most of the time I get a beep on the phone, and I have to pull over to see what they want. This time, Tracy caught me sitting still at a stop sign, so I could answer it. "Yeah, I guess so. What's up?"

"I just got home and my door is open. Can you come over and make sure everything is OK?"

"Be there in five. Don't go in. Get away from the house and lock your car."

"Thanks, I have already done that. I'm parked 200-feet from my place, in my car. I'm not going anywhere. I'll wait here until you show up."

I spun my BMW around the corner and sped down the roads to an address LT had given me earlier in the week where Tracy would be staying. From LT's description, I knew roughly, which place was Tracy's. I was not worried about picking up a police car on the way. In fact, that might be preferable.

Chapter 7

Mysteries

The time it took Martin to get to Tracy's townhouse, seemed like an eternity to her. She kept the motor running, while checking all the windows to make sure someone was not hiding on the street and sneaking up on her car. Her imagination was running in high gear. All those late night movie scenes were flashing in her memory.

Tracy spotted Martin's dark-green BMW in the streetlights as it swerved sharply around the corner at a brisk rate of speed. It pulled up in front of her place and Martin got out. Tracy pulled her car up into her driveway, and got out of her car, walking over to Martin. "Thanks for coming. I just did not want to walk in and surprise someone inside."

"Are you sure you locked the door?" he asked.

"Positive. Think we should call the police?"

"Well, if we make some noise, anyone inside will run quickly. My guess is they were gone a long time ago. Let's just take a careful peek."

We walked in and opened the partially ajar door. Inside, it was obvious that someone had been there. They must have been looking for something. Things were scattered all over the place. Fortunately, the furnishings were not Tracy's.

"Looks like Howard Long's place," Tracy said. "Think someone thought that I had something?"

"Well, if they did, that means they do not have it either," Martin replied. "I guess it is time for you to call the police."

"Did you hear that we had someone we thought was watching us today?" Tracy asked.

"No! Tell me more."

"Shawn spotted him at a couple locations. Photo got his picture and license number," Tracy told him.

"Change in plans, we'll call O'Riley. I have his number on my cell."

Thirty minutes later, O'Riley pulled into the driveway. "Anyone call for pizza?" he shouted as he got out of the car. It was late, and he was dressed in street clothes. "Martin, you owe me for this one."

As he walked in, he turned to Tracy, "Anything missing?"

"Not that I can tell."

"That's what I figured. Someone thought you had Howard Long's information. That's good and bad. It means that you may be in danger until we solve this thing. It also means someone is running around looking for the information, besides us."

"We may have a lead for you," Tracy told him. "We saw someone following us today from one location to another. We got his picture and license number just in case."

O'Riley looked puzzled. "That was careless. First mistake they have made. Where is it?"

"Our cinematographer has it. I asked him to forward it to us. I'll have it shortly. What do you think?"

"He was probably watching you, while someone was helping themselves to your townhouse. You got somewhere else you can stay for a couple days?" O'Riley asked.

"No, not really," she answered.

"I can take care of that," Martin told her. "My father has a visitor's guest apartment available at his place. No one is going to go looking for you at an old folk's home. It is rarely used. I'll give him a call and see if he can get the key."

O'Riley turned to Tracy. "If you can keep the old timers from snoring, you will probably sleep better there until we get a handle on what is going on."

Tracy reluctantly agreed.

When I called my father, he was just finishing his card game with the gang. "You want me to do what?" he answered.

"This is no hotel, how do you expect me to get a key at this time of the night? You know most of the residents go to bed at 8:00 pm, long before you guys even write the news."

"Thanks Dad, I knew you would understand. Give me a call as soon as you wake up the night guard."

Fifteen minutes later, he called back. "Yeah, it's available. I told them that a relative just came to visit and they needed a room. They bought it."

Tracy quickly bagged up her clothes and followed my car to the home. O'Riley stayed at her townhouse to let his people check for prints and lock up.

When we got to the center, we slipped her car into a spot labeled "visitor" in the garage. Then, we went up to my father's room to get the key to the guest room. When he opened the door, he commented, "You did not tell me she was good looking. Heck, half my gang would have given up their rooms for her."

I knew I was in trouble from that point on. The next words out of his mouth to me would probably be "When you going to get married?" My father was always a little too direct.

The guest room was always ready for guests of the residents. It was fully furnished, and the only thing that was missing was a loaded refrigerator. I stole some extra things from my father's for the night – including a couple beers. I figured Tracy needed something to get her to relax and fall asleep after the events of the day.

Tracy checked out the room as she brought her suitcase inside the door. The carpet was the standard blah off-white used in all the rooms. However, the furnishing they used for the guest room had a sort of western look to it using the colors of the desert southwest, browns and turquoise. The fabric on the furniture and the throw rug both used this color scheme and it was followed through in the bathroom towels and bedspread in the bedroom. It actually looked warm and friendly. Definitely different from my father's room. Both rooms had their unique décor aimed at different requirements.

After settling her into her room, we sat and talked for an hour trying to figure out what was happening. One thing was obvious, there was a story out there looking for someone to find it. Tracy was still shaking from the experience.

The next morning, Saturday, LT called a meeting first thing. I picked up Tracy and we got there just in time for the meeting. LT had a terrific nose for stories, and this one was tingling every nose hair he had left.

"What's the report on the picture and the license number," he shouted.

"Rental car, rented to a fake ID.," I told him. "I called O'Riley on the way in and caught him in his car. He said he stayed at Tracy's place until midnight, with the crime lab. Place was as clean as Howard Long's. Someone was exceptionally good."

"What about the photo?" LT asked.

"Still running it through facial recognition. O'Riley said he put a push on it since it was their only clue to the whole thing."

"Stay on O'Riley, Martin. He knows you and will work with you. Tracy, we need to keep someone on you all day long. Whoever this nut job is, he may think you have the info he needs and try to get it from you. Shawn and Photo, new assignment: I want you two to cover Tracy like a blanket. Get crowd shots everywhere you go and one of you hold onto her elbow at all times. I know that will be a difficult task to ask of the two of you. They made one mistake, let's see if they are dumb enough to make another. Martin, if you need any photos at your locations, I'll send them over for a quick shot. Any questions?"

Tracy was still a little shaken by the thought of someone going after her. Under the circumstances, she was glad that LT told her crew to have Tracy as the priority. She also thanked me for coming over and getting her a place to stay.

I warned her, "The old gang at the home might be more of a menace to you than the bad guys." She laughed. It felt good for her to laugh and relieve some of the tension.

It was a quiet Saturday. Most of the action in town was usually saved up for the late crew on the weekends. Tracy did not mind. Her mind was racing fast enough all day, and wherever she went, she was constantly looking around to see who might be hiding behind a bush.

Unfortunately, they did not spot anyone trailing the crew. If they were, they knew enough to do it from a long distance. I suggested to Tracy that she leave her car at the home for the next few days. I could pick her up and drop her off using my father's fob for the garage, which I had programmed into my car. Once inside, no one would know which room, or where she went. If they were following me, they would think I was visiting my father. It made sense.

I took her home that evening and made sure she got into the garage under the unit without anyone following us. Since the parking place she was using was marked "Visitor," I had my father change spots with her. He met us downstairs, and Tracy moved her car into my father's parking place. When we got up to the floor, "the gang" was there to make sure Tracy got to her room OK. "Really, Dad. Isn't this a little much?"

"Can't be too careful. Besides, all the guys wanted to meet our new guest. Can't blame them. Well, as long as she is in 'your' arms, I guess we can go back to playing cards."

I gave my father a look. I knew what he meant. Well, with all the attention, if any stranger did come up to the floor, the gang would know about it. That was one consolation. It was not worth the effort to try to tell them that Tracy was just a co-worker.

After making sure Tracy was safe in her room, I headed back to my father's place. The card game was just breaking up.

"I thought you old timers went to bed at 8:00 pm. That's what my father has been telling me."

That got a chuckle out of them as they were going out the door. As the last one went out, he turned to me and said, "What's the matter, did she kick you out tonight, and you have to stay with your father?"

My father snickered. "In my days, a beautiful gal like that would not be worrying her little heart out by herself."

"Yeah, that's why she is here. She knows all you old timers would come panting if she even sneezes in her room. I think she knows she is safe," I told them.

"So, what did you come back here for?" my father asked.

"Need another favor," I told him. "Do you still keep in contact with Uncle Al?"

"Yes, once in a while we talk. Why?"

"His son is still in the FBI, isn't he? I need a favor."

Sunday was as slow as Saturday. When I picked up Tracy, we kept an eye out for anyone that might be following or observing our car too carefully.

The rest of the day, it was Shawn and Photo's turn to keep an eye on her.

About 2:00 pm, I got a call on my messenger. It was FBI Agent Mark Lawson.

"Martin, this is Mark Lawson, I got a call from my dad asking me to get in touch with you. How are you doing? I see you on the news every once in a while, so I know you are still kicking."

"Mark, thanks for calling. It's been a long time since we saw each other – perhaps 15 years?"

"About that. Last time I saw you, I threw you a pass and you caught it just seconds before an old oak tree jumped in front of you."

"Don't remind me. I still think you threw that intentionally toward the tree so you could steal the girl we were chasing. By the way, how is Linda?"

"She's terrific; I'll tell her that you still remember her. So what's the occasion?"

"Mark, I have a murder, two break-ins, a stalker, and missing link to a possible cover-up, and may need a little more firepower than the local police."

"My, you have been busy. Sounds like police work so far. Not sure I can just jump in."

Well, Mark, they are stalking one of our reporters and broke into her place the other day. She was going to meet with the dead man, just before he turned up shot. In addition, the files he said he had have turned up missing. The only lead we have is photos of the person who has been shadowing our female reporter."

"Like I said, sounds like police work. You know we can't just jump on their toes. Can you find me anything – like crossing state lines?" Mark asked.

"You know that water pipeline involving Canada, Wisconsin, and Minnesota. It appears it is the core in the middle of this mystery."

"That's a stretch. What do you need?"

"Well, Mark, like I said, we have a picture and a name of a dead man, Howard Long. What we need is a link between them or at least the name of the man in the picture."

"Can we keep it on the QT? At least, until you have someone ready to be arrested?" Mark asked.

"I'll even promise not to tell Linda about some of the wild times we had before you got married."

"Pushing it, Martin. Send me the name and photo. No promises. I'll see if we have a match."

"Thanks. You won't regret it."

"Already am Martin, already am. Say hi to your old man. Always liked him in spite of his son."

"Same to you. Take care."

I knew if I called Mark directly, he would have blown the situation off. However, having the request coming from our fathers, now that carried a little more weight. I knew the FBI's database was larger than the one at the police department, even though they always claimed to share all information. If nothing else, they had a more powerful computer for running a facial identification.

I did not mention it to O'Riley. If we got some information that was useful, I would have to find an excuse for Mark Lawson to share it with him.

After a few accident reports, and a report of a brawl after the football game, Sunday's log closed down early.

I met Tracy after she was done with her assignments, and we stopped off at a restaurant for dinner on the way home. It gave us a chance to relax and talk without all the hassles. It was hard to believe all this had happened in only one week.

We stopped at a steakhouse close to the home. It was quiet, as many of the regular customers had already left. There was an empty table in the corner and we talked as we slowly ate our meal.

It was the first time I actually had time to look into her eyes and see what they looked like. From the time she arrived, it had been one wild ride on a rollercoaster in the dark. Now, it felt like I actually had time to see what Tracy was all about. There were softer parts of her personality when she was not just a reporter digging out facts. I suppose she felt the same about me.

You would think the place was packed. The service was that slow, but we did not mind. We sipped on some wine and I started to know a little bit of her history. Tracy told me that she never wanted to go into journalism. Her teacher in high school forced her to help work on the school newspaper. After that, it just came naturally. She grew up in a small town in northern Minnesota, Ely. Went to the University of Minnesota in Duluth, and was hired right out of school by the local TV station to help cover local events. It had all been too easy. She had not been forced to move from one small town to another trying to break into a major station.

That was why, when the opportunity came along to take the short-term position in Minneapolis, she wasn't sure if she should leave. However, it offered her the opportunity to see the way a larger station covered an area, and would tell her if she wanted to pursue it, or go back to the smaller station. "So far, this feels more like a horror movie than a learning experience," she told me.

I tried to tell her that this was not the normal routine. "If you were in Duluth, it might have happened there. Howard Long was going to meet you at Grandma's Restaurant. What if you found him in the ship channel?"

"You are right. I can't let this block my vision. It is just hard when you wake up in the middle of the night, wondering about a creak in the floor."

"Well, if you're worried, I'm sure one of the gang would gladly sleep on your davenport and keep guard on the door."

"Thanks. But, who would wake them? They probably snore so loud that they can't even hear the fire alarm. No, I'll sleep better when and if we can put a finger on what is going on. I appreciate you having dinner with me. It gives me a chance to relax before heading back," she told me.

"Glad to do it. It gets lonesome at my place occasionally when we finally have a day off. Most of the time, I get home in time for a quick shower and six hours of sleep.

"Well, they must have finally found some road kill, here come our steaks."

The food was fabulous. The chef must have picked out a couple of their better steaks for us. We wondered if it was because they saw our TV logo on my shirt, and they were worried we might be there for rating their restaurant. They probably figured that if we got succulent steaks, we would give them a good referral.

We didn't leave until almost closing. During the time we were there, there had only been two other customers. Neither seemed interested in where we sat. Both of us were still a little overly on guard.

When we arrived at the home, I stayed until almost 11:30 pm. When I left, I gave Tracy a kiss on the cheek, and told her to sleep tight.

Monday morning came early. After picking up Tracy, we had a short meeting at the station before hitting the street. Still no news on our mystery man.

LT kept up the vigilance on Tracy. Until he had some word as to who was watching her, she had two people at all times.

We were busy all day. Normal busy. No new sightings, no phone calls from O'Riley, or from Mark.

By the end of the day, we were starting to wonder if the opportunities to crack this thing wide open had passed. It had been a couple days now without any new leads. If they were smart, they would just leave and go back into hiding.

I drove Tracy back to the home, and we ordered a pizza delivered to her room. It was a safer place to sit and talk, with the exception of the gang that was tracking everyone in and out of the floor, including me.

To get rid of them, I ordered two extra pizzas. I knew they were better than the ones they had at the Castle, and figured if I dropped them off at my father's place; the others would follow their nose directly to his apartment.

We spent the evening talking. She kept asking me questions about what it was like when I was growing up. It brought back some pleasant memories; including when my father and I used to go sit on the riverbanks and fish all day.

I stayed until after the evening news. Tracy liked the wall unit that was similar to my father's. She did not know that she could program it to have different pictures all day long. When I got up to leave, Tracy asked me if I had to go. She was enjoying the company. Regretfully,

I told her that I needed to get some sleep. She gave me a long kiss and said, "Thank you for the evening." It caught me by surprise. I wasn't expecting a long kiss.

I wondered all the way home, what if I had stayed longer?

Tuesday morning, when I picked her up, she gave me another kiss. "Just wanted to remind you that I enjoyed being able to sit and talk last night," she told me. That kept my mind spinning all morning.

It wasn't until 1:00 pm that my mind snapped back to attention. Mark Lawson called. He had been out of town yesterday and got back to the Minneapolis office late this morning. On his desk was a file on our mystery person – Luke Carpenter. Apparently, they had a hit on the facial recognition program, and traced him to a group of people who worked out of the state of Wyoming. They were mostly ex-military people that worked for a security firm, S&G Security, located there. The question was; what was he doing in Minneapolis, shadowing a reporter that had not been on the national news?

"Any word on a link to our dead man?" I asked.

"Working on it. You know it takes time. One little step at a time. The history you gave me on your dead man appears to be right on. Good credentials, well off, nothing I can see about him to lead you down a blind alley. If there was a file, I'd like to see it. He must have had something on someone. Give us a day or two."

"Thanks Mark. I'm not sure how to let O'Riley know about this."

"Sit on it. Until we get another link, he still has nothing to go on. Then, we can talk."

"OK, thanks again."

Well, we finally got a name to go with the face. My guess was that Mark was digging in deeper than he let me know. When I saw Tracy this evening, I could let her know the news.

61

Chapter 8

Packages

At the end of the day, while I was waiting for Tracy at the station, one of the mail boys came by and handed me a package.

"Can you give that to Tracy?" he asked.

"Sure, I'm waiting for her right now."

"Good, it looks like it has been all over the country," he replied.

I checked the package. It was addressed to Tracy Saunders, in care of her station in Duluth. Apparently, they had it for a couple days and then forwarded it to her here in the Cities. I assumed they heard she had changed addresses and figured it would be easier to send it to our station for her.

As I sat there waiting for her, I could not help but wonder what was in the package. Something she ordered from an online catalog? It probably wasn't something from a close friend. They would know she was in Minneapolis. On the other hand, perhaps they didn't.

When Tracy showed up, she gave me a smile and asked, "Well, what are you hungry for tonight? My treat. I feel a little more relaxed than I did last night."

I almost forgot the package that was sitting on the chair next to me. "How about Chinese?" I asked her. As I got up, I saw the package. "Oh, this came for you."

She looked for a return address, and not recognizing any names, tucked it under her arm as we left the station.

We picked up some food to go, and decided to eat it back at Tracy's. So far, the arrangements to use the guest room were working out OK, and the home had not insisted on her staying only three days. They would probably face a mutiny by the grey-beard gang if they insisted she move out.

Both of us were starving by the time we got back. We dove into the boxes like two hungry teenagers, who hadn't eaten in weeks. It had been a while since I had egg rolls. They tasted superb dipped in the soy sauce. The Szechuan Beef was a little spicy. It was a good thing that they packed a lot of rice with the meal. I guess that's what the asterisk meant that was on the menu. I was surprised that Tracy liked it. When I asked, she told me that her aunt got her used to spicy foods. Apparently, they would get together every couple of weeks for some rather highly seasoned foods.

We were almost done eating, when I mentioned, "Tracy, you're not like most of the other women I know. Most of them would have opened their packages long before they would stop to eat."

Tracy laughed. "Actually, I forgot about the package. I keep wondering why someone would toss my townhouse."

When we finished eating, she picked up the package and opened it. "I don't remember ordering anything lately," she told me.

As she opened it, her eyes opened wide. Inside the package was another folder with four folders and papers in each of them. There were no names, cards, or letter inside.

When we looked at the first folder, it was obvious. This was the information Howard Long was planning to give to Tracy. Somehow, he must have figured someone was following him, and, in his haste, stuffed it in a mailing envelope and sent it to the only address he had for her – the station in Duluth. It sat there until someone figured out where to forward the envelope to her.

We thought about calling O'Riley, but decided in the morning was soon enough. It would give us time to look through the information and see if indeed there was something wrong.

There were a number of pages that obviously were not put in the kind of order one would expect for a presentation. We had to look at each piece of paper, trying to figure out the puzzle Howard Long had just given us. It was almost like taking a jigsaw puzzle and throwing it up in the air. As soon as you can figure out the master picture, you can start putting the pieces together. The only problem – what was the picture he was trying to show us?

We spent an hour looking at the pages when I decided to tell Tracy about my conversation with Agent Mark Lawson. We had a name to go with the face. Now, we might even have a story.

We decided to call Mark. This looked more like FBI work than police work. His people could put the story together faster and more complete with the knowledge they had available.

"Mark, Martin here. Sorry to call this late, got a minute?"

"I told you that you needed to give me a day or two to research your dead man," he said grudgingly.

"Just thought you might like first crack at the dead man's files. They arrived in the mail today, and we have them in front of us right now."

"Like I said, I love talking to my favorite cousin whenever he calls. You got an address and some cold beer, so that we can look at these files?"

It didn't take Mark Lawson long to roll across town and into the home. The longest part was getting into the building and by the gang that met him at the elevator. The main door was not set up for visitors late at night. Unless you had a passkey, it took forever for someone to let you into the building. Once inside, Mark figured he would find the room easily.

However, when the elevator opened the door to the 3rd floor, he was instantly greeted by a couple of older men with gray beards. They wanted to know why he was on the 3rd floor. They were not about to let him pass without an explanation. This caught Mark by surprise. He wasn't expecting a grilling from a couple of old men.

I had forgotten to inform Mark, and he obviously was not prepared for our casual security detail.

Chapter 9

The Mystery Deepens

The files were a set of papers collected from several sources and not necessarily in any definite order. It was as though the sender had stuffed the papers in a file and mailed it immediately. That might have been exactly what Howard Long had done.

While we were waiting for Mark, I had taken the papers down the hall to my father's room, and used the new printer I had purchased for him. I was sure he would never make use of its capabilities, but I got a decent deal on a printer that would copy, scan, and transmit data.

I told him, I needed to copy something for work. He was involved in a TV show and just pointed to the printer. Ten minutes later, copies of the pages were all up-loaded to my storage.

"You spending time with our guest?" he asked.

"Just trying to keep her safe," I answered.

"Just wondering if you needed to bring her a bottle of wine?"

I looked at him. "Good idea. It has been a long day. She might need something to help her relax before going to bed. Thanks!"

As I was letting myself out the door, he stated, "Don't be late for work in the morning."

I got back to Tracy's room and showed her the bottle my father had sent over. I told her, I thought she might need something to take the edge off for getting a good night's sleep. I did not mention my father's comment.

A few minutes later, I heard Marks voice out in the hall, trying to explain that he was visiting a friend. I quickly opened the door and rescued Mark from my father's gang. I told them, it was OK. He was a friend of my father's as well.

Tracy got a chuckle out of all the commotion it caused in the hallway.

After Mark arrived, I introduced him to Tracy Saunders.

"Tracy, nice to meet you. It is always enjoyable to put a pretty face to a name," Mark told her.

Just like the old Mark I knew, always flirting with the girls.

I showed Mark the papers we found. As he shuffled through them, he was impressed. Howard Long had sent us a number of pieces of information.

When we sorted through the papers, and found some stories about the chemicals used to eliminate the Asian carp from the rivers. It was almost like looking back at old history. There were also some papers from some chemical companies and from mining companies in North Dakota. These looked like everything Howard Long could pick up in his history with the mining company. The question before us was; how were they related, and who did not want them to be found?

After spending over three hours sorting papers in piles by topic and by date, we had an idea of what Howard Long was trying to tell us. Just not why, or what to look for.

Mark figured that somehow Howard Long had found a link between the stable chemical used on the rivers, and why it became unstable and contaminated all the rivers. Nevertheless, that was only part of the story. It did not explain the other papers and why they were mailed to Tracy.

Since the chemicals were used by several states where the waters had become contaminated, the link gave Mark the lead he needed to claim FBI jurisdiction. He was relieved to find it. As bad as the contamination was, it did not appear to justify murder. There had to be other things in the papers that were more important.

"OK, looks like we found evidence of the smoking gun," he told them. "I am still concerned that someone was following you. We need to throw them a curve until we can figure out the whole story. I know it is late, but I think we need to get your old friend O'Riley up to date, and get his blessing to release some stories."

They put in a call to Lieutenant O'Riley.

He answered, "Yeah, this better be good this late in the evening."

"Sorry, this is Martin Berman and Tracy Saunders; I also have FBI Agent Mark Lawson here. We found some information and Agent Lawson wanted to include you in seeing what we found."

"Oh, OK! What have you found?"

"Hi, O'Riley, this is Mark Lawson. Apparently, your dead man, Howard Long, mailed a package to Duluth just before he was killed. The station up there sat on it for a day or two, then mailed it to Tracy. She just got it this afternoon. When we looked at it, it looked as though Howard Long felt there was some connection between the river contamination and the pipelines. I'm not sure why it involved murder, but I am hopeful we can find the leads.

"I need a favor. I want to throw a curve at whoever it is that is following Tracy. They think she has the information. Let's change the ballgame. I think we should let them think she has all kinds of information, and it was turned over to the FBI. That should make her safe and get someone truly worried about what we have.

"It might take a few weeks to figure this whole thing out, and I do not want someone else getting murdered in the meanwhile."

"OK! I see your point. You are hoping to catch their tail, so we could find out who was involved," O'Riley told them.

"I ran the photos that Tracy had. We found him. He works for a security outfit out of Wyoming – S&G Security. If we let them think we do not have any leads, we can tap their phones and see what else they are doing."

"OK. What do you want me to do?" O'Riley asked.

"Let's release the name of Howard Long, and put in there that a package was received by the FBI that appears to have been sent just prior to his death. That ought to get a few phone calls moving."

"No problem. I'll put out a news blurb right now. Anything else?"

"No, I just wanted to make sure you were not feeling left out of the loop. Give me a couple hours before you send the blurb out. I need to put a monitor in place. I'll give you a call in a day or two and we can sit down and go over the information we pulled from the papers. They are a real mess. Looks like he dropped them, and then stuffed them in the envelope in a big hurry."

"Alright, thanks. I'll look forward to seeing what you have." With that, O'Riley hung up.

"That should keep him from getting mad that you called me," Mark told Tracy and me. "OK, if I take the papers and try to sort the facts out of them?"

"Can we get a copy?" Tracy asked.

"Yes, but for your safety, lets hold off on the copy until we know someone is not going to trash your apartment again. Right now, we have them guessing. I'm hoping there might be a clue in here as to where additional information is hidden."

I did not tell Mark that I had scanned the papers, and had them in my private storage bank on the internet. He was right; we did not want any copies left in Tracy's room for someone to get their hands on.

We thanked Mark Lawson for coming over so quickly. As he left, we still did not know what was actually in the notes. He told us, he would keep us up to date. It felt like we had just handed over the keys to a brand new car without ever getting a chance to drive it.

After Mark left, I turned to Tracy and said, "Think you are awake enough to take a short look at those papers? I was not about to give him the only copy."

She gave me a smile. "How about a glass of your father's wine, while we start attacking all those files?" she replied. "Every time I think of finding Howard Long in the alley, it makes my stomach churn. Doesn't it bother you?"

"Well, if I had met with him, and he was bringing me information, I would probably feel that way too. I guess I've gotten used to most of the killings we report on. Some of the gruesome killings, and when there is a child involved; now those are much harder to forget. They take a while."

While Tracy found two glasses, I set up the wifi attachment on my tablet, so we could download the images from my data storage bank, located on the internet on a massive public storage area called the cloud, and projected the images in the large TV/video unit on the wall.

The FBI would probably have a team of people working with a fine-tooth comb, looking for key words and theories. For us, the best we could do would be to put up four pages at a time on the wall and see if they were related. The question was where to start. Which page was meant as the beginning of the story?

We looked at page after page, trying to sort out the verbiage and trying to find the probable links. About 3:00 am, after looking at each page three times and finishing off the wine, Tracy and I decided that our eyes could not take it much longer. Scanning between the pages was much harder than I thought. I kept hoping to find some hidden page numbers.

However, the longer I looked at the pages, I started to realize that this was not the conclusive report that Tracy was hoping for. It was just a teaser that Howard Long was bringing to her, to show her the areas on which he had additional data. The water shortage was only one of several topics covered. Now, the question was, how were each of these topics related, and where was the supporting data that Howard Long claimed to possess?

Finally, our eyes were getting so blurry that we knew it was time to call it a night. I turned to Tracy, and said, "Think it is time to call it off until tomorrow?"

"I suppose you are right. I was hoping we could solve this thing before the FBI and police did. I genuinely hoped that Howard Long had mailed everything to me in the envelope."

"So did I. Maybe, with some sleep, we can find a clue to what else is hidden in the pages; just do me a favor, don't tell the press about the pages."

"Martin, aren't we the press?"

"Yes, I just always wanted to say that instead of hearing it from someone else."

Tracy laughed. "You want to sleep here since it is so close to morning?"

"Aren't you afraid that your security gang is still waiting for me to leave?" I asked her.

"I think they are probably sound asleep by now." With that, she leaned over and gave me a kiss. "Thanks for all the help this week. You're right, if I got this package up in Duluth as Howard Long had planned, I'm not sure what would have happened."

Now I wished we had stopped earlier in the evening. The alarm would go off way too soon. I was starting to enjoy working with Tracy. I was not sure if it was my father's wine or not, but right now, I was not going to argue about the invitation to stay the night.

"You have an extra pillow I can use on the sofa?" I asked.

"I think the bed is a lot softer," she gently replied. She was right.

We were both dead tired. I think I fell asleep while Tracy was talking to me.

My cell phone went off at 8:00 am Wednesday morning. It was LT. Fortunately, we had just gotten up and were awake – well sort of.

LT had just seen the wire about Howard Long by O'Riley and wanted to know what was going on. He thought we had an agreement about not releasing his name. I filled him in on the details of last evening, and how we now had Mark Lawson from the FBI working with us.

"You sure Tracy is safe at the senior center?" he asked.

"Right now, I think she is well protected." I told him. "How is the action this morning? Can you cover things, while we take one more look at the papers?"

"I thought you said you turned them over to the FBI?" LT commented.

"You know me better than that. I scanned them first. Don't tell anyone. We looked at them until our eyes were bugging out last night. If things are quiet, it would be nice to take a second look this morning."

"OK, I'll call if things get heated. Maybe I can use the day as an excuse to see how well Shawn has trained Photo. If I go with them on a couple calls, I should be able to see if we want to keep him around or cut him loose at the end of his internship. I'll call you around noon."

"Thanks LT; I'll let you know if we find some clues."

I did not let LT know that I had slept over at Tracy's last night. I decided that I should get a change of clothes out of my go-bag, along with my razor and tooth brush, and clean up at my father's place. I could probably borrow some eggs for breakfast at the same time. It would give Tracy a chance to take a shower before I returned. As I slipped out of the apartment, I gave her a kiss and whispered, "Thanks for letting me stay last night."

As I walked down the hall, I was met by one of my father's friends – Hank. "Have a good time last night?" he asked as I tried to quietly slip into the elevator.

I could see from the twinkle in Hank's eye that he was looking for a reaction from me. Since I really did not want to get into a long discussion about it, I just gave him a smile. I figured he could fill in the words.

When I picked up my clothes and went to my father's apartment, my father was waiting for me. "I figured that apartment of yours was too far to drive last night," he said. "Well, did you have a good time? Hank told me you spent the night."

I explained to him that we looked at papers until 3:00 am. Then, when we could not focus on them anymore, we fell asleep.

"OK, that accounts for from 6:00 to 7:00 am," he answered. "What about the other hours?"

I did not answer. Whatever I said, I knew it would just dig the hole deeper. "Can I use your bathroom to clean up? Oh, also, do you have a few eggs I can borrow?"

"You want them served too?" he replied. "Actually, I don't have any eggs. I usually meet the guys for breakfast; that is when we are not on guard duty. Want me to have one of them pick up a couple plates of eggs and bring them up?"

"You think they would?"

"Well, not for you. However, for the cute gal, I think they would consider it," he shot back at me.

"OK, thanks Dad. I owe you for this one."

By the time I had shaved, brushed my teeth and changed into some clean clothes, there was a knock on the door. "Room service," one of his gray-bearded friends said as he opened the door.

I looked. He had two heaping plates of eggs, sausages, fruit and a roll.

"Sorry, I ran out of hands to carry two glasses of orange juice," he told me. "I'll go back for them and bring them to your hideaway."

After thanking him, I took the plates back to Tracy's room. When she opened the door and saw all the food, she smiled.

"Dad's friends wanted to make sure you were not hungry," I told her. A few minutes later, our orange juices arrived.

I enjoyed sitting and talking to Tracy as we ate our breakfast. It was a lot better than grabbing a roll and coffee on the run.

We started in on the papers again after we finished eating. There just had to be something in them that was meant as a lead for us to pursue. If Howard Long knew someone was after him, and quickly put these in the mail, he must have wanted to leave a clue for us to follow.

After an hour of looking at the same pages, I asked Tracy, "Do you have the envelope that they came in? I don't remember giving it to the FBI."

"Yes, I think I threw it in the corner. Want me to look?" she answered.

Tracy searched through some trash in the corner and came back with a crumpled up yellow envelope. "Is this what you're looking for?" she asked.

As I checked out the envelope, I noticed that there was no return address. On the opposite side of the envelope, was a possible address: Starlight 0643A, St.Cloud. I showed it to Tracy. "That's not his address is it?"

"No, the address we checked out earlier was a rural route number. What do you think it is? Think he had a second address?" she asked.

I grabbed my cell. After doing a search for Starlight, I got a long list of hits. Then, for the fun of it, I combined it with "storage." It came up with a cloud server, which you could pay to have data stored on-line on the internet. Ten years ago, all that information would have all been stored on the hard drive on someone's laptop. "I think I've got it," I told her. "I think Howard Long gave you the address of his storage location and made it look like a return address."

We grabbed my netbook and typed in the server. Now, what was the password? I looked at Tracy, "Any ideas?"

This was going to be harder than finding the server. We tried several easy things – no luck. Initials, parts of names, project names, none of these worked.

We were about to give up and call Mark Lawson at the FBI, when we tried, St.Cloud. Just the word as written on the envelope, with no space between the period and the "C." To our amazement, it worked. We were in!

The question was, in to what?

Chapter 10

Clues

Tracy and I decided that we would scan through the information before letting the FBI or police know what we had found. Hopefully, Howard Long left us a clue.

The server had a number of files on it. We opened them one by one, hoping that somewhere Howard had left a compiled letter explaining how everything was related. So far, it looked as if everything was in Howard Long's head. He had a lot of data that was an expanded version of what we had looked at last night. It was going to take hours to put it all together.

Actually, I was not as upset as I could be. It would be a legitimate excuse to spend more time with Tracy. If it was too easy, we could have wrapped this up over the weekend. Just to be safe, I copied the files to my server on the cloud. It would be safe there just in case someone found Howard Long's notes somewhere else. Then, I called LT.

"LT, Martin here. We found something. When we looked at the pages, we could not find any links. However, in Howard Long's haste to mail the pages to Tracy, he left a clue on the envelope. It looked like a return address, but it was an address to an on-line storage. We figured out the address and password. It has about fifteen folders in it."

"Great! Did you figure out the mystery?" he asked.

"Well, that's the hard part. We haven't had a lot of time to search. So far, I was looking for a summary or something tying it all together. If the clue is there, it is well hidden. I think we just went from 30 pages to 300 pages. However, it is progress. How are you doing?" I asked.

"Slow morning. So far, I'm handling things. If you need the rest of the day to put it together, I think I can handle it. Just stay close to the cell."

"Thanks, LT. We'll stay close to the car if you need us."

"Make sure you keep Agent Lawson in on your information. I don't want them mad that we hid information from them."

"I'll give Mark a call," I told him.

Tracy asked if we could look at a few more of the files before we called Agent Mark Lawson. There had to be some links, and she was determined to find them. The files had a lot of detailed information on each of the events in the original envelope. We started with the file on the poisoning of the rivers. Maybe that one had a link to the proposed pipeline. Maybe not!

After spending over an hour on the one file, I decided I better call Mark Lawson and let his people work on it from his end as well.

"Martin, good to hear from you. Got another crumb for us to look at?" he answered.

"As a matter of fact, I think I have a few loaves of bread for you to assemble."

"Oh, that does not sound easy," Mark said, "what do you have?"

I told him about the envelope and the on-line server. As I gave him the address and the password, he typed it into his computer. "Wow, you hit the jackpot, congratulations. Exactly what do we have here?" he asked.

"That's the problem. We're not sure. I was hoping your boys could tell us."

"Well, I hope we find something quickly," he said. "It is going to be hard to justify a lot of hours without telling someone what to look for."

"We understand. Let us know if you find a key to the whole event." I thanked him for the time and effort.

When we finished talking, Tracy mentioned, "I think I might have found some information that might be part of the story."

I leaned over. "Let's hear it."

"Well, your father might be right about the rivers. There is a section in the report about the elimination of the exotic fish from the rivers. To prevent their spread, it said that the DNR suggested a number of things to slow them down. Unfortunately, the EPA and the legislature did not react quickly. By the time they reached any agreements, it was almost too late. The methods were like putting a plug in a dam five minutes before the ground below it gave way.

"According to the report, the DNR came up with the idea of poisoning out the rivers. It took almost three more years before the Department of Natural Resources of the other states involved, and the EPA, all agreed to the same solution.

"Then, at the last minute, the state legislature insisted on a cheaper, less tested equivalent chemical.

"I guess the outcome is well known by now. The chemical did not break down as quickly in the water as claimed. It had residual effects."

"OK, that I understand. What's the link that would get Howard killed for the information?" I asked Tracy.

"I'm not sure. I did see some names in the report. The one that stood out was Senator Bill Epstein. Apparently, he was in the state legislature at the time and was on the committee that approved the procedure."

"Yeah, him and probably nine to fourteen others on the committee. Besides, no one held them to being the experts. The manufacturer was ultimately held responsible for the problem, as I remember."

Tracy went on, "There is a lot of chemical jargon in here about the chemicals used and why the chemical did not biodegrade as quickly as it was supposed to. I'm not a chemist, so if there is something pertinent here, we will need an expert in the field to tell us."

"That sounds like Mark Lawson's people," I told her. "What else is there?"

"I don't know. It took that long just to figure out that information. I think we need to keep a flow chart as to the events, dates and names to see if there are any links," Tracy suggested.

It sounded like something you would see on a television show, where the crime scene investigators had this whole wall full of information, and strings drawn between the links of information and suspects. I sent Mark Lawson a text message with the information we found so far. It might give him a starting point to find the next link.

Tracy and I took a short break before working on the next folder, so we decided to take a walk around the courtyard to get a change in scenery. As we opened the door, I saw my father sitting on a folding chair down the hall.

"What are you doing? Taking turns watching us?" Tracy asked.

"Just doing our job. You know, there's not a lot of excitement around this place. You have to grab your chances."

"Thanks, Dad. I appreciate all you and your gang have done. We're just taking a short walk to stretch our legs," I told him.

We went downstairs and out into the courtyard. It was a mild afternoon, and the building blocked the wind from the courtyard. With the sun shining off the buildings, it was probably ten degrees warmer in there than in front of the building.

Tracy asked, "Martin, do you get cases like this very often here?"

"No, thank goodness. I've seen cases where someone was going to give the police some information, only to turn up dead. But, this is a first for me. Definitely takes you out of your normal frame of mind."

"That's for sure," Tracy told me. "I wonder how the police deal with it all the time."

"I think that's why they have shrinks on their payroll. I would rather report on the problems than get in as deep as they do. Think how they must feel when they have to let someone go that they are sure just killed someone."

"It was nice of your father to change his routine and get this place for me," she told me.

"I'm sure your folks would do the same."

"They died about seven years ago in a plane crash, in Africa," Tracy said. "They were visiting a mission and the small plane they were riding in crashed."

"I'm sorry. I didn't know."

"I wouldn't have expected you to. It is nice to see the relationship you have with your father. In fact, his whole gang has been great to us."

As we were walking, Tracy turned to me and suggested, "We should do something for them to show our appreciation. Got any suggestions?"

"When we get back, I'll talk to my father. Maybe we can have some delicious food delivered in, and they can eat it at my father's apartment. He has more room than you do for sitting."

When we got back to the room, after talking it over with my father, I ordered in chicken Kiev dinners from a local restaurant along with a couple of pies. I figured their special pies would buy us a couple more days of protection and leverage with the senior center for staying there. No one was going to argue with a bunch of old men about staying a few more days.

We spent the afternoon looking at the file on North Dakota. What was so significant about that file, that Howard Long had included it in the envelope and had a large file on the server?

It was long and tedious work. There were several articles, which he had copied about drilling for oil in western North Dakota. What that had to do with water in Minnesota was a mystery. They started about 2001, about the time Howard Long had gone to work for one of the companies.

To get the oil out of the ground, they had developed a method of injecting the layers with either water or a gas, to force the oil out of the substructure and into the pipes. The methods he described worked remarkably well and cut the cost of the operation considerably.

Due to the massive amounts of water needed, they had looked for an alternate method to push the oil out of the formation. The alternates they found were using some of the excess natural gas, and injecting carbon dioxide, CO_2, into the ground.

There were a number of technical papers on each method along with reviews by the EPA, Department of Energy, and DNR. They were a little above our pay grade for understanding all the terminology. However, it did give us a starting point for another flow chart, list of names, and a question mark between this one and the water problem.

Perhaps, there was something there in the reason for changing from water to a gas, other than requiring too much water. We made our chart.

At dinnertime, we joined my father and his gang at his apartment. It was a little cozy, so we took the chairs from Tracy's apartment and made do. Everyone enjoyed the food. It was a break from the standard meals served by the center.

Hank was the only one that did not load up on the vegetables that were included. When Tracy asked him if he wanted more, he told her, "I'm saving room for the other odor in the room."

His nose was right; it was the pies that finished off the meal. We had ordered a lemon and an apple pie. To the lack of our surprise, the decision of the day was whether to have hot apple pie with ice cream or lemon pie. It looked as though we might have to draw straws for the pieces of apple pie until Tracy finally ended the argument. She ended up cutting the pies into small pieces so everyone could have a piece of each. It left everyone happy and full.

When we were finished, everyone wanted to know what we were doing, other than sleeping together last night.

Tracy blushed. "It's not what you think." Then, she told them that she could not say very much about it. We did not want the information to get out about what we knew and did not know. They understood, but were still curious.

I told them that a guy was murdered trying to get us information about the proposed pipeline. I also told them that he said he had information we should know about regarding the poisoning of the rivers. So far, we had not found a link between them.

"How can you not find a link?" my father asked us. "If you kill the fish, don't you think there is probably something in the rivers that could kill people?"

"Maybe," Tracy answered, "but why didn't they spot the problem years ago? If that was the problem, you would think they would have started the pipeline ten years ago. I think it was tested, and they felt it was safe for humans."

"They said you could fish the rivers the next year too, didn't they?" my father responded. All of his friends agreed.

They had a point, but it did not explain the North Dakota link or why Howard Long had to be killed. There had to be something more. We did not want to give them too much information that might get spread to everyone in the center. Neither Tracy nor I knew all of them well enough to know if they would keep a secret.

After dinner, I called Mark Lawson to see if he had found any links. I was hoping he would shed a little light on the chemistry and technical information.

"Mark, Martin here, any news?"

"You don't give a guy a lot of time to work, do you?" he answered. "I have two guys working full time on it. Hopefully, they can find a lead before I have to cut them back.

"We started tracking all the names in the files. So far, we have a number of hits."

"Good!" I told him.

"No, not so good," he replied. "The reason they were hits was that they were linked to the obituary pages. We are trying to find the reasons for their deaths, but it takes a day or so. I can tell you that one person, from your North Dakota oil file, was in a car accident. Another, a fellow who worked with the coal industry in one of your other files, died of unexplained causes. There are at least four others. I have people tracking them down."

"You think that Howard Long figured out their deaths?" I asked.

"Don't know. They might all be explainable. He might have been researching their deaths just like we are, and that was why they were in his reports. On the other hand, it might just be a coincidence that they died. Just don't know."

"How about the technology?" I asked.

"Yeah, it's a little above my education also. I have someone looking at it. Let you know if she finds something."

"OK, thanks. I'll give you a call if we see anything also."

The conversation had been short. Perhaps others had been killed over the information, and not just Howard Long. Was there a link to the company in Wyoming that was watching Tracy?

We had not noticed anyone watching her since we moved her into the center.

Maybe they had simply not found her yet.

Chapter 11

The Missing

I called LT and filled him in on the day's progress, or lack of it. I was surprised that he did not give me a long discussion about him having to give up a day to be out in the field. Apparently, he enjoyed the change in routine. However, he wanted to make sure that I was back on the job tomorrow.

When we discussed the possibilities that there might be other suspicious deaths, LT agreed that Tracy could work out of her apartment tomorrow to see if she could find any more links in Howard Long's papers. If would be safer than having her out on the street, at least until the FBI could check out the dead people on their lists.

LT agreed that if someone was following her, they probably lost her in the move. As a result, he suggested that I would have to make sure it was obvious I was visiting my father, and not someone else. They might be watching my apartment trying to see if I would lead them to Tracy. With the word on the street stating that the victim had been identified as Howard Long, they would probably be more careful in letting someone see them.

That evening, Tracy and I worked until just before 10:00 pm on the files. Then, Tracy suggested that we could watch the evening news, and if I wanted, I could stay at her place until morning. With all the talk about dead people on the lists, she really wanted the company.

I certainly did not mind the idea. I had wished I could have spent more time with her last night. So, I agreed.

Thursday morning, I got up early. I needed to head back to my apartment, clean up, repack my go-bag, and put in a full day's work. LT had been courteous enough to give us some slack. However, I could feel the pressure that he wanted me back on the turf, and him in his office. At least Tracy was getting the opportunity to check out a few more of the files we discovered.

As I pulled into my apartment garage, I checked around for anyone that might be watching. So far, so good. It looked clear. If anyone did see me, with my bag in hand, they might have thought I just got back from an out-of-town assignment. I repacked my bag for several days, just in case. I think it was wishful thinking.

When I got to the station, LT had both cinematographers join me for the day. His day with Franklin Wahlbusher – Photo, went good. He decided that he would evaluate him again after a few weeks. For the meantime, he wanted one person shooting the crowds every place I went. If someone was watching, he wanted to catch their image.

Our first assignment was to report on a new set of laws that went into effect three months ago. Six months ago, the legislature was so upset by the way people were driving that they insisted on some severe measures to either get the public to change their driving styles, or be forced to lose their license.

The first of the laws concerned people talking on cell phones while driving. To fix the problem, they appointed a commission that came up with an easy fix. The police and the legislature had been trying to limit the cell phone use in cars and trucks for the past 15 years. It was determined by the legislature that all cell phones had GPS's built into them, since just before the year 2000. Finally, the commission settled on a simple upgrade of the cell's software, which could be done on line. You could program the cell such that it did not work, except to beep, if it was moving faster than 5-mph. A federal law was passed forcing all companies to reprogram their phones.

As a result, for the past three months, people in cars could not talk or text from their moving cells. It was time to get reactions now that the heated arguments were over.

The second of the laws was a state law adopted by the federal government. The no-cell law would help because too many drivers were ignoring the laws, and accidents were way up. However, the legislature wanted to eliminate the bad drivers, and if it would cut down the number of cars on the road, it might help congestion, as well.

The new law that was passed three years ago, so that car manufacturers could make the necessary changes, would require tickets for breaking laws such as not making a full stop for a stop sign and speeding. It was combined with not using turn signals, drinking and driving, and not giving pedestrians the right of way. As part of the law, sensors were implanted at intersections and on roadways that sent a signal to the cars computer, telling it if there was a stop sign or what the speed limit was. If the car was speeding or not stopping for a stop sign, the communication monitor would use a picture phone to send a picture of the driver and the car's ID to the police department. It prevented caravans of cars and trucks from ignoring the speed limits. Now, the drivers would automatically be issued a ticket. It would assist the cameras already installed on the roads.

To put some teeth in the law, drivers were allowed only two tickets before their license was revoked for six months. Then, if you got two more tickets, it was revoked for five years. If they were spotted driving on a revoked license, it was an immediate year in jail.

As a result, driving styles changed overnight when the bill became law. Accidents went down as well.

This morning, our job was to interview random drivers about the changes. We would catch people either at stop signs or at parking areas, and get their opinions about the new law, and how it affected driving.

Photo and Shawn Peterson traded off shooting the person interviewed and randomly shooting the crowds.

By noon, we had completed ten interviews and were off covering other events. When we reviewed the crowd photos, we were not able to spot any reoccurring observers.

Surprisingly, most of the interviews were positive. Some people had argued that cameras should not take random pictures without the owner knowing it. However, the public had noticed the improved driving habits, even though everyone wanted the improvements in someone else and not in their own driving.

As I was finishing the piece for the news, I thought about the other night when Tracy called and said someone was in her townhouse. I'm sure I was caught on several cameras. Hopefully, the law allowed for emergencies and the press covering events. I had a feeling I would find out in a few days.

I gave Tracy a call to see if she had any additional successes. She told me that Agent Mark Lawson had called her and asked her a few more questions about her discussions with Howard Long. In the process of the conversation, he mentioned that the person that had followed me after Howard's death, Luke Carpenter, was found dead in Wyoming.

Coincidence? Maybe, maybe not. He was checking on it. He suggested that I keep low for a couple more days.

I told Tracy I would bring dinner after my shift. She reminded me to watch out for anyone watching me. When I finished the call, I called LT and told him the news about the man from Wyoming.

"My nose is still twitching about this case," he told me. "As much as I need her in the field, I'm not going to ask her to stick her neck out. I promised her boss I would take care of her. Think you can handle things," he asked.

"Yes, as long as Tracy is checking out leads, she is still productive to us," I told LT.

"OK, keep me informed. Oh, O'Riley called for you. I told him, you would get back to him."

"Thanks. I'll let you know if anything new comes up," I told LT as I wondered what O'Riley had discovered.

I gave O'Riley a quick call.

"Martin, thanks for getting back to me. One of the officers caught me in the hall today. He knew that we worked together on projects. He said your name was on a list of traffic violators. Apparently, you were speeding the other night. Just wanted to let you know that I took care of it. I explained the circumstances to him."

"Thanks Lieutenant, I owe you one for that one."

"Just help me solve this murder," he replied.

"Working on it. Got the FBI looking into a few more murders that may or may not be related. Heck, you might get a promotion over this thing if we can ever figure it all out."

"Remember to keep me informed so that I'm not the last to know," he said.

"I promise."

At the end of the shift, I stopped at a different restaurant and picked up takeout. I did not want to be caught in a pattern. After I left, I made four right turns – went around the block to see if anyone was following me. When I was sure it was clear, I drove over to my father's place and into the garage. Then I took the food up to Tracy's apartment.

My father's chair was occupied by one of his friends. I waved as I got off the elevator and headed toward Tracy's apartment.

When I reached her door, she greeted me with a smile and a kiss. "Thanks for bringing supper. It is nice to have company."

That got my heart pumping. Yes, I could get used to this kind of treatment. "Do you always greet men at your door with a kiss?" I asked her.

"Only if they come bearing gifts," she answered.

We had sweet and sour pork for supper. Somehow, it tasted better than the last time I had picked it up. Even the egg rolls were fresh tasting. When we finished eating, Tracy showed me what she had discovered.

Agent Lawson had given Tracy just enough information on Luke Carpenter that she was able to find an article on the internet about his death. It was simply a death notice, so she used her reporter skills and contacted the funeral home that had submitted the obituary.

The mortician gave her the information about the cause of death and police officers involved in the investigation. It gave Tracy the leads she needed to follow up on Luke Carpenter's death.

The official cause of death was a blow to the head caused by a fall. The investigators concluded that Luke Carpenter was hiking on a remote trail in Wyoming, and either tripped, or slipped, causing him to lose his balance and hit his head. He was found by another hiker, and the coroner determined that he had been dead for about two days prior to them finding him. Only a couple photos were taken, and they were in the file. The officer who wrote the report informed her that an Agent Lawson had contacted him also about the case. "He asked me if I knew what the special interest was in a hiking death. He is going to email me the report as well as the photos."

As she said it, she glanced at her cell. "I guess he did. I see I had a message from him."

"You didn't tell him why you were interested in him, nor where you were, did you?"

"Not a chance. As far as he knows, I'm still in Duluth."

"Good. Too many people showing up dead for my liking," I told her. "I just hope one of Carpenter's enemies doesn't find out you contacted the funeral director."

We looked at the report and photos. There was nothing in the report showing the exact rock Luke Carpenter hit that caused his death. All we could see was a gash on the side of his head.

"Can't rule out murder based on this report," I told Tracy.

"I hope your Agent Lawson is as good as you think he is," she answered. "If not, I might need a lot more of your protection."

"Maybe I can ask Mark to go on vacation for a week. That way I can give you my personal protection a little longer," I told her. That got a wink and a smile.

I told Tracy about my conversation with O'Riley, and suggested that we forward the report about Luke Carpenter to him. "We need to have him feel like he is in the loop. Besides, I think he will be a little more concerned about your well being after seeing the report."

We sent it off to both O'Riley and LT.

Tracy and I spent the rest of the evening going over documents from North Dakota. The flow chart was starting to get filled up, and we still had several other folders to cover. As we were looking at one of the pages, I called my father to touch base.

"You didn't need to call," my father told me. "I know where you are." His gang had kept track of all movements in and out of Tracy's apartment.

"Thanks Dad. I just wanted to say hi. We're still working on this case."

"It's not the case I'm worried about. Don't forget to get some sleep."

"Working on it, Dad. Just knock if you need anything."

When I hung up, Tracy asked, "Is your dad OK with my staying here?"

"As long as you give them a smile each day, you're gold."

We worked the North Dakota file forward and backwards. There was information in there about the waterflood they were using to extract the oil from the formation. The oil was located deep below the water table, so contamination of the drinking water should not have been a problem. Several wells in the area were checked periodically to make sure there was no evidence of increased levels of hydrocarbons in the water supply.

This went on for over three years. Apparently, all the reports submitted to the EPA were within agreed tolerances. However, Howard Long had copied a report showing some increased levels of contamination. It was in some of the wells in the waterflood area as well as a few wells where gas was being injected.

Tracy and I were unsure whether this information had been sent to the EPA, or whether the EPA had excluded the information. It was something we could follow up on later.

After a few documents, we found a seismology report for the area. It showed that the area had only minor tremors. We figured this report was required to prove that the waterflood was not putting undue pressure on the rock structure causing earthquakes.

It was a lot of technical data. Without knowing what we were looking for, it was like trying to find a needle in a haystack. Only, in North Dakota, that haystack would probably be blowing in the wind.

We quit just before the 10:00 pm news. I wanted to see how my report on the new traffic laws looked. It was a perfect time to quit. Tracy was starting to see spots from all the data she had looked at today. They ran the story right after the national news.

"Wow, you got some great interviews," Tracy told me.

I was trying to figure out if she was genuinely impressed or just trying to make me feel good. However, she was right. Most of the people were in a pleasant mood and did not mind talking on television. The story was just what the department of transportation wanted. It justified the fight they had run for several years to get the laws enacted. It was astonishing that they could not get it done earlier. It seemed like the special interest groups ran the legislature. Every time they proposed a law, some group would shoot it down.

After the news, Tracy asked me, "Any chance you can stay with me a few more days, until we solve the murders? I'll sleep better if I know someone else is with me. I still feel sort of creepy."

I was not about to say no. I just leaned over and gave her a kiss. "I'll stay as long as you wish," I told her.

I went down to the car and grabbed my go-bag. I had enough clothes in there for several days. When I came back up on the elevator, I waved to my father's friends.

Tracy met me at the door. She had a light blue, short silk nightgown on, with thin straps on her shoulders. I was glad one of my father's friends did not escort me to the door. It unmistakably defined her slender curves.

Let's just say that for the next hour, the bed was very cozy. I'm not sure which side of the bed we were on; all I knew is that there was no room between us.

When the alarm went off Friday morning, it was nice that I did not have to run home to get a change of clothes and get cleaned up. By the time I finished shaving and brushing my teeth, Tracy was up and partially dressed. She was just missing a pair of pants.

While I was checking my cell for messages, we discussed some options for Tracy to look at during the day. I suggested that she tackle one of the folders we had not looked at in the past. So far, we had a possible link between two dead people and Tracy. We needed to put a link on a couple of Howard's projects and the pipeline. If we could accomplish this, there was hope that we might link all the things together.

Tracy gave me a kiss as I got ready to leave. "Keep your eyes open," she told me.

When I got to the station, LT had a meeting. He wanted to know what we had found, and to see if we had made any progress. Actually, he wanted to know if there was anything we missed that he could supervise.

After reviewing the facts with LT and Shawn, we concluded that we were making progress. Soon, we would have to wait for the FBI to finish their evaluation. In the meanwhile, Tracy would hopefully finish looking at the other folders and try to complete her flow chart.

Shawn, Photo and I left for our morning assignments. Today, it looked as though we needed to cover a car crash that killed three teenagers, a legislature meeting, and school closing discussion. About 10:30 am, while covering a tax committee meeting at the legislature, Photo gave me an elbow to the ribs.

"Look over at 9:00. The guy in the brown shirt. I'm not positive, but I think I saw him yesterday when we were interviewing people at the car ramp."

I looked over his way. There were about 20 people waiting for the post meeting interviews. The man in the back was trying to keep from looking too interested. "Did you get some good mug shots?" I asked.

"Yup! I'll get a few more and compare it to my shots from yesterday." Photo slipped off to the other side of the room and took a few more pictures from an angle that looked like he was shooting the speakers.

When it was over, the man slipped out early and disappeared. We compared pictures in the van as we drove to the school which the city had proposed closing. About half way there, Photo nudged me, "There, see, in the back by the trash can. It's the same person."

Sure enough, he was right. "Good eyes," I told him. I asked Photo to send the picture to Agent Mark Lawson and O'Riley. They could run a quick scan on the picture, and see if they had a match to our mystery person. With any luck, maybe they could recognize him.

Now, we had at least one person to have an eye open for. Was he watching us, or was he looking for Tracy? One thing, we were not going to lead him to her.

At the end of the day, I picked up some dinners and headed over to Tracy's. I made sure no one was following me by making a number of turns into small streets before heading back to the Castle.

When I got to her apartment, I knocked on the door. It was silent, no one answered.

Chapter 12

Bubbles

When Tracy failed to answer the door, I almost started to panic. That was until I spotted one of my father's gang. Hank was pointing down the hall. Tracy was in my father's apartment. Now, I was ready to panic.

Upon reaching his unit, as I went inside, I found Tracy and my dad deep in conversation at the table. Tracy greeted me with a smile. "Martin, your father and I have had a delightful conversation. I needed some groceries, and he went with me to pick them up in the store downstairs. It made a needed break from looking at all those files. I carried up a few items your father needed as well."

I looked at the table. My father had dragged out some old pictures of me, and had obviously shown them to Tracy.

As she got up from the table, my father said to her, "Thank you for making my afternoon so delightful. If you need anything else from the store, make sure you let me know."

"Thank you John. It was pleasant to get out of the apartment." With that, Tracy walked over to me, "Smells yummy. What did you pick up for dinner today?"

"Good question," I answered, "I hope it's not crow."

My father just gave me a smile.

We headed back to Tracy's apartment. I could hardly wait to hear the stories my father had been telling.

While we ate supper, Tracy filled me in on her couple of hours with my father. It sounded like he had told her the abbreviated version of my life story. I was glad I was only 37 years old. Otherwise, she would probably have to go back tomorrow to get the rest of my life history.

I had to sit through the review of the day's stories, with my teeth clinched. My father had gone into more detail than normal. Tracy found out about all my childhood adventures – from tipping over the canoe at camp, to having my date for the senior prom dump me the day before the prom, to my changing majors in college twice, and my not dating anyone for the past three years. I was starting to wonder if it was possible to get unrelated to one's father.

Tracy was enjoying the discussion. She could see that I was getting redder and redder in the face as the stories progressed. Then she said, "Don't worry, he didn't say anything that would make me think anything less of you."

That snapped me out of my "kill mode." I was all set to try to bribe Hank into tripping him down the stairs.

I think the food was OK. However, to be honest, I actually did not pay attention to it.

I changed the topic as quick as I could.

"So, did you discover anything other than my past today?"

"I checked one of the other folders like you suggested," Tracy told me. "It started out with some articles about power plants in Japan. I'm not sure how that was related. Maybe Howard was documenting the history of the processes. Anyway, it was about injecting the CO2 gases from coal plants back into the ground. The companies claimed that it almost eliminated the emissions from the plant."

"I think I remember hearing about how the CO2 processing had allowed them to use more coal from the western states," I told her. "Did anything stand out to you?"

"When we finish our food, I can show you the files I noted for unusual things you might like to see."

Tracy cleared the table, so we would have more room for spreading out our already enormous flow chart.

Tracy showed me that the leading western states in coal production were Wyoming, Montana, and North Dakota. Another pattern was showing up. These states and Minnesota seemed to be the center of all of Howard Long's files so far. The flow chart had a few outliers, like the report from Japan. However, most of the lines were concentrated in the four states.

She informed me, "The report mentioned that the Japanese had pioneered the use of safe coal technology after the problems they had with their nuclear power plants in 2011. The massive earthquake and tsunami shut down over half of their total energy production. They had to quickly upgrade their old coal fired plants to meet demand. The US had complained that the emissions were carrying acid gases all the way to the North American coast, affecting the old growth forests.

"The studies they completed in Japan showed that they could trap the CO_2 emissions and inject them deep in the ground. Much of this was accomplished with deep wells that were slant drilled into the ocean bottom, and ended up over 5,000 feet deep. Since Japan was a volcanic island with solid rock under the surface, drilling on an angle into the ocean bottom allowed them to drill deep without having to drill through 5,000 feet of rock.

"Wasn't it rock in the ocean as well?" Tracy asked.

"I suppose so. Although you do have the advantage of the coastal sands and the fact that the water gets deep quickly. I think they probably saved some money drilling into the seabed rather than straight into the bedrock."

Just then, Tracy's cell rang. It was LT. He was calling to let us know that he had heard from O'Riley. The photograph we had sent him of the person in the crowd was a false alarm. One of the capital patrol officers recognized the individual in the picture and questioned the man. He was a capital pollist. His job was to measure public reaction to issues including how people felt about the legislature. He was at the news conference doing just that. When asked about the other location, he said he was downtown shopping, and just happened upon our crew doing interviews. He was curious and decided to listen in on a couple to see what the public reaction had been, and whether or not the public was still upset with the legislature.

It looked as though it was a case of our crew overreacting to a common face. LT suggested to Tracy that she start getting back into the groove tomorrow. Saturdays were usually light, and her crew could keep their eyes open for her.

Tracy was relieved. She did not like the thought of someone watching her movements. Perhaps the pressure was truly off after the FBI had released the story. There had only been one suspicious person spotted in several days. Getting back in the field would mean that work would slow down their file search. Soon, she would have to move out of the Castle and back to her apartment. Tracy was still nervous about the thought. I could see it in the expressions on her face.

I talked to Tracy about moving back to her apartment. She asked, "Do you think I could wait until Monday to move back?"

I told her, I thought it would be fine. Since we were going to have less time to research the files, I suggested that we set up a meeting with Agent Mark Lawson later in the week to compare notes.

The news from LT took us off our concentration on the report, so we decided to take a break and eat a snack before going back to the serious items. Tracy had picked up some ice cream earlier in the day, and this looked like a good chance to cool off our taste buds. On top of that, it was my favorite flavor, mountain blackberry. Apparently, this was another of my father's revelations.

While we were eating the ice cream, Tracy asked, "Your father seems to have adjusted to your mother's death, and appears to enjoy living here. However, he said the only problem is that you never get a chance to come around for a visit. How come?"

"You know how it is being a reporter. Your schedule becomes hectic and keeps you on the go. It makes it hard to make solid plans on things. About the time I think I can spend an evening with him, I end up working late."

"You managed the past few days to find time to be with me," she replied.

"Don't forget, my father has his gang also. If I came over too often, it would probably break up their routines, including their card games. Besides, I call him almost every day."

I was becoming a little uncomfortable with the topic so I suggested that we finish with the coal technology and see if there was something else in the files.

Tracy finished telling me what she had found. "Like I said, the Japanese showed everyone that they could make a clean burning coal power plant. To the people in North Dakota, the thought of using substantial amounts of coal again for electricity sounded like money in the bank. Most of the coal was coming from Wyoming and Montana for the power industry. The coal in North Dakota was a lower grade of coal, which is called lignite. It is a soft coal that is somewhere between a hard coal and peat in characteristics.

"The problem with the coal is the moisture content. The moisture content can vary all the way up to 65%, and has a higher ash content than bituminous coal, which is the standard soft coal. Because of the moisture content, the emissions from the plants that burn it contain higher amounts of CO_2. That means that the power plants had to deal with the EPA requirements on green house gases.

"If they could successfully inject the gases into the ground, they could build power plants near the coal sites and transmit the electricity to the power grid.

"According to Howard Long's files, a fair number of the owners of the coal fields changed hands in a single year. Then, after the power company got the go ahead from the EPA, they built a large plant along the North Dakota/Minnesota border, and another near the eastern edge of the Black Hills, where they could supply western South Dakota, and western North Dakota with electricity.

"Some of the CO2 was sold to the oil companies. It was cheaper and safer than pumping natural gas into the rock structure. As a result, a number of pipelines crossed the western North Dakota, Montana, Wyoming region. It looked as though everyone was coming up a winner in this case."

I stopped her, "Why do I get the feeling as if there is a fox just watching the chickens out in the farmer's yard getting fat?"

"You might be right. Here, let me show you a couple of reports." Tracy put the reports up on the screen. They were technical reports from the one pipeline company talking about pipe leakage.

"Did they have some leaks?" I asked.

"Apparently, they had a few. Although, I could not find a lot of documentation from the power companies indicating that they ever had a problem. Look at these couple of pages."

The information was hard to get an exact hold on. However, it was talking about a pond near Williston, North Dakota, which had bubbles rising from it. The report stated that the birds tended to fly around the pond and did not use it for drinking or chasing bugs. A farmer – Kurt Norstrom, had complained that his cattle were acting strange, and he had decided to keep them away from the pond."

"Anything else in the report?" I asked.

"Just that a section of the pipe was replaced. I wrote down the name of the farmer in case we wanted to follow up on it."

"Good. There must have been a reason Howard Long saved the information. What else is there?"

"Well, I did see a note that there had been an earthquake. They checked their pipes just to make sure they were all OK."

"Did it damage any?" I asked.

"The report stated that they had intentionally put enough jogs in the line so that any shifting of the earth was absorbed without the stress it would have on straight pipes. Apparently, they were prepared for earthquakes. It is intriguing though. Remember the seismograph chart we saw from the oil company? Over a three-year period, they did not show any events above a level two. This report seems to indicate they had something stronger. If they designed their piping for earthquakes, you would think there might have been a history of quakes, to cause them to waste the extra piping needed to prevent a large quake from breaking the pipes. Do all pipeline companies lay pipe this way? What do they do for pipes that go down deep into the ground?"

"Flag both of these on your flow charts, along with the pond episode. Howard may have started to put two-and-two together. Maybe the old boy did have a bigger picture than we thought. We still have to tie it all in, somehow," I told her.

We spent another hour looking at the files. We were starting to make progress. However, it was just way too slow. I was impressed by the thoroughness that Tracy showed in doing her research. She did a marvelous job sorting out the critical facts from a report without losing track of the small details. From my contact with her prior to her coming to the Cities, I did not realize how talented she was in digging out the facts for a report.

When the news was about to come on, we quickly shut down the video system's display of my files and stashed the flow charts. Tomorrow was another day. We needed to stay up-to-date on the activities in the Cities. Just in case one of our assignments was related to a report from the day before, we needed to be able to write a new report that would blend with the old one. It would not look right if one reporter filed a report on a subject, only to have the next one file an entirely different approach.

In addition, I wanted to enjoy some of the time with Tracy, as long as it lasted.

After we turned off the news, we went in and snuggled in bed. I was just starting to relax and enjoy the moment, when Tracy asked, "How come your prom date dumped you the day before the prom?"

Chapter 13

Information

Why is it that when you are snuggling in the bed and starting to relax, a simple question can change the mood in seconds? The question, "Why did your prom date dump you the day before the prom?" hit like a lightning bolt out of the sky on a clear day. It took a while to explain it.

Saturday morning started with early activities for both of us. After stopping for a quick bagel and coffee, we rolled into the station. LT was waiting there as we arrived. He had the morning assignments set for us, and it was obvious that he was attempting to keep Tracy away from large crowds. Her assignments were mainly small events where her escorts could keep an eye on both her and the onlookers.

He gave Tracy several local news assignments. She would cover the new play equipment at a park, a neighborhood group that was protesting the clearing of trees for a new set of stores, and the ground breaking for a new senior center in St. Paul.

LT had me cover a report of some sports stars that were arrested for a wild party the night before, and then cover any noteworthy events that came up during the day.

At lunch, I gave Agent Mark Lawson a call.

"Mark, I thought you would be out on the golf course trying to get in a couple more rounds before the snow season showed up?"

"Well Martin, I know this is hard to believe, but some of us work hard protecting the rest of you."

"Mark, we have been working on the files for the past few nights. Just wondering how you were coming, from your end, on solving the mystery?"

"You mean you didn't give me the only copy?" he asked.

"Sorry, I scanned them first, just in case you spilled your coffee on them."

"And, with all this, you want whose help?" Mark asked.

"OK, anyway, we started a flow chart of the files. Found some minor links, but so far, there is a lot of information to fill in between the lines. I was wondering if you wanted to get together later in the week and compare notes?" I asked.

"Thanks, but can we move it up a few days? By the end of the week, we'll probably have it solved and be on a different case."

"Your boss standing right next to you?" I asked Mark.

"Heck no! If he were, I'd have to act civil to you. How about Monday evening?"

"Sounds good. My place?" I suggested.

"See you Monday, about 7:00 pm."

I was hoping we would have had a couple more days to look at all the files and plot the crossovers. However, maybe Mark's team had some links to add to our discoveries. I figured I would tell Tracy about the meeting when we returned to the station later in the day.

When I arrived at the station around 5:00 pm, Tracy was already there. She had been talking to LT about the research we had been doing and the partial successes we had seen so far. I mentioned to them that I had talked to Mark earlier in the day, and he had requested a short meeting at my place Monday evening to review the information. It sounded OK to Tracy.

LT asked, "If I bring the beer, can I join you? I'd really like to see if we have something developing or if we have missed the opportunity."

"Never pass up a free beer," I told him. "Want to arrive early and have some takeout while we show you what we have? I'm not sure what Mark has, but just in case we decide to hold something back, we can get you up to speed on what the files look like."

Let's make it 5:30 pm," LT said. "I'll let you put some quality takeout on your travel expenses since we are talking business."

We left the station quickly to pick up a dinner and head over to Tracy's townhouse. When we arrived, we took one look at the place, and decided that it might take the rest of the night, and the next day, just to put everything back the way it was before the intrusion. The police had disturbed many of the things that the intruders had missed when they went through the place with a fine-tooth-comb looking for prints. The police had only officially released the townhouse earlier in the week.

"Want to stay at my place?" I gently asked her.

"You wouldn't mind?" she asked. "I'm not sure I could sleep tonight if I was alone in this place after seeing everything all over the floor."

We picked up a few of her things and headed over to my apartment. It was not as clean and elegant as the room at the Castle, but it would allow Tracy to get a pleasant night's sleep. We had probably pushed the three-day limit on the room at the Castle way beyond their limit; otherwise, I would have taken her back there.

We grabbed the takeout and brought it back to my apartment. I did a quick cleanup, while Tracy set out the food. Fortunately, the place was reasonably clean from my staying at Tracy's the past few nights. She took one look and said, "Not bad for a guy's apartment. It could use a little color here and there though."

Once we gobbled down our food, we quickly set up my video system and looked at a few more files before the news. Both Tracy and I wanted to get through as many files as we could, before we met with

LT and Mark. The reminder of Tracy's messed up townhouse put a little more enthusiasm into finding the culprits.

We opened the file on the power plants in western Minnesota. Like the plants in North Dakota, they were coal-fired plants using North Dakota coal instead of the more expensive Wyoming coal. The public had argued against this plant for decades. When it was decided that they could pump their CO_2 into the ground and prevent all the greenhouse gases associated with coal plants, they were finally given the go ahead to erect the plant.

The coal-fired power plant was exceptionally large in size. It produced most of the electricity needed for western Minnesota, eastern South Dakota and eastern North Dakota. From everything I could remember, it appeared that this plant had been an enormous success. Once the right-of-ways were finished for the power lines, it created the power needed for the region at a reasonable price.

The plant was running at almost zero emissions. The CO_2 was both sold and piped to industrial users, or it was pumped directly into deep wells that took the gases 2,000 feet below the water table.

When Tracy and I looked at Howard Long's files, we saw it covered the controversies before the plant was constructed, discussions on emissions, permits on the deep wells, and general operating conditions. It appeared that all the EPA requirements were met. Just like the plants in western North Dakota, the process was keeping the plant within the required limits for coal-fired power plants.

There were several technical papers. We filed them into different folders – those we read, and those that needed further examination. Most of them in the latter file were the hard data type files that were slightly beyond our expertise. So far, we did not see the crucial problem that Howard Long had led Tracy to believe he had found.

There was one intriguing comment in one of the reports that got our attention. Apparently, lignite coal has a very high moisture level that causes problems with transportation and storage. It was probably the reason that they wanted the plants close to the sources of the coal. They were concerned about shipping the coal by train and leaving a car filled with coal sitting on a siding for a couple months until the plant needed it. This would not be a problem for a major plant close to the coalfield. However, if the coal was shipped to a minor user, the problem could exist. The last thing they wanted was publicity caused by of a fire linked to the coal.

The nighttime news came on. It was filled with most of the items Tracy and I had covered during the day. So far, it looked as though it had been quiet in the evening hours. Usually, the wild life started about bar closing time on Saturday evenings. That meant we would probably be following up on a few robberies, shootings, and accidents in the morning.

After the news, we put away our equipment and got ready for a short night's sleep. It seemed like morning was coming earlier and earlier every day. With all the research we had been doing, our minds were racing all night long.

At least tonight, Tracy was not waiting for us to get into bed before asking me questions about my old girlfriends. She nuzzled up close to me and whispered in my ear, "Thanks for letting me stay with you."

I turned and gave her a kiss. "You can stay as long as you need to," I told her. Truth be told, she could stay as long as she could put up with me. I was enjoying the opportunity. It was well after midnight by the time we fell asleep.

The next morning, Sunday, I realized that the bathroom in my place was unquestionably smaller than at my father's Castle. Once Tracy spread out her things, there was very little counter space left for any of mine. The three-quarter bath off the bedroom did not have any counter space.

Somehow, we made do, got something to eat on the way to work, and reported in just in time to get the assignments.

There had been two shootings, three minor robberies, and one of the drunks ran into a bus stop, flattening the place last night. LT divided it up between Tracy and me, giving Tracy the robberies, so that her cinematographer could protect her.

By noon, we had it covered. Videos were relayed to the station and the editors could have the afternoon to finish the job. We hung out at the station, and used the computer there to open the folder on the cloud and look at a few more files, while keeping an ear to the police scanner. Fortunately, it was quiet all afternoon.

About 5:00 pm, we pulled up stakes and headed back to my apartment. As we stopped to get some food, I realized that LT would probably put two and two together tomorrow when he came to hear Mark. It would be hard to hide the fact that Tracy was staying with me. I did not want to lie to LT.

At dinner, Tracy and I discussed what we were going to say tomorrow night. First on the agenda, what to say to LT. I was not quite sure how he would look at it. I was hoping he would understand, with all Tracy had gone through, and with her apartment in a mess, that it was safer for her to stay with me. Well, the logic sounded convincing, just didn't cut the mustard any more than it did with my father when I was staying with her at his Castle.

We decided that we would deal with it tomorrow. Hopefully, LT would not say anything. After we were finished eating, we would put the information we found this afternoon into the flow chart, and see if we could make any assumptions that LT and Mark Lawson could also find.

"With the schedule you keep, do you ever miss going to church on Sundays?" Tracy asked.

"Actually, I do. For a while, I tried to go on Saturday night, but, I found I was usually on the wrong side of the city, and by the time I arrived, the service was halfway done. I keep hoping, when the rest of the crew gets well, we can go back to having a few days off now and then. How about you?" I asked. "Do you take Sunday mornings off?"

"Our schedules were more flexible in Duluth," she told me. Usually, I could go to an early service and still cover the news in the morning. Also, the other stations and mine would share information, so if we had something urgent, we could check to see that one of our other colleagues was covering the same time block."

"So, do you prefer Duluth to the Cities?" I asked.

"I'm still looking at the fringe benefits."

Just then, my phone rang, "Hey, you so busy chasing that gal that you don't call me anymore?"

It was my father. He was right; I had missed calling him yesterday and today. I guess he genuinely did care if I called him every day. I apologized and told him that we were meeting with Mark Lawson tomorrow night, so I might not get a chance to call him then either.

"That's OK. I'm planning on lightening Hanks billfold tomorrow night. The gang is coming over for cards. You still seeing Tracy? Oh, that was a dumb question. Say hi to her for us. Tell her, we miss seeing her."

"Thanks Dad. I'll tell her. Thank your gang for watching over her. I'll call you Tuesday."

Now, I had two people that did not know Tracy was staying with me. It probably would not stay that way very long.

Tracy and I spent the next two hours setting up things for tomorrow night. We knew that we would not have time between the time we got off shift, and LT showed up for dinner. I started thinking, *"What would LT like for dinner? I needed all the things I could, to keep him on my side."* I decided some Italian sandwiches might be in order. It would go with the beer LT was picking up. Our breath just might be a little overpowering for Mark. So, Tracy suggested, "Just ask for some light on the peppers."

It sounded like a good suggestion.

We quit early and just sat on the sofa, talking about the past week. Tracy was tired out and put her head on my shoulder as we waited for the evening news to come on. It didn't take ten minutes before she fell asleep. I put my arm around her and just held her tight.

I was honestly hoping all of this did not have to come to an end tomorrow evening, after LT was here.

Just before the news, I woke her up. "Sorry, thought you might like to see how your stories were aired."

"It felt good to take a nap, I hope you didn't mind."

"I enjoyed holding you close," I told her. Then, she gave me a kiss.

I don't know about Tracy, but the kiss got my attention. I was wishing they could cut the news early tonight, perhaps for a movie, and we could get back to that moment between us. I would even volunteer my stories to be cut.

Unfortunately, it ran the standard length. As soon as they cut to the weather, we shut it off and wandered to the bedroom. We didn't need an electric blanket to warm up the bed. Apparently, Tracy was enjoying the moments as much as I was.

The next morning, we got up a little earlier than normal. We needed to straighten things up for LT's coming over in the evening.

Chapter 14

The Boss

All Monday morning, I was concerned about having LT over for dinner. I just was not sure how he would react to knowing that Tracy was staying at my place. Surely, he must have realized that we were arriving in one car each day. I wondered if Tracy had mentioned anything to him about it.

I picked up Tracy about 4:30 pm at the television station, and stopped for takeout before heading to the apartment.

LT arrived right on time – 5:30 pm. We sat down and ate the sandwiches that we had picked up, combined with the beer LT brought. I took out a jar of pickles and chips to have with the sandwiches. About half way through the meal, LT asked Tracy if she was staying at my apartment.

"Yes, Martin was kind and offered me the chance to stay here for a few days. I wanted to move back into my place from the Castle, but I had not been able to as it would take a couple of days to get my townhouse back to usable condition once the police crime-scene crew cleared it. Since it was evening when we left the Castle, Martin said I could stay with him until we cleaned it up. With all the work on the investigation and long hours, I have not had the time to get back and spend the time needed," she told him.

"Well, I guess we did push the hospitality of the senior center as far as we could," LT stated. "I'm sure Martin is taking care of you the best he can."

I breathed a sigh of relief. So far, LT appeared to be letting it ride, and not pushing the issue. As long as it did not interfere with our work, he would probably stay out of it.

During the next hour, we showed LT the way the files were when we received them, and how we had gone through only about half of them.

"That looks like something a team of people needs to work on," he said.

"Yes, that's why I brought in Agent Mark Lawson.," I told him. "If there is a smoking gun, his team will surely find it."

"Did you and Tracy find anything that looked suspicious?" he asked. "There must be something, or they would not have killed Howard Long over it."

"So far all we have seen is slight problems in production reports," Tracy answered. "All plants have problems, so I'm not sure we have found what we are looking for. I am hoping Mark Lawson can fill us in on the man from Wyoming, and whether he was murdered or if it was just an accident after he was following me."

LT told us, "If they do not come up with something, I am afraid this may be one of those reports that we might have to let die a slow death."

Mark Lawson showed up at 7:00 pm. When I greeted him at the door, he commented, "Smells like I should have come earlier."

LT handed him a beer. "Glad you could make it. We were just discussing the fact that most of the files are rather technical in nature."

"That's what my team told me also. Show me what you have, and I'll try and fill in some of the blanks," Mark told us.

Tracy and I showed LT and Mark the flow chart we had put together. It showed a few of the projects Howard Long had investigated, and links to people and locations.

"Unfortunately, as you can see, there does not seem to be anything that would cause someone to murder two people," I told them.

Mark looked at the charts. "I'm impressed, not bad work. I take it; you did not get to all the folders."

"No, we have to work occasionally," I told him.

"Well, let me add some fascinating links to your charts. Let's start with our dead man in Wyoming. When I checked on him, they claimed he died hiking in the hills. Fell on the trail and hit his head.

"The pictures I looked at did not seem to confirm a serious injury. In that remote area of Wyoming, a local doctor signed the death certificate. Surprisingly, only a few people attended the funeral, with no big outpouring of emotions from the company he worked for. If you died tomorrow, don't you think the office would be upset and at least make a show of emotion for you at your funeral?

"Our office had taps on their phone lines before the accident. There was barely a mention of the accident on S&G Security's phone lines.

"The company moves people around. However, they communicate to them using scrambled communications. I still have a person watching them.

"From what we can find out on Howard Long, there are no integrity problems with either him or his files. If he said he found something, he probably did. Why they killed him is truly a mystery."

"You said there may be others that died?" I asked Mark.

"Your report on the farmer near Williston, who had CO2 bubbles coming out of his pond; about a month later they found him dead on his farm. I looked at the autopsy report. He had several ailments. None of them should have killed him. The report listed a high level of hydrogen sulfide in his system. That could have affected his nervous system, and been an attributing factor to his death. The question we had was where and how he was exposed to the gas?

"In the same report, we found several other names listed in the files. One of the people from the pipeline crew was involved with a mysterious car accident on a straight section of farm road. He ran off the road. The car rolled when it hit the ditch and he was killed. Accident? He fell asleep at the wheel. It was the middle of the afternoon. The accident report just listed it as a one-car rollover. It happened around the same time as your farmer's death.

"Then there was the head of the DNR. He was traveling to northern Minnesota in a small airplane. The plane ran out of fuel half way up there. The commissioner and the pilot were both killed. Reports said it was an experienced pilot who would never have left without a full tank of fuel."

Mark handed us a file on each one of them. By themselves, they looked like accidents. If they could be linked together, they spelled murder.

Mark told us, "My guess, off the record, is that I have my work cut out for me for some time. I think the farmer had an accident, not as sure on the pipeline worker though. My guess is that he discovered something someone did not want anyone else to know about.

"From the records we have obtained, and from Howard Long's notes, it said they replaced a section of corroded pipe on the farmer's property. I'm not a pipe expert. I can just barely tell the difference between my garden hose and a metal pipe, so I'll leave it to my experts. Why did CO_2 corrode the metal pipe? Where did the farmer run into the hydrogen sulfide? Was it in the pipe, and that was why it corroded?"

"Looks like your people have a lot of work to do," LT told Mark. "You still have not found the vital connection to our water pipeline. I hope you can find the key to the mystery. If you do, please make sure you let us know. For now, I'm afraid I need to drop this project to a lower level of importance for spending time on research. We just don't have the personnel."

He turned to Tracy, "Sorry, but if we get another solid lead, we can look into it. However, until then, I'm not sure our time is well spent chasing it."

"I understand," Tracy told him.

Then, LT excused himself from the group and headed home. It had been a long day for him, as well.

Mark asked, "Are you going to drop it?"

Tracy replied, "Only on the surface. Someone killed Howard Long and tore apart my townhouse. I think they deserve a little more investigation, even if it is just evening work."

"One thing I forgot to mention," Mark stated. "One of my investigators found that occasionally the western North Dakota plants would mix some Wyoming coal into the mix to increase the Btu's. The emissions were supposedly shipped to the coalfields for injection, whenever this was done. Apparently, they could use it for making coal slurries, which they would draw from smaller deposits. You think they could have run it in the wrong pipes? Just a thought. The Wyoming coal contains sulfides."

"Sounds like you have a question," I told Mark. "Are you going to follow-up on it?"

"Yeah. If it was the cause, they just might want to keep it quiet. That and the pipeline guy that just happened to have Benadryl in his system when he went off the road. I checked with his relatives. They said he never took any antihistamine pills. I'm still wondering how he got it in his system if he never took the drug."

"You think someone might have slipped it to him in a drink?" I asked.

"Well, if he was tired from working long days, and someone put a slightly higher than normal dose in his system, he might have lost his attention while driving," Mark stated. "It is just hard to prove at this point. Witnesses are going to be hard to find.

"I'm doing a background on all the names in Howard's files. Maybe there are links. Maybe there are more missing people. We'll see. If I find something, I'll let you know."

I thanked Mark for letting us know what they had found. We knew it would be a long shot for him to come up with a quick solution.

However, we still had some hope. He captured a few pictures of our flow charts before he left.

"I'll give these to my crew. Maybe it will give them some ideas."

After he left the apartment, Tracy turned to me, "Is it OK if we spend the rest of the week looking for clues?"

"Only if we work together," I told her.

That got me another kiss.

Chapter 15

More Investigations

After Mark Lawson left my apartment, Tracy and I agreed we would continue looking at the files, at least until the end of the week. Unfortunately, that meant working every evening and probably not getting the amount of sleep we needed. It also meant that Tracy would not have time to straighten her townhouse this week. As long as LT did not complain, it was OK with me.

Tuesday we were back to work as normal. LT was convinced that Tracy was no longer in danger, and we split the load evenly between us. Shawn was working with Tracy, and I asked him to keep a close eye out without telling LT that he was doing anything unusual.

He told me that LT had already given him the same message.

* * *

Mark Lawson sent one of his investigators, Butch Thomas to North Dakota. He wanted to know a little more about the piping of CO_2 to the oil fields in the Williston area. Specifically, he asked his person to check on the type of pipe used and where the pipes were laid.

He gave his specialist the whole file on the power company and told him to keep the security on the FBI laptop on at all times. He did not want a stolen computer giving away any information on what they were looking for. However, he knew that Agent Butch Thomas needed to know all the facts in case he could put some of the links together based on what he found.

With all the oil field work completed in the past ten years, the pipeline company had been extremely busy. By the end of the day, Mark's investigator had found someone from the pipeline crew that had worked for the company long enough to remember working on the initial CO2 lines from the power company to the Bakken oil fields.

The man, a pipeline engineer named Josiah Simmons, told him that he worked the field ever since the rock fracturing technology was introduced, and injection of CO2 was used to force the oil out of the rock structure.

"You see, the rock structure down there is extremely tight. The porosity of the rocks is exceptionally low. Normally, the oil would just flow out of the structure. If it needed a little help, we would use a waterflood injected into a few wells. That would give it the pressure needed to force it up the main pipes.

"With the Bakken Field, because of the tighter porosity, they found that gases, like CO2, would penetrate the layers better than water. The oil extracted from each well leveled off after a couple years, even with the waterflood. Fracturing the rock structure at the end of the well with small amounts of explosives, and using natural gas or CO2 injection into the wells helped increase the production, pushing the oil molecules out of the layers."

"Did you work with Kurt Norstrom?" the agent asked.

"You bet, for about five years. Too bad. He was a skilled worker. Really hit us hard when he had that car crash. I guess you just can't work all those hours without sleep."

"Did he seem over tired to you?"

"Not any more than normal that I recall. We were all putting in long shifts."

"Josiah, do you remember what jobs he was working on at the time of the accident?" Butch asked.

"Yes. I had to finish them for him. We were replacing some corroded stainless pipe up by Williston with coated stainless pipe. It was strange; they were running dry CO_2 gas at a low pressure of about 50 psid. That pipe should have lasted for years."

"Do you remember if Kurt Norstrom had a cold, or was taking something for an allergy?"

"Not that I can remember. Pretty dry out here. Unless you are allergic to sand, sage or tumbleweeds, there is not much else out there."

After interviewing some of the other pipeline workers and family members, agent Butch Thomas could find no support for the Benadryl in Kurt Norstrom's system. The need to replace stainless steel pipe with coated stainless for CO_2 was underlined in his report. He also included the question, "What caused the corrosion?"

By evening, Mark Lawson had the report on his computer. So far, it was just as he suspected. He sent a note back, "While you are up there, check to see if they have had any earthquakes in the past ten years affecting the oil fields or pipelines."

* * *

Tracy and I had supper. After talking to my father and convincing him that Tracy was doing OK, we started looking at the files from western Minnesota that we had filed earlier, and not had a chance to examine.

The files listed all the technical information that was just what one wants to read just before bedtime! Flow rates, parts per million of gases, Btu's, percent efficiency, and disposal rates. With a dozen pages like these, who needed sleeping pills? Why did Howard Long keep all the data? Surely, he could have whittled it down to the important pages.

Tracy thought he might have been trying to maintain all the data just in case he missed something; someone else could go back and find the relevant numbers.

About 20 tired yawns later, we found a sheet that had a paragraph underlined. It was a mineral composition of the surrounding rock structures. One of the materials listed on the file was low-level uranium, which was contained in one of the deep rock layers.

119

Obviously, Howard Long felt this was important. On the other hand, did he simply find it unusual and underline it? We would probably have to talk to a geologist to know.

We finished the unread files, not discovering any smoking guns.

"Howard did not do you any great favors by sending you the papers or the link to these files," I told Tracy.

"There must be something here. He was too knowledgeable to just give us nothing and make us spend weeks looking at it."

"You mean like we are doing right now?" I asked.

Tonight, watching the news was a welcomed break. All that data was getting hard on the eyes. Besides, tomorrow was another day.

Wednesday afternoon, Agent Mark Lawson received a call from his field agent, Butch Thomas.

"Butch, what's the weather like in North Dakota this time of year?" Mark asked.

"You must have looked at the weather report," he told Mark. "Canadian front moved in today. It's snowing like crazy. You would think it is December rather than the beginning of October. Thought you might like some intriguing information, so instead of counting each snowflake, I thought I'd give you a call."

"Let her rip," Mark told him.

"I did some checking on seismic tremors in the area. This area is fairly steady for high country. Apparently, they had a decent one in 1986. Minor shaking in 1975 and 1993. Then in 2015, they had a level 5.5 in the area. That one caused some sour taste in the drinking water in several wells that had to be treated with carbon filters. The quake must have caused some fissures in the rock structure.

"The earthquakes in 1975, 1993 and 2014 were located in western Minnesota. However, they were felt all the way out here. You thinking that the quakes are part of your case?" he asked.

"Never know until the fat lady sings," Mark answered. "Good work. You driving or putting your car on the commuter car and taking the com-rail back tonight?"

"No thanks! I think I'll wait until morning when the snow stops. Not sure there are any roads open out here anyway. Early snows tend to bring icy roads."

"Stay warm," Mark told him as he disconnected. He knew that Butch was old fashioned and preferred driving to taking the rail.

If it were Mark, he would prefer the comfort of the rail.

Ten minutes later, Mark called Martin. "Martin, got some news for you. Remember your comment about earthquakes in the Dakota's? I just got a call from my man out there. They had one in 2015, which caused trace oils in several water wells. In addition, in 2014, there was a significant one near Morris in western Minnesota. Is that what you were looking for?"

"Perhaps! Maybe we are tightening those strings on Tracy's charts. Anything else?"

"Martin, you know I would tell you if there was. Our pipeline worker had no history of allergies or using antihistamines. One of his co-workers was interviewed. He also said he was surprised that the pipe would corrode with the level of CO_2 they were pumping. That help?"

"You're getting warmer. I'll let Tracy know.

"Oh Mark, did you know there was low level uranium in western Minnesota?"

"Whoa, you must still be working nights. Good information. Is it connected to the power plant files?"

"Not sure yet. Howard had it underlined," I told him.

"I'll tell my investigator to stop off on his way home from Williston. At least it is not snowing in Minnesota this early in the season."

"Thanks; keep the info coming," I told Mark.

That evening, Tracy and I decided that we should take a second look at the western Minnesota files. If they had some earthquakes, perhaps they had the same conditions that they had in North Dakota where the oil was seeping into the drinking water wells.

It took the whole evening, but Tracy finally spotted one line in one file. It noted that normal radiation levels were found in western Minnesota. It listed another file that was not among the files we had. The question now was where to find it.

Our best guess was that it would have been filed with either the EPA or the DNR. The date on it was August 2016. With a file number, we hoped to be able to locate it. However, our searches on-line came up blank. Tracy put it on her to-do list for Thursday – call the DNR and EPA.

The next morning, between assignments, Tracy called both the EPA and the DNR to see if they had the file.

The EPA was the logical choice for locating where the file might have been sent. However, after a few calls, Tracy was told that there was no match for those file numbers in their system for that time period. She decided to pursue the DNR.

After lunch, she called the Minnesota Department of Natural Resources. It took four transfers to get to an individual that was knowledgeable of the DNR's archive filing system.

"Yes, I think we have that file in our system," she was told. "I see the title of that folder in the log of files reported by a power company out in western Minnesota."

"Can I get a copy of it?" Tracy asked.

"I need a "sign off" by the commissioner, but that should not be a problem," she stated. "Well, maybe it will be. I just tried to open the file so I could send it to the commissioner for approval. It appears to be empty."

"Do you have a backup?" Tracy asked.

"We should. Let me call you back in an hour. I'll have one of our technical people pull the backup disk."

Tracy waited patiently for two hours. Finally, she called the woman back. "Hi, this is Tracy again. Did you locate the backup copy?"

"I'm sorry, we cannot find it. You know, this was filed just before we changed administrations. With the new DNR commissioner coming in, it is possible that people were moved, and the backup was not done during a short period."

That was not what Tracy wanted to hear. "Please give me a call if you locate the missing file," she told her.

When she disconnected from the DNR, she called Martin.

"Martin, good news and bad. I found where they sent the file. They sent it to the DNR. The bad news is that after it was logged in, they lost it, along with the backup copy."

"Sounds a little convenient doesn't it." I told her. "Let's talk about it tonight."

Chapter 16

Possible Connections

That evening over dinner, Tracy and I discussed the missing radiation level file. It wasn't until she mentioned that the person she talked to at the DNR said that it was lost around the time that they changed DNR commissioners that a bell started to ring in both our minds.

Was this the missing link we were looking for? It might not be "the link," but, it might be the start of the links that bring answers to what Howard Long was trying to tell us.

I gave Mark Lawson a call.

"Well, it's dinner time, and it is only Thursday, so you must have found something," Mark answered.

I gave him the file number and told him about how the DNR had lost the file just after the change in DNR managers.

"You mean, just after the plane crash," Mark stated.

"Does that arouse your interest at all?" I jabbed Mark.

"Enough that I might let this food get cold. Good work."

"Anything from your man on the ground?" I asked.

"He confirmed that your geology report was correct. There is a layer of uranium containing ore under parts of western Minnesota. They deemed the concentration was too low to mine. The deep wells went far below that layer into what they felt was a salt layer. It should have been safe for storing the CO_2 gas."

"And?" I asked.

"Don't know. I wonder if the earthquake had the same effect in Minnesota as it did in North Dakota. CO2 gas wants to rise doesn't it?" Mark asked.

"That's why it is called a greenhouse gas. It gets up in the upper atmosphere," I told him.

"We'll check to see if there are any reports of bubbles in ponds out there," Mark told me. "I'm sure Butch would love to head back out there and see if the snow might be heading into western Minnesota."

After we were finished talking, a thought occurred to me. How did the man from Wyoming, Luke Carpenter, know to watch Tracy? The only people who knew that Tracy had any contact with Howard Long were the local police, the sheriff's department in St. Cloud, the FBI, a copywriter from the Duluth station, and our station. No one else was aware of what Tracy or I knew. LT had told us to drop it. Even LT did not know that we had possibly found one link, even though there was no proof.

Did someone have an inside track to the information? Was this the reason that no one was following us? If so, all they had to do was sit back and see if we were getting too close. So far, we were just starting to scratch the surface. We had no idea what was below the paint. If we started to get close, might we be in danger?

Tracy did not like that thought. She felt safe with me. However, someone could break into my apartment, just as they did hers, and take what they wanted. What if they tried to break in while we were here?

I called Mark back and told him about Tracy and my conversation.

"She might be right," he told me. "Too early to tell without any facts leading to any individual. However, if we start to get close, someone might want both of you out of the way just like the two people on our current list."

125

It was not what we wanted to hear. "Think we should see if the Castle has an opening?" I asked Mark.

"I can't protect you from here, and if you are concerned about the police, it might be a better choice. Why don't you give your father a call in the morning and see if he wants house guests."

I agreed. Tomorrow, I'll make the call.

That evening, Tracy snuggled up even closer. I could tell that the thought of an insider was bothering her. To tell the truth, it sounded rather creepy to me as well.

In the morning, we discussed whether we needed to pack up or wait. I suggested to Tracy that so far, we were far from having direct information that might implicate any individuals, and I thought we could wait until after I talked to my father, and even then, later today or tomorrow would be acceptable. Since tomorrow was Saturday, the workload would be lighter. Tracy told me that she would be nervous all day.

On the way to the station, I called my father. "Dad, how are you this morning?"

"Well, when I looked in the mirror, I was still vertical. What do you need at this time of the day?" he asked.

That was direct. I guess I don't call him in the mornings terribly often. "I need another favor. Can you get that room back for another week? Mark suggested that it might be beneficial to stay out of sight just in case someone out there is watching us."

"I thought you said the danger was over? he asked. One bedroom or two?"

"One would be fine. Thanks. Let me know if you get the key."

I turned to Tracy, "He'll figure out something. He's terrific at convincing people to do whatever he wants."

"I'll feel safer over there, Tracy told me. "With all the people that live at the Castle, someone would be nuts to try to break in. Martin, do you think we will figure this out before my short term loan to the station is up?"

"I don't know. This one is not an easy case even for the FBI."

Mid-morning, I got a call from my father.

"It's all set. I've got the keys."

"Thanks Dad, we'll see you after dinner."

When I called Tracy, I let her know that we could move in tonight. She was pleased to hear it. She suggested that we pick up some beer for my father and his gang when we stopped for groceries.

After our shift, we stopped off at a Mexican restaurant for dinner. Then, we packed up at my apartment, picked up groceries, and moved back into the Castle.

When we arrived at my father's place, he asked, "You want guard service, room service or just turndown service?"

Tracy showed him the case of beer she had purchased for him.

"Oh, I suppose that means you want all three," he joked.

We hauled our clothes and supplies up to the room, and we were settled in by the time the evening news came on. It did not give us time to do any research this evening. I could see by the expression on Tracy's face that she felt more secure staying at the Castle. She looked more relaxed than she did earlier in the day. I could not blame her, I felt more secure here as well.

Tracy dragged a couple beers out of the grocery supply, and suggested that we have one to relax. Then we watched the news, before heading off to bed.

I was starting to realize how much quieter it was at the Castle than at my apartment. I had not paid attention to this fact earlier, with all the things that were going on. However, after I made sure my alarm was off at my apartment, I got to thinking; I don't remember hearing the neighbors at the Castle. I guess the older building I am living in was constructed before they had standards for sound insulated walls. One thing for sure, the Castle made for a quieter night's sleep.

As soon as the news was over, it was lights out. It is remarkable how concerns and stress can leave you exhausted.

Saturday mornings were always lighter workdays than the rest of the week. You would think that people would be partying all night on Fridays after work. However, as it turned out, Friday's were heavy restaurant nights. Saturday night was when people hit the nightlife, so the media coverage would take most of Sunday morning to mop up the nighttime stories.

I made a suggestion to Tracy, if she had a quiet time during the day, she and Photo could head over to her townhouse for a few hours to straighten it out. Shawn and I could handle things unless something grandiose came up. Two hours of room straightening by both of them would make the place look a lot more respectable. Besides, she would not be there alone. Tracy decided it was an excellent idea.

Just before noon, Tracy and Photo picked up a sandwich and headed over to Tracy's townhouse. Photo knew the situation and did not mind helping put things back in the cabinets and vacuuming the floor, while Tracy straightened out her bedroom. They made sure they did not have anyone on the street observing their arrival. So far, the street was empty.

By the time they finished cleaning the place, it looked presentable. Now, if anyone new searched her place, we could tell the difference. They finished just in time to cover another traffic accident. This one knocked down a power pole, shutting down the power to one of the malls.

It had been raining all afternoon. The cool temperatures of fall were slowly dropping. By the time the shift was over, I was ready for either a hot shower, or a plunge in the hot tub located by the lap pool at the Castle. I was not sure if I was overly tired or just exhausted. However, with the rain, I could still feel the chill straight through my

128

body. Unfortunately, I had not packed my swimsuit before we moved, and I doubted that Tracy had either.

I picked up Tracy at the station, and we zipped through a drive-thru to pick up something to eat. Neither of us felt like finding a formal restaurant to eat dinner. We ate as soon as we got back, for both of us were cold and hungry from all the activities of the day.

After eating, I told Tracy that I wanted to take a long hot shower before looking at any more files. I was still cold.

The pulsating stream of water was just starting to warm up, and the steam was starting to rise out of the top of the shower when I heard the door open. A couple seconds later, Tracy asked, "Mind if I join you in that hot shower?"

How do you say no to a beautiful woman that is slowly taking off her clothes so that she can brush up against you in a hot shower? You don't.

She climbed into the shower and gave me a kiss. "Warm enough for you?" she asked.

I could feel my blood flowing, warming up every part of my body. Her kiss alone had started to warm up my blood. As we stood there, the soap from my body was slowly rubbing off on her soft skin.

Even though we had snuggled in bed for the past week, this was the first time I had seen her fully naked. She was bathed in the light of the shower. Her body was as perfect as the smile on her face.

We took turns rubbing the soap over each other and then rinsing it off.

When we emerged from the shower, the chill from the cold rain was definitely gone from our bodies. The mirror was totally fogged up. Even the fan couldn't pull the steam out of the bathroom. I was not sure if it was from the hot water or the body steam emanating from our shower. We put on the thick robes supplied by the Castle for guests, and went out to the sofa to discuss everything we knew about the case.

It took a while before we got back to discussing our project. I found it hard to concentrate when someone was rubbing her soft leg against mine.

An hour later, we forced ourselves to slip into some casual clothes so that we could start discussing some of the "what-if's" of the information we had. If it wasn't for the lingering concern for our safety, it could have waited for another day. However, we desperately needed to find some links in the files if we were to solve the mystery, and there had to be some links in these files.

We took each electronic folder and tried to come up with as many possibilities as our minds could concentrate on.

I started with the power plant in western North Dakota. If the pipeline was the key, who would have gained or lost the most by exposing the problems?

We started listing all the possibilities on a new file on the computer: Did they use a cheaper quality pipe that corroded through? Did they switch to Wyoming coal to increase output without checking the emissions? Did someone make a mistake and send the plant emissions to the wrong wells?

Then, we looked at the outcomes: How much money was involved with using non-coated steel pipes? Were there other pipes with the same problem? Was hydrogen sulfide gas mixed into the CO_2 to save money on purchasing a separate stripper for the sulfides? Did the hydrogen sulfide gas kill the farmer? Where did it come from? Was it from a corroded pipe? Did the earthquakes open a route for the gas to reach the surface? Was the hydrogen sulfide or CO_2 gas responsible for the oil traces in the drinking water? On the other hand, was the earthquake responsible? There were a number of outstanding questions without clear answers.

Next, we looked at who gained: Did the pipe supplier pocket the difference, or did the plant save money by using non-coated pipes? Did burning Wyoming coal save the plant money in efficiency? If someone discovered a serious problem, who stood to lose the most money, the power plant, pipeline company, or the oil companies? On the other hand, was it someone in the EPA or DNR protecting their bad decisions?

The list went on and on. Hopefully, if we did the same analysis for each folder, a common question or result would show up somewhere. If we could find something in common between the folders, we would have a start. We could only imagine what the FBI might be finding with their resources. If they put some muscle on the files, they might be spotting the smaller details that were going right over our heads.

For now, the list was an impressive start for a night when we started out cold and tired. Now, we were just plain tired.

Tracy and I shut it down about 9:45 pm, watched the news and slipped off to bed. After that shower earlier in the evening, I had the feeling that Tracy was dropping the hint that she might be interested in more than getting an early night's sleep.

I was right. The goodnight kiss took much longer than normal, and both of us seemed to forget how tired we had been from the long week. After warming up in the shower, and now warming up in bed, it was close to midnight before I got to sleep.

Chapter 17

Options

The next morning, I was awakened by a soft, warm body pressing tightly against me, and a gentle kiss. "Good morning," Tracy greeted me. "Hope you had some good dreams last night."

It took me by surprise. Was she assuming I had dreamed about her after last night, or had I been talking in my sleep?

Sunday morning was a typical Sunday. Lots of news to mop-up from the night crew. They had been kept busy with the typical bar fights, shootings, and accidents caused by drunken drivers. Obviously, the new laws for drivers had not entirely solved the problems. There was also a group of people that were upset because a concert was cancelled at the last minute. That was always good for a few interviews.

We picked up a few assignments at the station for each of us to follow up on, and hit the streets. It would keep both of our crews busy until well after lunch.

When I was sending a set of reports back to the television station for editing, I sent off a note to Mark Lawson with the latest of our what-if possibilities. I figured that his crew was going to have more time to put the timelines together than we did. Hopefully, in a couple days, Mark would have some idea whether any of our thoughts and research was leading to something or not.

In the afternoon, Tracy got a call from her manager in Duluth. He was wondering how the opportunity to work at a larger station was going and if she had a feeling for when our regular crew was coming back from the disabled list.

While she was gone, the station in Duluth had been using two journalism students from the University of Minnesota in Duluth. Tracy's manager was trying to let her know that not only was she missed, but also, he wanted her back as soon as she could.

Tracy told him she had heard that it would be another two or three weeks before the recovering reporter was cleared to get back to work. He was just starting physical therapy, and the decision on returning to the job depended on how long it would take the soreness to leave his neck and spine after his surgery. If everything went OK with physical therapy, he could probably start limited work in a couple weeks, before being cleared for coming back full time.

"Well, keep us informed," her manager told her. "We need to figure out our schedule up here as soon as we can."

It was becoming a dilemma for Tracy. What had been an opportunity to experience the big city life had left a number of questions deep in her mind. Did she prefer the gentle life of Duluth to the Cities? Was there a permanent spot available here if she wished to stay? What about Martin? Was there something there, or was it just an "opportunity" of the moment? Like a breeze blowing a drapery back and forth, these questions lingered in her mind throughout the afternoon and into the evening. Somehow, she needed to come up with the answers. No one was going to give her a crib sheet for those questions.

When I met Tracy at the station and we headed out the door, she asked, "Think we can find a quiet restaurant for dinner tonight and leave Howard Long's case alone for an evening?"

"Sure, I know a lovely place about ten miles away where we can sit and relax. Have a tough day?" I asked her. She looked as though all of her normal enthusiastic expressions were drained from her face. Whatever was bothering her, I figured she needed time to relax and work through them.

I took her to a small family owned restaurant in Long Lake that I had found a few months ago. It was quiet, good food, and the waitress was not constantly pushing to turn tables and get more people seated.

We found an empty table in the corner, and had a glass of wine while waiting for our orders. I decided not to push Tracy about her problem. I figured she would tell me when she was ready.

As we were relaxing, my eye caught the activity at a table on the other side of the restaurant. There were people at only four tables this evening. I was watching a couple with what looked like a two-year-old girl. She was exceedingly well mannered, and the couple was making sure that she had something to eat that little girls like. When the server would come over, the little girl would play bashful, then give her a big smile as she walked away.

I told Tracy to watch her. I figured it might give her a break from whatever she was thinking about. I was right. The little girl proved highly entertaining.

When our food finally arrived, Tracy looked more relaxed and was enjoying her food. She had ordered a seafood platter, and it was just as she liked it – without a lot of breading on the shrimp and scallops. I ordered the fried chicken special.

We ate slowly and relaxed before heading back to my father's Castle.

When we arrived back at the Castle, Hank greeted us at the elevator. "About time you two showed up. We were about to send out the National Guard. Thought someone had kidnapped you."

Tracy laughed. "Sorry Hank. I didn't realize we were supposed to call ahead with our schedule." She gave him a big hug.

Hank looked a little flushed. "Just make sure you let Martin's father know your schedule," he said. "As long as I get a hug, you're OK coming in late as far as I'm concerned."

"Thanks Hank," Tracy told him.

It was obvious that Tracy was becoming a favorite of the gang.

When we were back in the apartment, I asked Tracy what was on her mind. I was surprised that she did not want to dig into the couple of folders of Howard Long's, which we had not had time to examine.

"I got a call today from my manager in Duluth," she told me. "He wanted an update on when I could come back to my job. I have been thinking about the conversation all day."

"What did you tell him?"

"I told him, it would be two or three weeks before Jake Schwartz would be medically cleared to come back to work, provided he did not have any problems with rehab."

"That sounds about right," I told her. "Have you decided if you want to go back or stay?"

"That's the problem. There are too many things going on. I guess life is never an easy route with easy choices. What do you think I should do?" she asked.

I told her, "Unfortunately, it is not my decision. I'm starting to get partial to those goodnight kisses. Besides, what's my father and Hank going to do if you are not around to twist them around your fingers?"

She looked deeply into my eyes. "I think you are part of my problem. I've enjoyed being with you the past couple weeks. I'm not sure what to do. If I decide to stay here in the Cities, I need to start discussing it now so I do not leave my manager in Duluth out on a limb. I don't know where things are going with the two of us. Everything is moving far too quickly."

I was at a loss for words. She was right; things had progressed too quickly. It would be far easier if she had a couple more months before she needed to make that decision. Neither of us knew enough about the other to make any long-term commitments. It felt like a wild, wonderful fling. We had spent the past weeks working together. We still did not know what made each other tick, or what skeletons were still hidden in our closets.

"Have you decided if you prefer working in a small market town or in the Twin Cities?" I asked her. "That part of the question is what you need to decide before you can make any other decisions."

We sat on the sofa in each other's arms the rest of the evening. Neither one of us had the courage to tell the other one that what we wanted is what we had now and for it to stay this way for a long time.

The next morning, LT caught Tracy in the hall as she checked with the editors for the daily assignments.

"I got a text message from your boss yesterday. I guess I'm not the only one who works on Sundays. He wanted to know about Jake's progress and when you might be able to head back. I didn't answer it yet. Figured I better chat with you and see what you want to do. I'm not sure if you want to try and stay in the Cities or go back to Duluth."

"Thanks LT. Things have been a little different than I expected with this assignment. I appreciate you asking me before sending him a message. You think there are any openings down here?" Tracy asked.

"Well, our budget is tight for the next three months. Then, I think we may be able to hire someone if you are interested. Otherwise, I know one of the other stations is looking to hire someone. I think you would fit in fine no matter where you would like to go."

"You make my decision even harder," she told him. "I can't imagine working for two better managers. When do you need to let Duluth know?"

"I think we can stall for a couple days. It's Monday. I can stall him until Thursday or Friday if you like. You have a bigger question. I'm more worried about Martin if you decide to head back to Duluth. Both of you have that look in your eyes."

Tracy gave LT a hug. "I know. Let's see what the next couple of days bring. I wish I had a crystal ball."

"If I had one, I'd loan it to you," LT told her. "Take your time. It sounds like a tough decision."

Tracy thanked him and headed off to find Photo.

Photo was in the editing room, cleaning his lenses. He figured Tracy would come looking for him once she finished talking to LT. When she arrived, he grabbed his gear and the two of them set off to check out their first assignments.

"LT ask you about staying or heading back?" Photo asked.

"Yes, well sort of," Tracy answered.

"I figured that. He was asking the editors about you earlier. They told him that they would like to keep you here."

"Thanks. That's nice to know," Tracy said with a smile.

"LT told me, I could stay on part time, while I was finishing my final quarter, and then go full time if I liked."

"What did you say?" Tracy asked him.

"I told him, he had to get you to stay first," Photo responded with a twinkle in his eye.

"You did not."

"You'll never know," Photo told her. "You need to stay to find out."

Their first assignment was to cover a conference committee at the state legislature. The discussion was about the shutting down of one of the iron ore mines in northern Minnesota. The mine had run out of high-grade ore twenty years earlier. Now, the low-grade taconite ore was about exhausted. That meant, 300 workers would be laid off and the Silver Bay shipping port abandoned.

Even though it was old news, it played well for the evening program. Everyone had a tender heart for the massive ore boats on Lake Superior, and pictures of the open ore mines were something most Minnesotans were aware of. Now, the discussion was what to do with the remaining mines.

Years ago, they had opened some limited mining for silver and copper in the same region. These mines were primarily underground mines, and the ore was processed near the area it was mined. As a result, the giant ore boats were not needed. If they shut down the iron mining, the boats would be limited to shipping grains, cement, and coal.

Tracy asked the state representatives a number of questions, hoping to get some fresh sound bites for the news.

From there, it was off to the Mall of America, often called "The Mall" by the locals. There was a press conference about to start on a new store that was hoping to move into the Mall of America. It required a large addition to the retail space to put the new store in a prominent location.

Photo got pictures of the drawings showing the location of the proposed store, and how they needed to change the outside appearance of the Mall to make it fit. These were beamed back to the station along with Tracy's report for the 6:00 pm news.

Shawn and I spent the morning at the Minneapolis courthouse.

A large bribery case was just finishing up and was going to the jury. Apparently, one of the leading construction companies had bribed someone in the state to build two new dams on the Mississippi River above Minneapolis. The concrete on the old dams was starting to crumble, and several companies had placed bids to replace them. Somehow, the amounts of the sealed bids had gotten out to one company, and they had submitted an eleventh-hour bid for the dams, which was just below their nearest competitor.

All was going their way until an auditor noticed that the envelopes had been resealed.

We covered the closing arguments and sent our reports to the station. It did not look good for the owner of the construction company.

As we were leaving the courthouse, I got a call from Mark Lawson.

"Martin, where are you?

"Just leaving the Minneapolis courthouse, why?" I asked.

"Meet me at the café next to the Guthrie Theater. We need to talk."

"When?" I asked.

"Now!"

I met Mark at the café. It was early, so the noon rush had not started.

"OK, Mark, what gives?"

"What are you and Tracy working on today?" he asked.

"Well, I'm covering the bribery trial at the Minneapolis courthouse, and I think Tracy was at the legislature this morning covering the mining issues, and at the Mall after that. Why?"

"We picked up some traffic on our phone taps this morning from S&G in Wyoming. They wanted you and Tracy monitored."

"Who did?" I asked.

"Not sure, but we know who is coming to follow you. I have a man waiting for him at the airport right now. It would help if I can get your schedule and Tracy's. If we lose him, we can pick him back up again quickly as long as he is tailing one of you. Right now, our plan is to have the man tailed."

"Are we in danger?" I asked.

"Not yet. Let's see what they are up to and if we can get more information out of them. Something that was reported on for this morning news must have caught their attention."

"Mark, those reports have not been run yet."

"I know. That's why we are meeting. We need to keep this confidential until we find out who the players are."

I told Mark I would let Tracy know and keep him up to date on our assignments. It would be hard to keep this information secret from our manager and co-workers.

I met Shawn back at the truck. "False alarm. The FBI had a report that we were investigating their use of private airplanes. I told him, it was a false lead. Someone was trying to lead them astray. However, if they wanted us to investigate them, just let us know."

Shawn and I took off to cover a few stories around town before the jury came back with a verdict.

When I picked up Tracy at the end of the day, we drove a couple blocks before I pulled over and parked near one of the lakes Minneapolis is famous for.

"Martin, why are we stopping?"

I explained my conversation with Mark Lawson earlier in the day. "I think we need to figure out a game plan. It would be best if we could cut down on our visibility once we are finished with work. That means we should probably head straight back to the apartment at the end of our shifts and not stop anywhere for dinner. The good thing is that Mark knows about the stalker and is getting the warrants to monitor all of his conversations."

Tracy was slightly shaken. "Are we in danger?"

"Mark does not think so, at least for now. I think we need to pick up food for a week. My Dad can pick up other items we need. Let's just stay flexible, so we can adjust if needed."

I checked the traffic and made a few random turns. No one was following us – yet. We pulled into a food mart and purchased what we needed. Then, we headed back to the Castle. Once again, we were cautious to see if anyone was observing us as we entered the garage or used the elevator.

After we unpacked, we stopped down at my father's apartment to inform him that someone might be watching us.

"You want us to put a guard on your door?" he asked.

He was serious. "No, I just wanted you and your gang to keep both eyes open for strangers. If you see someone, call Mark Lawson first, and then call us."

When we left his apartment, he commented, "Keep safe."

"We will," I told him.

After eating, we planned to spend the rest of the evening trying to read as many unopened files as possible. If someone was planning on watching us, we desperately wanted to know why.

Then, we would take a close look back at our schedules. Was the person in Wyoming really worried about something we reported on earlier today, or was it something in the news in the past couple days? Somewhere, there had to be information that someone was worried about us finding or remembering.

Chapter 18

Watching the Watcher

As quickly as possible after eating, we started on the remaining files. As we were working on it, a couple questions crossed my mind. If someone was watching us, we should probably eliminate the flow charts from our apartment. It gave them a roadmap as to what we knew, or what we were getting close to. Where could we put them? Perhaps one of my father's gang could store them for us. No one would look there.

The second item that was still crossing my mind: what was in this morning's coverage that could have caught their attention? We certainly needed to address it tonight before we went to bed.

The first new file that we opened from Howard Long was on mining in northern Minnesota. It had some articles on the early days of iron ore mining, and a number of clippings regarding the Reserve Mine trial, where the judge directed the mine to stop pumping tailings into Lake Superior. It seemed extremely remote that Howard Long was telling us that the old tailings were a serious problem for the water pipes. However, we were not throwing out any possibilities, just listing them.

There were also proposals in the folder on gold, silver, and copper mining that dated back to the 1990's. Apparently, the coverage Tracy had done this morning on the mining industry was not a new topic, just an update on what had been presented years ago as part of the mining future. I logged that thought into the back of my mind. Was that what our watchers were worried about?

The other file was all about the problems between Canada and the US with floodwater protection. On the northwestern side of Minnesota, a large amount of the watershed, along with water from North Dakota, flows into Canada. Efforts over the past forty years, to reduce the flood threat in the area, have always been hampered by international agreements. Canada wanted to restrict the flow rate of the water as well as try to reduce the sediment in the river. With a river that could flood ten-miles across in the spring, trying to control it was a significant effort. Whole towns were often at risk.

"Why couldn't they build a reservoir on that river and use it for drinking water?" Tracy asked.

"Well, unlike most rivers where they build dams, this one does not have a steep set of hills to help contain it. It is so flat along the Red River, that to build a reservoir, you would have to dig down to make one. Then, all the silt from the river would fill it back in, in only a few seasons. If you dammed it up by ten feet, all of the fertile cropland of the Red River Valley would be lost to flood land. That's why they did not include it in the pipeline project."

Tracy and I must have looked over fifty files before pulling the plug. There was a lot of information, but still, no roadmap. What were we supposed to be finding?

Just then, the phone rang. It was Mark Lawson.

"Just wanted to let you know we have our man, Scott Lenard, under surveillance. We have two people on him 24-7, and have planted a couple of bugs in his room, as well as in his supplies. If he sneezes, we shout gesundheit.

"Did you and Tracy discuss this morning's news conference? Just wondering what questions were asked or answered at the legislature. That has to be the key to our surveillance man."

I put our conversation on speakerphone.

"Tracy, Mark wants to know what you might have asked this morning, or what answers came up that might not have reached the news?"

"Hi, Mark. Thanks for the heads-up. I have been thinking this evening about what might have been said that would get someone's attention. Honestly, I cannot think of anything. They were discussing the demise of iron mining and the shutting down of the Silver Bay terminal. Nothing new there. That's been talked about for ten years.

"They also talked about silver and copper mining to help the unemployment situation. Those are underground mines.

"That's all I can think of," she told him.

"OK, if we pick up some verbiage from our guest, maybe we can put the crosses on the 't's and dot the 'i's. Something must have pricked their spines. We'll figure it out.

"Remember to send me a text message on each of your locations, so we can keep our surveillance up."

"You think they will slip up and say something?" I asked.

"That's the idea. They slipped up once, leaving their man from Wyoming uncovered; maybe they will slip up again. I'll call you if we see anything."

We were glad to hear from Mark. We needed the confidence that he was a step ahead of them, whoever they are! At least now, we had a name, even if we felt like fish in a goldfish bowl.

We sat and talked about the news conference until the evening news came on. Then, we both listened intently to see if there was something mentioned in the report that we missed. Unfortunately, if there was, we missed it again.

Tracy and I had a small dish of ice cream before heading off to sleep. We needed to settle all of our nervous energy.

When we got to bed, Tracy asked me to hold her tight. She needed the warmth and feeling that someone was protecting her to get a good night's sleep.

I gave her a passionate kiss and told her, "I'm here if you wake up and need a hug."

She just rolled over tighter to my body.

Come morning, I was sure neither of us had changed positions all night. We were still tight as possible to each other.

We felt uneasy that Tuesday morning, as we got ready to head for work. On the drive in, Tracy mentioned to me, "I wish Mark Lawson had given us a picture of the person that is following us. It would be nice to know who to watch for."

"That's probably the reason he didn't. If we saw him, we would probably tip our hat and he would know someone spotted him. No, we just need to make sure we are never alone, and stay in the crowds as much as possible. We'll let Mark and his people do their thing.

"Don't forget to text Mark on your locations. We don't want his people to lose us or the person they are following."

"I promise," Tracy replied.

That morning, both of us felt like we had been lying on an anthill. We felt the creepy-crawlies all day. The tendency was to keep looking around. However, that was the last thing we needed to do. If it looked like we were watching for someone, it would spook them into using other people that Mark was not following.

At this point in time, we did not know who to trust. Obviously, someone was tipping them off. Was it someone in our group? What about the new guy – Photo? I made sure he was working with me for the next couple of days just in case. I had worked with Shawn for enough years that I knew he would look after Tracy.

By noon, Tracy's stomach was twitching and turning. Tracy texted Mark and me that she and Shawn were stopping at a small diner. Tracy needed something to eat. "Maybe some soup and crackers will settle down my stomach. We'll probably be there for the next 30 minutes."

As they were ordering their food, Tracy noticed two men come in and sit at the counter. They ordered a sandwich to go. Then, before Tracy finished her meal, they left. She wondered if these were Mark's men that were keeping an eye on them. She thought that she could spot them again if they showed up anywhere they were the rest of the day.

When Shawn and Tracy left the diner, Tracy sent a note letting both of us know their next destination.

Photo and I were working on a traffic accident on the north side of St. Paul. Someone had crashed a motorcycle into a tree, after taking a corner way above the speed limit. Unfortunately, the tree won the battle. Photo got some video of the crash scene along with the skid marks on the pavement. You would think after seeing these on TV, people would slow down. All it took was a little sand on the corner of the street, and the motorcycle lost control. Fortunately, no one was on the corner, or they would have been killed as well.

I glanced around a couple times. I didn't see anyone that looked overly concerned about our crew. There were just a bunch of locals standing around observing the accident and the police.

We sent in the video and our report to our editor.

The rest of the afternoon went as normal. By 5:30 pm, both crews were back at the station, and we were starting to head to the apartment.

"Did you see anyone following you?" Tracy asked.

"I looked a couple times, but no, I didn't see anyone. How about you?" I asked her.

"Just two men at the diner. I'm not sure if they were following us or not. I kind of thought they might have been Mark's men. They just picked up a sandwich to go and left before we did. However, it could have been a coincidence. I just don't know."

I called Mark Lawson using my car's phone to see if he had any more information for us.

"Martin, don't you know you shouldn't talk and drive at the same time?"

That caught me by surprise. Were we under surveillance and he knew I was driving? We had just pulled over to the curb to call Mark. "Mark, any new information you can share with us?" I asked.

"Quiet as a church mouse," he answered. "Just be patient, they'll slip up. It is just a matter of time."

"Mark, were those two guys at the diner your guys?" Tracy asked.

"That obvious, huh. I split them up later in the day. I'll have to talk to them about it," Mark replied. "Just keeping an eye on you."

"Thanks!" I told Mark. "We'll be at the apartment if you need to get a hold of us."

When we got back to the Castle, we drove into the garage and went up in the elevator, keeping our eyes open for anyone who might be somewhere they should not be. So far, no one was in sight.

We got back to our floor, and noticed there was a note just inside our door.

Food in the oven.
Thought you might like something ready.
Dad

He had gotten his friends to pick up a couple dinners from downstairs and had them wrapped to go. They were still warm when we opened the container to see what he had gotten for us. Obviously, he had figured out our schedule as well. Or, had Mark let him know we were on the way? Either way, the food tasted delicious.

After eating, I called and thanked my dad, while Tracy set up the netbook. We were determined to find those missing links.

Somewhere in the files on the mines, there had to be something significant in that news conference that struck a bell. If there was, we wanted to find it.

We were deep in thought talking about the files, when there was a knock on the door.

Tracy looked at me and said, "Quick, duck the netbook, while I duck the papers." Then, she motioned for me to see who was there, while she stood around the corner near the bathroom.

Chapter 19

Watching

I guess it was a wake-up call to how tight our nerves were strung out. Both of us were in panic mode.

When I got to the door, I looked through the peephole and discovered my father peering back in at me. I laughed as I opened the door.

"What's so funny," he asked as he came in.

Tracy and I explained to him, "We thought you might be the bad guys. When we heard the doorbell, we scrambled to hide everything."

"Listen, you two are old enough to know that bad guys don't knock. Haven't you ever watched that TV? They always just break in the door. Besides, I have enough problems with the door latches in this building. I couldn't break in if I wanted to. I just wanted to come over and say hi. I haven't seen either of you for a couple days, and I was wondering if you two were still talking to each other."

"Thanks Dad. Just next time call first. If there is someone watching us, we don't want to get you involved."

Tracy thanked him for the food, again, and told him, "It was nice to have something warm and ready to eat when we came in."

"So, how long do you think you need to stay in this cave until Mark Lawson nails the guy?" my father asked.

"Don't know. Mark has his finger on the person's pulse. We are just hoping that they say or do something stupid, so we can figure out what this whole thing is about," I told him.

"OK if I have a look too? Sometimes an extra set of eyes can spot something you might have missed."

I looked at Tracy. "Sure. But, if you say anything, we will put a moat around your Castle and throw you in for the alligators."

We spent the next three hours looking at the last files and showing Dad the flow chart we developed. He was impressed. When we were about to put it all away, just before the news, he mentioned to us, "You know, everything you have there relates to pollution and injecting things into the ground. You need to concentrate on just those two items for an evening."

He was right. That was the common thread.

"Well, I think you have about worn out these old tired bones," he said as he got up to head back to his place.

We thanked him again for the food, and told him, we would try to do a better job of talking to him.

As the news came on, I was thinking about what my father had told us. If he was right, we needed to take a second look at that news conference the other day, and see what was in there about pollution or injection into the ground.

The Reserve Mine lawsuit was a case of pollution. Asbestos tailings were dumped directly into Lake Superior. The court made them dump the tailings on land, away from the water. The asbestos in the water was a fine layer that was originally dumped in at Silver Bay. However, by the time it settled to the bottom, it had redeposited itself miles in each direction. At the time, many locations, including cities and homeowners, were taking their drinking water directly from pipes on the bottom of the shoreline of the lake. I wondered if they ever did any follow-up studies of those people.

Now, with the announcement of the ending of the iron mines, except for large man made pits, which already were being converted to lakes by nature, there did not seem to be a lot of attention on the subject.

The copper mines were following shafts of ore that were small enough that strip mining was unproductive. As a result, all the people employed to run the big dump trucks and blast the rocks, were becoming unemployed; if they had not already lost their jobs in the past few years.

As recently as five years ago, the mines had switched over to a method first used in Arizona and New Mexico for copper mining. They would inject a fluid into the area and leach out the minerals they were mining. Then, by use of several chemical processes, they could extract the copper, silver, and some trace amounts of gold out of the solutions.

Because of the newer technology, a number of slant wells, wells drilled horizontally after reaching the level containing some ore, were already in operation. According to the press conference, they were going to expand their mining operations, which would have a positive effect on the unemployment in the area. The skills needed were different. Now, it was the drillers and the chemists who needed to work with the geologists. However, many new supply jobs were going to open up to keep up with the expansion.

I kept wondering what all of that had to do with Howard Long, when the weather report came on. They were talking about the unusually warm fall, and how the streams and rivers along Lake Superior were much drier than normal. That's when they put up a map of the area showing all the rivers and streams, and a thought hit me. Where is the Mississippi River?

Tracy looked over at me while I was digging out my netbook. "What are you doing now?" she asked.

"Just wondering where the rivers go in Minnesota," I answered.

I looked at a map done by the DNR showing the principal rivers and lakes in Minnesota. I had forgotten that the Mississippi River wove its way all around northern Minnesota before finally heading south as a mighty river. It started in a small lake near Bemidji, and snaked its way 493 miles all over the northern region, before reaching the Twin Cities of Minneapolis and St. Paul. Some of the towns along its path included: Bemidji, Grand Rapids, St. Cloud, Aitkin, Brainerd, Little Falls, Fort Ripley, Sartell, Monticello, Anoka, Champlin and Coon Rapids. There were at least a couple dozen smaller towns along the upper river, as well. Some of this explained why many of the lakes and feeder streams had been closed to fishing ever since the great carp invasion.

As I looked at the list, Grand Rapids stood out. It was also on the southern edge of the region where copper mining was going to start. I slid my map in front of Tracy.

"Did you know the copper mines were in areas that drained into the Mississippi River?" I asked her.

"No, I guess I never looked," she answered.

"It looks like they are either in the watershed that drains into the Mississippi River, or in the ones that drain into Lake Superior. I think we have some more research left for tomorrow night," I told her.

"I think you left one out. Some of those northern streams, up past Hibbing, flow into Canada. If you think there is something in the files about this area, it is going to affect a much larger area," Tracy suggested.

It definitely gave us a thought of something we needed to pursue. It might be a solid lead, or it might be a dead end. Tomorrow might give us an answer.

The lead was what the doctor ordered. It gave us the distraction from our followers and something new to think about, as we got ready for some sleep. Had it not distracted me, I am not sure if I could have fallen off to sleep. I surely would have had some wild dreams, with faces coming out of the woodwork watching me all night.

Now, I settled into bed next to Tracy, and reached over and gave her a good night kiss.

After that, I wondered, what would it be like if Tracy moved back to Duluth? Would it mark the end to this romance? How would she feel about it? Would we ever have time to see each other with Tracy in Duluth and me in the Twin Cities?

It took me a while to fall asleep. I kept wondering if there was anything I could or should do. I kept listening to her gentle breathing as she slept soundly, tight against my body.

Chapter 20

Detection

I woke to the sound of rain on the windows. For once, the weather report was correct – rain on Wednesday morning followed by a cool and partly cloudy afternoon. When I got to the station, I decided I would give our weather crew a tough time. It had been three days in a row that they had it correct. If they hit the forecast correctly the next day, they might have a better winning percentage than most of the Minnesota sports teams. I was wondering which one of them was taking credit for the unusually good luck.

Tracy and I got off to work in the soggy traffic. It made the morning commute just a bit longer. Once again, I was glad we were staying at the Castle. The underground garage was nice and dry.

When we reached the station, we were glad to see that so far the assignment board was listing inside tasks. Hopefully, it would stay that way until the weather front moved on.

I sent Mark Lawson a text message with our first assignments and locations. It was only then that I had a thought: why were Mark's men at the diner? Did that mean the person they were following was also there?

I decided to keep my mouth shut and not worry Tracy. At a stop sign, I sent Mark another text asking him the same question.

Water Pressure

Photo and I were half way to our first assignment when I got an answer. *"Remember, we are not following you."* So, I was right. I wondered what else Mark had found out about the individual.

As we moved through the traffic, I did some searches on copper mining in Minnesota, and watersheds in northern Minnesota. I figured I could read them over later in the afternoon if things stayed slow.

I was about to relax when we got word of a tanker truck turnover on the freeway blocking all lanes. I knew that would tie us up for the rest of the morning, and the rain would keep us cold and wet.

To make things worse, it turned out the accident occurred at the beginning of the curve into the tunnel in downtown Minneapolis. It took us almost 20-minutes to find a way to the crash site without getting tied up in traffic ourselves. It was a mess. After talking to the highway patrol, we were told that the only injuries were to the driver of the truck. He had sustained just minor injuries. In spite of the mess in the traffic, the rest was just minor fender benders as people tried to stop quickly on the rain soaked pavement.

Photo had to work hard to get pictures without getting the lens wet, and trying to maneuver to get the right angles that showed the problems. So far, I was acting as his spotter trying to find the shots. The story would be simple.

The accident kept us on location for almost two hours. Actually, we couldn't move any better than the traffic, until they opened a couple lanes each way.

For Tracy's assignment, she had found a nice dry location to interview the main architects of a building project. They were proposing some urban revitalization, and wanted the city to demolish two square blocks for their project. It gave her a pleasant break from the rain. The builders were from Dallas, and had a source of money already approved. So far, it needed a number of city approvals to go forward.

When Photo and I finally got out of the traffic, I received a message that the verdict was in on the trial from Monday on bid rigging. I had 30 minutes to get back to the courthouse. Fortunately, we were only 15 minutes away.

We arrived in time for Photo to set up his video camera for the reading of the verdict. It was a good thing the jury did not come back earlier in the morning. We would have had to tap into another station's feed to get coverage.

When the verdict was read, the courtroom erupted. After considerable discussion, the verdict was not guilty. Everyone had assumed the verdict would come back guilty.

We hung around and picked up some interviews with a few of the jurors. Apparently, even though the jury had evidence of bid tampering, the attorneys failed to prove who had actually opened the envelopes. As a result, the jury could not find proof beyond doubt that the defendant was involved in the bid rigging.

Photo had some fantastic shots, and we knew that this would unquestionably make the news along with the accident earlier today. If Tracy had a compelling story, it would probably finish the time segment for the news that night.

When we wrapped it up, we headed back to the station. On the way, I finished my internet search I started earlier in the morning.

About half way to the station, I wondered how the outcome of the trial would affect the development of the building project. With the bid rigging getting the airtime at the same time as the city building project, would the public be scrutinizing future projects? How about the city engineers? Would they be worried that someone was constantly watching them looking for cases of handouts?

Tracy's text message said that she was heading back early as well. Unless something came up, we had a chance of getting out of the station before 5:00 pm. That was the earliest we had wrapped up a day in a couple weeks. If anything else came up, the station would call either us or the evening crew to follow up on any new events.

On our way back to the apartment, I asked Tracy if she saw any of Mark's agents today.

"No, if they were there, they stayed hidden very well," she answered. "How about you?"

"I told her, with the big accident, anyone following them would have had to have a helicopter to stay close to them in the traffic. I suppose that's why Mark wanted us to keep them informed of our locations. There was no way any of his people could have guessed which way he would have exited the traffic jam."

I decided not to tell her about Mark's comment from this morning. I did not want to worry her more than she was already.

As we got to the apartment, Hank met us at the elevator on our floor. "Did your father tell you about the guy we shagged out of here this morning?"

It caught us by surprise. We had not heard anything from my father or Mark. "No, tell me more," I told him.

"You see, I saw this burly guy get off the elevator and start looking around. I hadn't seen him before, so I asked him where he was going. He took one look at me and said he was on the wrong floor. He took the steps down to the first floor and went out the main door. I was way behind him, so I don't think he knew I was following him. Then, I told your father. He called some guy to let him know."

"Good job," I told him.

Hank gave me a general description of the man before we headed back to our apartment.

As soon as we got inside, Tracy turned to me, "You think they were checking on our place?"

"Maybe. I think I'll call Mark."

157

I called Mark Lawson. When he answered, he said, "I figured you would be calling about now. Did your father tell you about your visitor?"

"No, actually his friend did. What happened?"

"We followed him to your building. Actually, we were hoping he might break in and take something. Unfortunately, your friend spotted him, and the man hightailed it out of there. Your visitor did leave us with a good phone message though. It might be almost as good. We still have him under surveillance."

"You mean you would have let him break into the apartment?" I asked.

"In a heartbeat. If we could catch him with the goods and telling someone else about it, we might have solved that link problem you keep talking about. He did make the mistake of leaving a message for someone, that he aborted his attempt to get into your apartment because some old guy was asking too many questions. I'm waiting for the message to be picked up as we speak. Can't wait to see who is involved."

"OK. Thanks for the info, Mark. Let us know if you get anything else."

"No problem. Get a good night's sleep."

I told Tracy what Mark had told me. Then, I told her about his comment this morning.

"When were you going to tell me about that one?" she asked quite abruptly.

"Relax, Mark told me, they had it under control, and did not want to get you worried."

I opened a bottle of beer for her and told her to cool down, while I fixed dinner and talked to my father. I figured my father might be just as riled up as Tracy. To my surprise, I was wrong.

"Hey son, glad to hear from you. So, what do you think of the old gang now? We shagged that guy out with his tail between his legs."

I didn't tell him what Mark had told me. I just thanked him for keeping a close watch on the place. Actually, I was amazed that the guy turned and ran. You would have thought he would have an excuse in his pocket all set expecting to run into people. Hank must have truly caught him by surprise.

After Tracy's nerves simmered down, we had dinner. Slowly, we got to the point that we could discuss the events of the day. It was hard for Tracy not to be in command of the situation. I told her that it was the same for me. We just had to trust that Mark knew what he was doing, and he was obviously on a strong lead right now.

Both of us wished that Mark could tell us who the man had called. We realized that Mark was monitoring things to see who actually picked up the message. It is one thing to call a number. It is another, to find out who is on the other end. If he could put a solid name to the number, we could put more names in our flow chart. Someone had to lead us to a person, or corporation, that had something to gain or lose if we put the puzzle together. We all felt we were just one lead away from finally getting the flash-of-light vision telling us what this was all about.

That evening, Tracy spent a couple hours looking at the files and the information we had assembled from them. While she was working on that, I was looking at the information I had gathered on the internet during the day. With everything that had happened, I had not had a chance to look at it earlier.

I decided that I needed a little more information from my father. I called him up and asked if he could join us for dinner tomorrow.

"Thursday. That's chicken day downstairs," he told me. "Besides, we play poker on Thursday. Hank and a couple others just cashed their checks. You aren't going to keep me from lightening up their billfolds are you?"

"OK, let me give you a choice: you can bring up chicken, or have the frozen lasagna we are having," I told him. "I need your help looking at some history. You think the gang can take a night without you fleecing them dry?"

"Alright, you twisted my leg again. Give me a call when you get back tomorrow."

"What's that all about?" Tracy asked.

"Just a hunch. I want to hear a little more about that carp issue. That's one subject my father knows extremely well. Hope you don't mind."

"No, we owe him a dinner," Tracy answered.

"I think Howard Long's files are a sort of a history lesson, showing us what happened in the past. I'm still not sure how it all relates, but I think my father is right, it is pointing toward underground pollution. Maybe the place to start is in the rivers and lakes. I still wonder if there wasn't another file that ended up in the wrong place, or we just missed the key to find it."

"I have been thinking the same thing," Tracy told me. "You think it was in Howard's house?"

"We may never know if it was. I think we need to relax tonight. If things keep ratcheting up, the next couple days might get interesting."

"Did you decide what you are going to tell LT? It's Thursday tomorrow. He will probably want an answer tomorrow or Friday at the latest," I asked her.

"I honestly don't know what to say. I wish all this other stuff would go away so I could concentrate on one thing at a time. How do you concentrate on making decisions on your job when you know someone is out there stalking us?"

I was hoping she would have said that she was trying to figure out whether the two of us were worth her staying in the Cities. "I understand. Somehow, you need to put these crazy people out of your mind, and concentrate on your own feelings."

She just looked into my eyes. "I'll let you know when I figure it out myself."

We just sat on the sofa holding each other's hands. I wasn't sure if there was something I should say or not.

After the news, we slipped off to bed. When I kissed her good night, she whispered, "Just hold me tight all night."

I gave her a long kiss. My hand gently stroked the small of her back while I was kissing her. She reached around and rubbed her hand up and down my back. Then, I whispered to her, "I love you."

She held me tight all night.

Chapter 21

Fishy Stories

When we woke the next morning, the sun was just starting to peek over the horizon. Somehow, we missed the alarm. It was a half hour past our regular wake-up time.

We jumped up and got ready for another day.

On the way to the station, Tracy asked, "Did you mean what you said last night?"

"Yes, I think I would really miss you if you weren't there."

She reached over and grabbed my hand. She didn't say anything. I guess she didn't need to say anything. Her hand said it all. She was feeling the same way. I could see that she was worried about what she would have to say if LT asked for her decision today. Tracy was quiet all the way to the station. She was hoping I would have repeated that I loved her.

When we arrived, I could see Tracy was relieved to see that LT was not in the office today. He was out of town, attending a meeting for the day with the network people.

We picked up our assignments and let Mark Lawson know where we were heading. I told Tracy to relax, Mark had our backs.

All day long, both Tracy and I kept an eye out for Mark's agents as we went on our different assignments, trying hard not to make it obvious that we were watching the crowds. We even kept an eye out to see if either Photo or Shawn sent any text messages to people we did not know. It would be hard to detect. However, if either of them went off to a corner to send a message, it might be a sign that they were letting someone know where we were going. We did not spot anything out of the ordinary.

At the end of the day, we headed back to the apartment for our dinner with my father.

"Did you make any decisions?" I asked Tracy.

"Not yet. I'll let you know."

The ride back was almost as quiet as the ride to work.

When we got to the Castle, Hank was at the elevator. "No visitors," he told us.

"Thanks Hank. We really appreciate it," I told him.

My father was waiting at our door. He had an enormous smile on his face. I had a feeling he was grinning just for me.

"Dad, I told you, I would call you when we got in."

"I saw your car turn into the garage. Figured I would meet you when you got up here."

We went in and got the table set while the lasagna cooked.

It gave Tracy a chance to clean up and change clothes for the evening.

At dinner, my father was unusually nice to Tracy. I wondered if he knew that she had to make some decisions soon. We had a healthy laugh at a few of my father's stories during dinner, and then moved off to the living room to talk about the history of Asian carp.

I knew most of the history of the carp. They had been part of a fish farm down south. When the Mississippi River flooded, they became

163

part of the population of the river. Unfortunately, they took over the local fish population. I asked my father to bring us up to date.

"Well, it took a couple years before the government started to figure out how serious the situation actually was. When the fish started to interfere with the tourist business, things got a lot more serious. They got into the Illinois River. When a boat came through, the carp would jump out of the water after feeling the pressure wave of the oncoming boats.

"It's one thing to see a fish jump out of the water. It's another to see a 20-pound fish jump three feet into the air. Well, the first time you took one square in the choppers, you figured out that traveling on the river was not fun anymore.

"The DNR's of the states along the Mississippi all looked to the Federal Government for them to do something. Everyone figured that they had time to figure out a solution. After a few years, by the time the DNR thought they might have a plan, it was too late. The DNR hoped that a few of the larger dams would be the stopping point. Guess they never figured on birds. The birds would catch some of the minnows and accidentally drop them above the dams. Didn't take too many. The ugly fish were all over the rivers. The Mississippi, St. Croix, Minnesota, and many of the feeder rivers were all invaded. The carp multiplied even faster than rabbits.

"Actually, the DNR was their own worst enemy. For years, the DNR was trying to eliminate all the small headwater dams that created usable lakes and rivers. Many of these were only a few feet high, but restricted the movement of spawning fish. So, before they knew the carp were coming, the DNR systematically started removing all these small dams. They were trying to get back to normal spawning along the waterways.

"Well, surprise! Next thing you know the carp were heading up the small creeks and rivers and right into the feeder lakes.

"The public was not very happy with the DNR. Actually, they should have been upset with the legislature. The DNR had been trying to head the carp off for several years. It was the politicians that were spending money on goofy things rather than solving the problem."

"Do you think they could have stopped the fish?" I asked.

"Probably not. But, if they had put an electronic charge in the water at a dam on the Mississippi River by Iowa before they moved up river, it would have slowed them down. What the DNR found with the birds probably meant the carp would have gotten around the dam eventually.

"It was just like the zebra muscles. Everyone blamed the fisherman. Then, someone did a study on a small pond that had no boats on it. The DNR found the muscles had been on weeds that the egrets, herons, and crows had carried into the pond. The same pond had Eurasian milfoil.

"Surprise, surprise. The DNR had claimed the boaters had caused that problem also. If they had spent the money fixing the problem instead of buying airtime on the television blaming us boaters, they might have found a solution. I suppose some of it did get carried in by boats. However, the birds did just as much harm. They just refused to tell the public for a long time. You know, it is hard to get funding to train birds to wipe their feet before going to another lake.

"It is much easier to blame people than look at nature. Darn, even the turtles were carrying the weeds from one lake to another when they were close by.

"Biggest surprise was when they found that the natural carp fed on the tiny mussels before they grew bigger. People along the St. Croix River were trying to tell them that for several years. In rivers with lots of carp, the zebra mussel population stayed in check. Lakes with few carp, they simply spread."

"You think nature would have balanced out the carp naturally?" Tracy asked.

"I don't know. Every time someone finds something, it seems that eventually nature takes care of it. Anyway, I think the politicians got their necks in a noose over this one. When the DNR wanted to poison out sections of the rivers and slowly bring back the fish, those air-heads insisted on doing the rivers all at the same time. In a way, it made sense. If they did it by sections, they might miss some and have to keep redoing the job.

"Like I told you before, some pea-brain politician insisted on saving the state money and wrote in a funding bill that a new chemical had to be used. The DNR did not have a choice. When they found that the chemical reacted with the trace herbicides that were seeping into the water from the farmlands, the chemists discovered that the reaction made a stable molecule that did not degrade quickly. Suddenly, it did not degrade with the UV light from sunlight. As it killed the fish, the trace chemical would be carried by the surviving fish up the river, until they died and the chemical was released once again. What a disaster. They took a state with excellent fishing lakes and rivers, and reduced it to less than half the fishing lakes they had before they tampered with the waters."

"So, is that the reason the DNR was working with the Native American tribes?" Tracy asked.

"Yes, it killed off half of their lakes. Nevertheless, many of them were isolated lakes where the DNR had not been allowed to dismantle the dams that maintained their shallow depths. Unfortunately, it looked like the birds would finish off those lakes too. When the Mississippi River was poisoned, it wiped out the best of the walleye lakes – Lake Winnibigoshish.

"When the principal source of fish died, and the birds left the region, what looked like a disaster, saved the small lakes."

"Did it kill off everything?" Tracy asked.

"No, they did something right. Whatever the chemical was, it attacked the digestive system of fish. So, the weeds and other aquatic creatures escaped the disaster. However, the fish that were over a few inches long died.

"Anyone want to buy an almost new boat?" my father asked.

We just shook our heads. What a sad story.

"So, who was at fault?" I asked.

"Air-heads," he answered. "Just those dummies we elect to protect our interests. You know, the guys without the chemical background that, once they become elected officials, are experts and try to save a buck here and there so they can spend money on their favorite projects. The guys that take out the cement head dams to allow fish to spawn. The guys we elected. I doubt that any of them anticipated the problems. It reminds me of the old question, who stole the teacher's apple? You going to blame the whole class?

"Well, it is the same way with the legislature. You could look at the legislative vote to see who sponsored the bill, and who voted for it. It might give you some clues. It won't tell you who was trying to convince them to vote their way.

"I remember our senator was one of those people who were pushing for action on the Mississippi River. He was in the state legislature then. Heck, everyone was screaming for action then."

"Are they sure that the water is safe for humans?" Tracy asked.

"Who are you going to believe? The EPA insisted that all the cities that took water from the rivers put filters on the pipes. Heck, I thought they were doing that before the problem. That's why I prefer water that comes from wells, where nature has 50 to 200-feet of sand above it to filter the water properly. There's no fish in that water.

"Still want to drink water out of Lake Superior?" he asked.

My father had a convincing argument. I was hoping he had a favorite enemy number one, someone we could see if they profited on the problem, but instead, it looked like all the other problems Howard Long had willed upon us. Only this one had significant results from someone's mistake.

Tracy and I had taken a number of notes from the conversation. We hoped that it might match up with something in our files. So far, the puzzle was simply making smaller pieces. Nothing we looked at seemed to put the face on the puzzle.

We thanked my father for the history lesson. Then, he left us to see who had won the pot. I knew he really wished that he could have been there to fleece the others in his gang. On the other hand, he felt like he might have contributed to our project. That was worth missing the card game.

Tracy and I talked for a while after he left. She told me that she truly did not want things to change between us. She was enjoying the time together as much as I was. It felt good to hear it.

I suggested a steaming hot shower to relax. She agreed. It is remarkable how a long hot shower can calm the nerves. It is a good thing that many of the senior citizens went to bed early at the Castle. We probably drained their hot water tanks.

We missed the news.

Chapter 22

Friday

When we reached the station, LT was waiting for Tracy. The two of them went into his office and had a long conversation. Unfortunately, I had to go on assignment. I would have to find out later what was decided. I left a text message for Mark. I sent another to Tracy – *"Let me know what you decided."*

I didn't hear from her all morning. I was not sure what that meant. Somehow, I was sure it was not good. I kept checking my cell to see if there were any new messages. Even Photo was wondering why I kept checking my cell. I decided not to tell him. I just made sure that I checked it every ten minutes, just in case Tracy sent me a reply.

At noon, I got a message from Mark. *"Need to see you, got some free time?"* We decided to meet at a donut house around 2:30 pm.

Around 2:15 pm, I told Photo that I had to meet with one of my sources. While I was gone, he could spend the time in the truck, finishing our stories for the day and send them to our editor. I figured from our conversation that Mark and I would only need 15 to 30 minutes.

When I met with Mark, the store was deserted except for the two of us. He told me that he had a few leads from tracking our stalker. His phone message from our building went to the same corporation, S&G

Security in Wyoming where the first person was from – Luke Carpenter. The good thing was that the phones were bugged, so the FBI was able to get a voice pattern of the person who answered as well as visual record of the people who were in the building that day. It took Mark's team only one day to pin the tail on one of their managers.

The other significant news was that the manager from S&G immediately dialed a person in Colorado. I did not ask Mark how the FBI traced that call. I wasn't sure he would tell me anyway.

Mark informed us that the person in Colorado worked for a consulting company. Now, Mark had another name and a company to add to the information we gave him on our charts. Mark's team was looking to see if these people were involved with any of the projects in Howard Long's files. If they were, we might have found the smoking gun. If not, we needed to keep the heat on. The group of them was obviously squirming over something. We needed to make sure we were staying close to the same places, so they thought we knew more than we did.

I thanked Mark for the information. It was what we needed. Now, I was anxious to join Photo and head back to the station. I wanted to know what happened this morning with Tracy.

We got back to the station before she did. I looked for LT, but he was not there. As a result, I tried to find something to keep me busy until Tracy returned. I still wondered who it was that was leaking information from our office to Wyoming. Was it one of our reporters, camera people, managers, or had it been someone on the police force? Right now, I wished I had someone to talk to about the case.

About 20-minutes later, Tracy and Shawn came in the door. They had a busy schedule and had just finished the last of their assignments. I mentioned to Tracy that she had not returned any of my text messages. She said, "Give me 10-minutes. I'll tell you when we get in your car."

On the way back to the apartment, Tracy told me all about the conversation she had with LT. He had apologized that Tracy probably did not have the type of opportunity she was hoping for when she filled in for Jake Schwartz. Between the investigation into Howard Long, the man following her, the break-in into her apartment, and Jake coming back a couple weeks quicker than they thought, Tracy's time at the job had been extremely chaotic. Even with all the events going on, LT told her that he felt she had done a superb job filling in. He hated to see her time on loan from the Duluth station go by so quickly.

Tracy said that she told LT that although she really liked working in Duluth, she would like to stay, if there was an opening. It gave her more freedom to investigate strange cases. As frustrating as this case had been, in Duluth they would not have had the manpower to allow her to investigate it.

LT had told her that he could not guarantee an opening. He told her that he hoped he would get an approval in a month or two for another reporter, but at this point, he could not guarantee the job. If something opened, she would be the first person he would call. He suggested another television station in the area, and told her that he would personally call the manager and give them his raving review of her work, but she declined.

"I really did not want to work for someone that I did not know, and a crew I was not familiar with," she told me.

"So, what are you going to do?"

I looked over at her to catch any expressions. There was a sad look in her face.

"For now, I have probably only this week until I have to head back to Duluth. Then, if something opens up, I can decide if I should come back or stay up there, I guess."

It was not what I was hoping she would say. If she went back to Duluth, with my working schedule, I would rarely get time to see her.

The ride back to the apartment was a quiet one. As we approached the Castle and I started my routine of watching for other cars that might be observing our coming or going, I remembered that I had not informed Tracy that Mark and I had met earlier in the day. I filled her in on the discussion, and how Mark had traced the calls to an engineering firm in Colorado.

We were finally starting to get a few breaks in the case. She was glad to hear that the FBI was starting to find the links that were so illusive. However, it was not the kind of excitement the news would have brought a few days earlier.

With the thought of Tracy heading back to Duluth, I realized that the desire to pursue the case on our end would probably fall off. If that happened, it would put the effort squarely on Mark Lawson's shoulders. In addition, if Tracy went back to Duluth at the end of the week, she would not have anyone to protect her. That was not a pleasant thought.

We arrived at the apartment and had a relatively quiet dinner. The frozen halibut we had radiated smelled good and was plentiful, but our minds were not on the food.

"It's not going to be the same at dinner time without you," I told her.

"It is a lot quieter in Duluth. With the winter coming on, I'm going to miss working with you."

"You think you might take LT up on that offer if he has an opening?"

"LT told me, he was hoping for the position. I'll have to see when and if he actually has the job opportunity in his hand. He might have it in a couple months, or it might be next summer. It will be hard to say. I'll just have to stay flexible."

After dinner, we sat and talked about the files and possibilities. No matter how we looked at it, it was just like hitting a moving target. Unless we could find the center of the target, we were just shooting at the wall with blinders on.

One thing we did decide on, unless something new came up, we would try and enjoy the few evenings we had left together before Tracy would have to head back up to Duluth.

We sat arm in arm on the sofa the rest of the evening until the news was over and got ready for bed. When we crawled into bed, we snuggled tightly into each other's arms hoping for a good night's sleep.

We did not hear from Mark Lawson on Thursday or find any hidden clues that were sticking out from a rare book on the shelf. I guess that only happens in the movies.

At the end of the day, we drove 30-minutes south of town and found a quiet restaurant for a meal. I figured that no one would be looking for us out of town. It gave us the time to slow down after work and talk without anyone else in our conversations. The longer ride in the car made a perfect place to wind down the day.

On the way back, we passed Buck Hill – a ski hill next to the freeway, which was starting to make preparations for the winter season. Buck Hill had their lights on and was doing maintenance on the lifts for the long ski season. With the lights on, the workers could see if they had the floodlights aligned properly for the new twists in their hills. Even though it was October, it was a reminder that in another month, winter would be upon us.

Tracy chuckled as she saw it. It looked like a small hill compared to the hills near Duluth. "I wonder how much of that water from Lake Superior will be used to put snow on the hill," she asked.

I hadn't thought about it. Most people were thinking drinking water. If you added in the other uses, that pipeline might be used for a number of recreational areas. We had not even added that dimension into our flow charts.

I guess our amateur status in solving murders was starting to show. One thing, at least we established a large enough question from all our research that the FBI got involved. Now it was Mark's problem.

Whether it was the uncertainty of the future or just exhaustion, it was obvious that it was taking the heated sparks out of the romance. It seemed that there was a lot more holding each other's hands and being close to each other than long passionate kisses.

By the time the news was over and we were ready for bed, I couldn't help but remember the hot shower we shared earlier. I'm not sure if either of us was ready to make the next move or not. The problem of both people being unsure with the situation is that nothing tends to change.

I figured that I needed to step it up a notch tomorrow night. It might be the last chance I will have to make a favorable impression, before she moves back home.

Chapter 23

Moving Day

Friday evening was spent more as a date than just another evening. The only difference was that both Tracy and I knew that tomorrow she would be driving back to Duluth, and except for sending messages back and forth, we would probably not be seeing each other for some time.

We took the time to go to a restaurant that was downtown Minneapolis. I picked one of the nicer restaurants, the type that still used white linen tablecloths. It was a special place for us to enjoy Tracy's last night in town.

We both had the house specials – bacon wrapped filet mignon with asparagus tips and a baked potato. It was cooked to perfection. The steaks were just barely pink in the center, and extremely tender. We followed it up by splitting a piece of carrot cake.

Tracy enjoyed the meal.

"Martin, thank you for the fantastic dinner on our last evening together before I head back. I think you picked the perfect restaurant."

"After all those takeout meals we shared, I figured that the least I could do would be to take you to a quality restaurant before you left. I suppose you will stay away from takeout for the next year."

"Well Martin, I might try some home cooking for a few days, until I get tired of my own cooking. I think it is the company I might miss."

I had to admit, it was the company that I would miss also.

After eating, we drove back to the Castle. When we got to our floor, my father and his gang were all in the hall waiting for us.

"We decided we wanted to say goodbye before you snuck out in the morning and we missed you," my father said.

Tracy was surprised. She knew that the gang was watching out for us, but now it was apparent how much they truly cared about her.

"I don't know what to say. I'm going to miss all of you, too. You don't know how much your watching over us has meant to us. Without your help, I'm sure I would have lost more than one night's sleep."

She gave each one of them a hug and thanks. Then, we headed into our apartment to pack up and spend one last night together.

The next morning, as I took Tracy's gear down to her car, Hank was still on-guard in the hallway.

"Hank, what are you going to do when Tracy's gone?"

"Well, Martin, she's the best looking girl in the building. I might just have to move to improve the scenery."

Hank always did have a sense of humor. Between him and the rest of my father's friends, you were never quite sure if they were serious or not.

When we had almost all of Tracy's things in the car, I escorted her to the garage and gave her a kiss goodbye.

"Promise you will stay in touch," she told me.

"Call me when you get back to Duluth, so I know you made it OK."

I waved as she drove out of the garage. Now it was my turn. Time to head back to the old apartment after a day's work. I left a few things in my father's apartment. I figured I could pick them up in the next day or two when I came for a visit. Then, I headed off to the station.

Jake Schwartz and LT were talking in the hallway when I arrived. It was Jake's first day back, and LT wanted to make sure that he knew that he was to take it easy the next week. Photo was given the job of carrying all of Jake's equipment and doing the driving.

"Well Martin, you can go back to reporting on jaywalkers," he shouted at me. "The "A" team is back."

I shot back, "Just don't trip over the curb. I'd hate to have to take over all your duties again. LT might decide he doesn't need you."

That got a smile out of everyone. It was good to see him back at the job. He looked pretty good. I wondered how many pills he was taking to keep his neck and back from hurting. I was sure that he was not going to let anyone know.

We all went into the assignment room and looked over the leads for the stories of the day. LT made sure that Jake did not let his famous ego get over his head on his first day back to assignments.

About 1:00 pm, I got a call from Tracy. She wanted to let me know that she got back to Duluth safely, and was all unpacked. She was hoping to review some of our files over the weekend, before she started back to work on Monday morning. I told her to take care and let me know if she found anything.

At the end of the day, I headed back to my apartment. It seemed shabby and lonesome after the past couple weeks. After putting my gear away, I called my father to thank him for all the help the past few weeks. I told him I would try to stop over tomorrow night, and we could have a pizza together. That way I could kill two birds with one stone – I could visit him and pick up my things.

I was exhausted from all the activity of the day. By the time I was done and got ready for bed, I just went to sleep. Tomorrow was going to be just another ordinary day.

Sunday morning, as I was putting things together for work, I noticed a couple items were not in the exact place I kept them. They were close, but just slightly ajar. It took me by surprise. I looked around the apartment, but I could not find anything missing. However, there were two items in the living room and one in the kitchen that were moved by a few inches. When I checked the bedroom, I noticed my stack of sweaters was in a different order than they were earlier. Someone had been in my apartment.

As I drove to work, I pulled over and called Mark Lawson.

"Mark, hate to bother you, but I moved back to my place last night. When I checked things over this morning, I realized that someone must have been in my place. There were several items that had been moved."

"You think it was the same person that went through Tracy's apartment? Any idea when they were there?" he asked me.

"Sorry Mark, all I can tell you is that it was probably in the past week. They made an effort not to make a mess and let me know they had been there. So, do you think they learned how to straighten up after themselves, or what do you think they were doing?"

"I'll send a man over while you are working. Don't tell anyone. We still have the problem of that leak. I think we are getting closer on this case, but we have a long way to go. Wish I knew who was giving them information on you and Tracy."

"Thanks Mark. Give me a call later if you hear anything."

The rest of the morning, I kept wondering why they did not trash my place like they did Tracy's. What were they looking for?

Around 3:00 pm, Mark Lawson called me.

"Martin, what's your plan for supper?"

"I'm having a pizza with my father."

"If I bring the pizza, can I join the two of you?"

"Mark, I'm sure my father would enjoy seeing you again. How about a pepperoni and mushroom?"

"Done. See you about 6:00 pm."

I called my father and told him we were having a guest for supper.

When I arrived at my father's apartment, Mark was already there. I could hear the two of them laughing as I went to knock on the door.

My father opened the door, and told me, "Mark and I were just discussing the two of you. He was telling me how he got you out of the way so he could catch this girl's attention. Did you really run into the tree?"

"Yeah, he never did apologize for that one."

I figured that Mark had some information that he wanted to tell me in a location where he knew it was safe. Since my father had protected Tracy and me for the past couple weeks, it looked like a good location to discuss what was going on.

As we finished the pizza, Mark told us why he wanted to meet with me.

"John, I hope you don't mind that I asked Martin to meet me here, but I needed a safe place to talk to him and I figured that if anyone saw him head here, they would assume that he was coming to see you.

"Martin, you were correct on your guess that someone was in your apartment. I sent a couple guys over there this morning. I had a hunch and had them scan the apartment for listening devices. They found three. That's why they didn't trash your place."

"Did you remove them?" I asked.

"No. We left them there. That's why I did not want to talk to you over there. I ran a quick scan of your father's apartment before you came. It's clean in here."

"What in the world are they looking for?" I asked.

"Whatever it is, it must be important. I think there is something out there that they are worried about and afraid we might know about it. That's why they bugged your apartment. Probably didn't realize you would move back into your father's place with Tracy. I didn't want to spook them by removing them until we find out who is involved."

"Can you do that?" my father asked.

"John, these people are remarkably talented. They have made a couple mistakes so far, and we are getting close. The bug is valid for about 500 feet. Whoever is listening has to be that close to Martin's place or have a relay within that range. That means they have to be in Martin's building or the one next to it. Now, we have to find a way to locate the receiver."

"Can you do that?" I asked.

"Maybe! We'll talk about that later.

"Let me fill you in on our friend in Colorado."

Mark told my father and me about their investigation into the stalker who was watching Tracy and me, and had tried to break into the apartment. The leads from bugging the phones at the security firm in Wyoming, S&G, had started the connection that now included the stalker, the manager of the security firm, Neil Paulson, and an engineer at a consulting firm in Colorado. All three were now under surveillance, and their histories investigated. Somehow, they had to be tied to one of the reports that Howard Long tried to tell us about. "If we could crack the link, the rest of the dominos might fall. The fact that they put a bug in Martin's apartment shows me that they are still worried about something else coming out.

"We are tracking the serial numbers on the bugs right now. My hope is that it will lead us to the vendor that sold them, and then to the firm in Wyoming. If we can get enough evidence of breaking the law, we might be able to get them to open up wider to get a plea."

"So, you want me to be a sitting duck?" I asked.

"That's right. If that doesn't work, we might even require you to have a conversation with someone that is juicy enough to draw someone out of the woodwork, just to see if you actually have something. I'll let you know."

"What about Tracy?" I asked.

"I think you should give her a call tomorrow during work on her cell. Have her call you back on another line. They may have tampered with one or both of your cell phones as well. Keep that in mind if you talk to anyone, including me."

That was an unnerving thought. It had not crossed my mind that someone might have cloned my cell. Unfortunately, with the right equipment, someone could clone a phone from over fifty feet away without you knowing it.

"If we need to talk, let's do it using random phones and not your regular phone," Mark told me.

My father sat there silently. It was not like him not to interrupt the discussion. I figured he realized this was definitely out of his league, and whatever Mark and I had planned, he would hear about it all later.

When Mark left, I spent the next hour talking to my Dad about the whole event. He was glad to hear that Mark was in control and I was not trying to handle things by myself.

"You know, you can always move in with me if you need to. There is room on the davenport."

"Thanks Dad, for now, I think Mark wants me as bait. If it gets too dicey, I'll take you up on the offer."

"Hank's got a gun if you need one," he offered.

"What's he doing with a gun in this place?"

"He said he bought it just in case the doctors ever told him he was losing his mind or had incurable cancer. He did not want to go the way either of our wives went."

"Thanks! Hopefully, things will not get to that point."

I left my father's apartment with the thought of Hank and his gun. I wondered how many other old timers kept guns hidden in the closets.

When I got home, I made a small note that I taped to my cell phone – Listening? It would be a reminder every time I picked it up. Then I took it off. There was still the issue of the mole. If it was someone at the station, I did not want the person to see my note and realize we were on to the bugs. I redid my note with just "??." It was just as good of a reminder.

The next morning, I called Tracy from a phone at the station. She was at her desk at work. I asked her to call me back at the number for the phone I had used, on another line. A minute later, the phone rang.

"Martin, what's going on? Why didn't you want me to call your cell phone?" Her voice dropped as she realized what she had just said.

"I met with Mark last night. My place has been bugged. He is not sure if our cell phones have been cloned or not. That's why I wanted you on a random phone line. Are you OK up there?"

"Yes, I think so. What is Mark going to do?"

"Looks like I'm the bait until we find out who is doing it," I told her. "Mark is starting to fill in the blanks; however, he would love to catch someone red-handed to get them to tell the whole story."

"I thought things were dying down," she replied. "There has to be something else that we have not found."

"That's what Mark thinks also. So keep your head and don't travel alone at night. If you need to talk to me, leave a generic message. I'll get back to you."

"Thanks! You stay safe," she replied.

I hated to leave her on her own. I was sure that she would not tell her manager, or other workers, since we did not know who was tipping our unknown friends off. That meant that she was extremely vulnerable. Her best defense was to stay alert.

* * *

Mark had his people attempting to connect any leads they could with the person in Colorado. Since the phone links led to him, he had to be intimately involved in this somehow. They looked into his financial history, work history, and even his college background. The same was done with the manager at the security firm in Wyoming – Neil Paulson. Mark hoped that there was a financial link between the two.

The case was an absolute puzzle. The worst part, it would not take too long before his department would be asking why he was spending so much time and money on the case. It would be hard to explain that it was a case about ?? – well so far, a case about nothing. All he had was a case of attempted break in and entry, illegal phone taps, and two unexplained murders. All of which were probably cases for the local police unless he could establish a solid tie-in.

* * *

When Tracy left her station at the end of the day, she was much more aware of her surroundings than she was normally. She did not want to think that someone was following her up in Duluth, but she did not have any reason to believe otherwise. When she got in her car, she reached for a Kleenex in the glove compartment. It was then that she realized that someone had been in there earlier. Her sunglass case was not on top the pad of Kleenex. It was on the side. Someone had gone through her car looking for something. Had they left a bug in there like they did at Martin's?

On the way home, she stopped at a gas station and used their phone to call Mark Lawson.

"Mark, this is Tracy. Just wanted you to know that someone went through my car today while I was at work. The things in the glove box were out of place."

"Great observation. You on a secure line?"

"Yes, I stopped at a gas station."

"Good. Did Martin talk to you earlier about the bugs at his place?"

"He did. That's why I figured I should call you when I noticed things were disturbed in my car."

"Tracy, do you think there are any surveillance cameras on your parking lot?"

"Yes, there are a couple of them."

"Good, I'm going to have one of our people look at the footage in the morning. Meanwhile, you watch your toes and keep alert for anything out of place. If you are worried, stay with a friend."

"Thanks Mark. Let me know if you find anything."

"Get a good night's sleep," he told her.

183

Tracy went home and cautiously went into her apartment. Everything looked OK. Just to be safe, she decided she would not call anyone about the case using her phones in case they were bugged.

When Tracy got to the station Tuesday morning, she saw a technician's truck in the parking lot. When she got to her desk, she saw that they were working on the surveillance system. Her only hope was that it was the FBI, and not someone else erasing their tracks. Then she saw a note on her desk. It said, *"Smile – Mark."* He had just left an enormous clue for her.

The technicians worked on the system in her building and in one across the street. They were upgrading the software.

Later, when the FBI agents examined the images, they realized the individual that had entered Tracy's car had hidden their face. It was as though the person knew where the cameras were, and made sure their face was very well concealed, and their vehicle was parked out of view. Since the FBI had a time signature on the video, they checked a couple other surveillance cameras in the immediate area for cars or trucks. If they were lucky, someone might be spotted just before and just after the person entered Tracy's car.

They were in luck. The traffic camera just down the block had two cars that both entered the area and left the area at the correct time. There was no guarantee it was the person they wanted, but it gave them a lead. If they did not have the right vehicles, using the traffic cameras from that spot and another light in the other direction would probably give them about 100 more cars and trucks to run leads on. Their hope was on the first two.

It took some keen research, but the second car going through the stoplight met the requirements. It was a white, Chevy rental car out of the Twin Cities. It was in both sets of pictures, before and right after the break-in. Another bonus! The picture taken at the light heading south after the break-in, showed a clear view of the driver in the car complete with the car's license number. The FBI agents sent their information to Mark Lawson with a new candidate to watch.

Tracy was still shaken when Agent Mark Lawson called the station around 4:00 pm. He left a message for her to call him. Tracy's heartbeat skipped at least two beats as she read the message that the secretary handed her.

"Mark, hi, this is Tracy. Did you find anything?"

"Like I said, they may be experienced, but that does not mean they are good. We got a time signature from your camera at the station. When we correlated it to the stoplight cameras nearby, we came up with a car coming and going. Best thing, it was a rental from the Minneapolis airport. The driver wasn't even smart enough not to smile for the street camera. We're running recognition software on him right now. Any idea what they were looking for in your car?"

"No. I can't find anything missing."

"Well, let's assume that they are doing the same thing to you as Martin – bugging your places. They might be hoping that you would call Martin with some information while you are in the car."

"You think I'm safe?"

"Can you stay with a friend until we finish our investigation?"

"I have an aunt who lives out on Minnesota Point. I can call her."

"Good. Let me know her number if you stay there. Meanwhile, take a few extra turns like Martin showed you. It might just slow them down. However, if you spot anything odd, drive to a police station or fire department. That will scare them away."

"Thanks Mark. I hope you catch them soon."

Tracy called her aunt, Linnea Hastings. After Tracy told her aunt that she needed a place to stay for a few days, because someone had broken into her place, her aunt told her that she would love some company. She could come over immediately. Tracy could stay in the guest room any time she wanted it. It was just what Tracy wanted to hear. She drove home, packed up clothes for a couple weeks, and moved in with her aunt.

Tracy's aunt's house was right on the beach along the point that separates Lake Superior from the large harbor, where the giant boats were loaded and unloaded. The nice thing was that it had a tuck-under three-car garage. Her aunt was only using one of the spaces. That meant she could drive right in and close the door behind her when she returned each day.

The guest bedroom was on the second floor, which had a spectacular view of Lake Superior. This was a view that tourists paid over $200 a night just a few houses away at a Bed and Breakfast. If she had to move out of her apartment, this was more like a vacation spot. The kitchen was in the front of the house and had a good view of the street.

The historic ship-channel lift-bridge slowed down access to the area. It was the only way in or out of Minnesota Point. Located at the other end of the point was a park and an open shipping channel without a bridge. As a result, it was considered a fairly safe neighborhood.

Her aunt was glad to have the company. With the cold coming on, the park was empty of picnickers as the tourists were gone, and it was starting to get very quiet along the beach. Instead of having to listen to the cold wind off the lake, now her aunt would have someone to talk to. Tracy's aunt lived alone in the house ever since she had it built about fifteen years earlier. After her husband died, and she collected on his insurance policy, her aunt decided that she wanted a house with a view. And, what a view it had.

Knowing it would take some time for anyone to find her, Tracy got a good night's sleep that night. Unless they followed her from work and came across the lift bridge right behind her, it would be hard to find where she went. Tracy made a mental note to herself: *"Go past the house and through the parking lot at the condos. Then, watch for anyone that might make the same turns she made."*

186

The question that was still weaved through her mind: *"Why were they brave enough to bug Martin's and her apartments? What would happen if they got bolder and broke into her aunt's home, while either of them was there?"*

* * *

Chapter 24

Following Leads

Wednesday was a busy day for Agent Mark Lawson. The software scan of the driver's face in Duluth came up with a hit. Now, they had another character in the cast of "what is it?"

To Mark, it showed a problem, which he was slowly becoming worried about. The bad guys were getting bolder with each attempt to find out what Martin and Tracy were looking at. Mark was getting worried that they would realize that Martin and Tracy did not have any real information and just disappear in the sunset. If they did, they would never find the killers. Worse yet, whoever was behind this thing might just try to create an accident, where their problems – Martin and Tracy, simply disappeared.

It was time to find the weakest link in the people they had identified, and figure out their weaknesses. If they could force one person to open up, they might be able to get the information that would end the whole investigation.

Later in the day, Mark called a meeting at his office with his crew to look over the investigations into the leading characters of the case. So far, they had identified four figures in the investigation. They had the manager in Wyoming, the engineer in Colorado, the person who tried to get into the apartment at the Senior Center, and now, the person they identified while trying to break in to Tracy's car.

After the car break-in, Mark's agents found bugs in both Tracy's car as well as in her apartment. This person of interest was clearly experienced in his occupation. Whether this person or someone else bugged Martin's apartment was still a question in their minds. Someone was paying considerable money for professional eavesdroppers.

He and his team needed to find something that would lead them to the deaths of Howard Long in the alley in Minneapolis, or Luke Carpenter out on a trail in Wyoming. If the FBI could connect them to one of Howard's files, it would just be icing on the cake. Maybe Martin was right; maybe they could follow the leads all the way to a US Senator who was involved in the fish problems.

Mark's field agents had been busy for the past couple of weeks. Now, they finished running the life history of several individuals, looking for links and looking for something that tied them to one of the projects in Howard Long's files. One person had popped up, the individual who had broken into Tracy's car in Duluth, Ken Payton. He had graduated from the same college in Washington State as Luke Carpenter. Both were in the same history and business classes. They were also on some of the same intramural sports teams. Both entered the Marines instead of continuing college their junior year.

"OK, looks like we have a start," Mark told them. "How do we link them in the present?"

The agents looked over the files. Payton and Carpenter were employed as consultants. Bank accounts showed payments in the past couple years from a firm in Idaho - Bent Mountain Inc.

"Any links between the Wyoming firm and this one in Idaho?" Mark asked.

His finance expert pulled up a few screens and pointed to a deposit. It was from the firm in Wyoming - S&G Security, to the firm in Idaho - Bent Mountain Inc.

"Any way of identifying what it was for?" Mark asked.

189

"Sorry, I'm still trying to understand how this firm in Idaho exists. It is there on paper, but when I looked on the internet, I can't find them."

"You mean they don't advertise?" Mark asked.

"No, I mean the address is a P.O. Box. Same with the internet links. Just a location on a public server."

"OK, that's a start. Let's keep digging. How close was Ken Payton to Luke Carpenter?" Mark asked.

They looked at the files. It appeared they were close friends in school and in the army. After that, both people had sketchy history files. They scanned credit card histories, IRS histories, and motor vehicle histories. Both seemed to come and go a number of times without a real sense of why their accounts went dormant for months at a time.

"OK, let's leave our mystery man. How about our other individuals," Mark asked.

They discussed the links for which they had support in the files. Mark's lead field agent, Butch Thomas, carried the conversation. "The engineer in Colorado, Peter Skiff, is connected to the Wyoming firm by the wire taps. When we checked on this individual's history, we found he had worked for a number of engineering firms in the past, most noticeable, was a firm that designed piping networks for power plants."

"Can I make a guess? How about one in western North Dakota that burns coal?" Mark suggested.

"You get the prize," Mark's agent told him.

"How about the other projects on our list?" Mark asked.

"Sorry boss. No connections that we can find. We looked as hard as we could to find a link," Butch told him.

"How about the person we tailed all over town after he left the Senior Center?" Mark asked.

"We have a name and a driver's license. His history only goes back three years. Then, nothing."

"Oh, just what the world needs, a ghost that shows up when he wants. You mean his facial scan comes up blank?" Mark asked.

"Just like he popped into the world from another planet."

"OK, that may mean he worked for the CIA, or some other agency. I'll see if I can pull some favors and get some info from them on this one," Mark told his team. "We still have nothing on the firm in Wyoming but connections. Any suggestions?"

The group consensus was that either the man from Tracy's encounter in Duluth, Ken Payton, or the man from Colorado, Peter Skiff, needed to be approached and leaned on severely. They had gone as far as they could on the files and leads. Now, they needed a break. One of those two individuals had to know more. The engineer might get off by saying someone designed the wrong pipe. The man from Duluth had the most to lose if they pinched him. He was their target.

Since the time they had ID'd Ken Payton from the video cam in Duluth, they had him on their radar screen, and were monitoring every movement he made. They had picked up his trail at the Minneapolis airport when he returned his car. From there, they tracked him to Sioux Falls, South Dakota. He was living in a townhouse on the southern edge of town. He did not seem to have a standard pattern of movement, meaning that he probably did not have a 9 to 5 job. For the most part, he appeared to stay home with the exception of restaurants, trips to the grocery store, or to a local bar. Mark decided to pick him up tomorrow, when he was on the way to the local bar. If he made any statements, he would not have the defense that he had been drinking, and his statements were forced out of him by interrogators.

Early Thursday afternoon, as Ken Payton approached the Tower Bar near his townhouse, two FBI agents met him in the street. They told him that he was under arrest and read him his rights. Then, they escorted him to the local FBI office, where Agent Mark Lawson was waiting to talk to his mystery man.

Ken was playing it very casually. He was not sure what the FBI thought they had on him, but he was fairly confident it would not stick. Since no one had caught him red handed breaking the law, he assumed that they were on a fishing trip. He was right.

Mark started out by trying to make Ken Payton believe they had a solid case on him for illegal invasion of privacy, illegal eavesdropping using bugging equipment on an individual, stalking, and breaking and entry.

If Mark could make him believe that they had a case, Ken might talk to get a reduced sentence.

The questioning went on for several hours. Ken Payton was shown pictures of his car, with him driving it in Duluth. He was made to believe that they had additional camera images of Ken Payton leaving his car to bug Tracy's car. They also told him that they had traffic camera images placing him near Tracy's apartment at the time it was bugged. So far, if they were making him worried, he did not show any evidence of it. Ken Payton just sat there and did not even break a sweat.

After four hours of interrogation, Mark decided it was time for a break. He was hungry. He figured if he left Ken Payton to sit by himself in the room for an hour, it would give him a little more time to wonder what else the FBI had on him that was keeping him in the room. So far, all they offered Mr. Payton was water.

Ken just sat there for the next half hour. The video camera in the room appeared to indicate that he didn't seem to be worried in the slightest. Then, they could see a small crack in the expression on his face. Ken Payton was wondering what the FBI was actually looking for. Placing a bug in a car did not seem to warrant the attention he was getting. What else did the FBI think they had on him?

Mark and his colleagues gathered in a separate room with a video projection of the interrogation room. "I don't think you are getting to him," one of the FBI agents told Mark. "He needs to feel he is threatened, and so far, he knows that we don't have enough on him to do much more than a slap on the wrists. In the old days, we'd bring in a sturdy brute of a guy to scare the heck out of him. This guy is so cool that even those tactics would probably not shake him."

Mark nodded his head. "You're right. I was hoping he might be the weakest link, but now I'm not sure. One problem, if we cut him loose, he will tip off the rest of them. We may never get another decent lead."

He sat and thought about it for a couple minutes. "Unless!"

Mark jumped to his feet. "Let's just put a little more on the table and see if he bites."

As Mark opened the door to the interrogation room, he shouted down the hall for one of his men to prepare the release papers. Ken Payton was glad to see Mark come back into the room. Now, his hope was that Mark was going to give up, and show him out the door.

Mark sat down at the table and in a relaxed mood, told Ken Payton that he decided if he did not want to cooperate and offer up some new information, he was going to turn him loose, and not offer any protection for him.

That caught Ken Payton by surprise. "What do you mean not offer any protection? I don't need your protection."

"Really, I thought you might reconsider considering the history of your employer."

"What do you mean?" he asked.

"Your old friend, Luke Carpenter, screwed up. I heard they found him on a trail in Wyoming. Where are they going to dump you?" Mark asked.

"What do you mean?"

"Luke screwed up and left a trail. They fixed the problem by eliminating him. I think we'll bring you back to the Twin Cities, and let you go from there. When you walk out with a big smile on your face matching the one on our faces, you think they are going to believe that you just had a free trip to Minneapolis? We just might want to let a few people know we let a suspect go who was bugging cars and apartments. News spreads. Think your people will believe you?"

Mark had just put a real doubt in Ken Payton's mind. He knew that Mark was right. This employer did not like loose ends or mistakes.

Even though the FBI had not gotten anything on anyone else that he knew of, they might not realize it.

"What are you suggesting?" Ken asked.

"Are you still happy with your current employer after what they did to your old friend? If you gave us some help, we might be able to work out a deal. If I were you, I wouldn't even worry about spending a short time in jail. Did your employer torture people to find out what they said, before they dumped their bodies?" Mark asked.

"How much time in jail?"

"Depends on how much help we get. Your decision. Right now, I'm leaning toward forgetting the time for eavesdropping and let your people deal with you. Oh, we would charge you, just to let them know we caught you red handed. Then, with a few people watching, we'll just let you walk out the front door of the Federal Building."

Mark leaned back in his chair. His years of experience taught him that Ken Payton had just bitten on the hook. Now, he didn't need to pressure him for a decision. He had until they released him for Ken Payton's panic button to be pressed. Just to make sure the point was well taken, he offered one more incentive. "Interesting way you were paid for your work. Took my men three days to track down the electronic money transfers."

Mark noticed the expression change on Ken Payton's face. He was taking the bluff.

Ken Payton just sat there. He did not like the fact that the FBI knew about Luke Carpenter, and now they had connected Luke to him. That meant that the FBI had been on this case for some time. If they had broken the money transfer history, it would only be a matter of time before they started to make connections to other operations of the group.

All of Ken's feelings of elation that he would be released soon were now gone. Ken Payton knew that Mark had him right where he wanted him. On top of that, he was still upset by the way his employer handled Luke Carpenter. They could have simply sent him on an assignment out of the country for a number of months. That was the way they normally eliminated all connections to a job.

Mark stood up and looked at Payton, "Take your time. We'll let you sleep on it overnight, and then, I'll give you a free trip to Minneapolis in the morning. Oh, sorry, no phone calls." He picked up his notebook and headed for the door.

Ken Payton just sat there watching him.

As he reached the door, he called Mark back. "OK, if I work with you, I need something in writing ahead of time."

Mark just eased back into his old chair. "I can arrange it. But, you'll have to give us a start so I can talk to the DA."

"OK. I heard a rumor that they were going to eliminate that gal in Duluth on Halloween. Some kind of accident. That give you a start?"

"That just starts to warm my interest. I'll have the DA send me an authorization. Then we can talk," Mark told him. "I know the DA. He's going to have a bunch of legal stuff in the agreement to make sure your memory stays sharp. You help us, and we'll make sure you are safe."

"Just make sure it says I have immunity to prosecution," Ken Payton demanded.

When Mark walked out of the room, his agents asked him, "You going to post some protection on your reporter in Duluth, or pull her out?"

"That's a good question," he answered.

It was tempting. If Mark knew that they could protect her and know where the threat was coming from, they could catch someone in the act. However, there was no guarantee the bad guys knew where Tracy was staying. They could be planning on something while she was on the job, instead of at her aunt's place. In fact, it might be planned for Tracy's house.

Minnesota Point was not the most convenient place to protect someone. There were only a few places for Mark's people could be placed without being noticed. If they guessed wrong, they would need other people in place protecting Tracy. Ken Payton had heard the rumor. He did not know who, how, or where.

Whatever they did, Halloween was less than a week away. Mark needed to make some decisions and inform Tracy of the threat. If he informed the local police, he still didn't know where his leak was coming from. Word could reach the wrong people.

Mark had caught the Federal District Attorney as the DA was heading home from the gym in Minneapolis. After a short discussion, the DA agreed to fax Mark an agreement offering limited immunity with several statements of requirements needed to keep the offer in force. In less than an hour, Mark had the agreement. The DA also agreed not to inform anyone in his office about the detainee or the offer.

When he put it in front of Ken Payton, Mark stated that he needed a little more up-front information before the DA would allow Ken Payton to sign the agreement.

Ken read it over. "It says limited immunity."

"Yes, that's the common term the DA uses. You have to understand, he does not know how many people you might have killed. If he gives full immunity and finds you shot the governor, he'd probably be out of a job."

It sounded logical. The truth was, they actually did not know what other crimes Ken Payton had committed and did not want to excuse him from everything.

"OK, what else do you need to prove? I'll work with you."

"Give me a few bones to show me you are willing to help. Then we can sign it. However, if you go back on your word, there are enough out-clauses in the agreement that the DA will have you on the street in a heartbeat."

Ken Payton reluctantly proceeded to give Mark a history of some of the operations he worked on in the past few years. Under the circumstances, it was the only thing left for him to do.

The information he gave Mark was enough that Mark hated to stop the conversation for the night. So far, Ken Payton had started to connect some of the dots. Mark had enough information to keep his agents working for the next month.

Chapter 25

Protection

Friday morning, Ken Payton was transferred from Sioux Falls to a private holding area that the FBI had available in Minneapolis. It would allow him to be semi-comfortable, while the FBI gathered information from him and protected him at the same time. For the world, Ken Payton had once again simply vanished.

Mark met with Payton again right after lunch. "So, do the accommodations meet your approval?

"Yes, thank you. It is a little better than the holding cell in Sioux Falls. How long are you planning on keeping me here?"

"As long as you are cooperating and our case is going forward, we'll keep you safe and snug here. No one will find you here if that's what you are worried about."

"Thanks. You are right; my life might be shortened if I was out on the street right now."

They sat and talked the rest of the afternoon. Mark had his recorder going to make sure nothing Payton said was omitted.

Ken Payton explained how he was given projects from the manager of the security firm, Neil Paulson, in Wyoming. The manager had been successful over the past ten years in recruiting Marines that were leaving the service. He was extremely selective and made sure the individuals were highly loyal, and well trained in clandestine operations.

Ken was approached by Neil Paulson about a month after he and his long time friend, Luke Carpenter, were discharged from the service. Both had been surveillance specialists. When Ken was approached, he recommended his friend Luke to the firm. Both were hired.

They were required to break all communications with each other as part of the agreement for both of them to be hired. The firm did not want friends talking about operations. To get around it, they set up a special code, and used a public cloud-server to send messages when they needed to talk to each other. Their military training had taught them how to communicate without others knowing what they were doing.

"How many specialists did they hire?" Mark asked.

"Don't know. They would never tell us. Luke and I figured there were probably six of us. When we heard about an operation, we would try to figure out who did it. Our best count was six. We were a separate operation from their regular security firm. It allowed us to hide under the disguise of the rest of the firm. I don't know if they have replaced Luke or not."

"So, what you are saying is that you, Luke, and this guy, Scott Lenard, which we photographed in Minneapolis, all worked for S&G Security," Mark told him, showing him the photograph of the person that attempted to break into the Senior Center."

"Yeah, I guess. I didn't even know his name. I saw him once a few years ago when they were switching people on a job. The firm made sure we did not get a full picture of anything. It was their way to maintain protection of what they were working on."

Mark was wishing that Ken Payton knew who the other three people were. It would make it easier to find them and get the rest of the picture.

"Which case was that?" Mark asked.

"A few years ago, that guy was asked to get a field engineer away from a pipeline project he was working on in North Dakota. The firm was worried about something in the design and wanted the engineer out of the way. They asked him to make things look like an accident. Well, he got to talking with him at the local greasy spoon. After talking to him for a while, he managed to spike his drink at lunch.

"When the engineer was driving to another location, he went off the dirt road and rolled. Our man was following him from a ways back to make sure he fell asleep while driving. The plan was to have him drive off the road and get banged up when the car hit the ditch. They were only expecting the accident to sidetrack him, figuring that he would be off the job for a few months. Somehow, something else happened, and the accident killed him. I guess he forgot to put his seat belt on. Next thing I knew, our man was pulled from the operation and sent on vacation. I was asked to take over."

Mark showed him a picture of the pipeline engineer on his netbook. "That the engineer?"

"Yes! How did you know about it?" he asked.

"We have been working on several things for some time now," Mark told him.

He was excited to get a positive ID. Apparently, Ken Payton did not know why Neil Paulson had him on Tracy's tail. They were never told the story behind their tasks. This might make Mark's work a little more difficult. At least they had a solid line between Ken Payton, the pipeline worker, and now the firm in Wyoming. Mark's superiors would look at this, and start giving him a little more slack in investigating the case.

When Ken Payton took a restroom break, Mark called his office. He instructed his people to put a larger effort on the financial traces of the Idaho and Wyoming firms. They needed to find the other people involved to solve the cases. His hope was that there might be an internet trail of the finances. Mark told them he was looking for three to four individuals.

When he came back, Ken Payton told him about a job that he was sent on a few months ago. It was in Texas. The job was to destroy all the files and computer data at a house in Dallas. Mark was given the name and address of the location. Ken Payton told him that he discovered a hidden file taped to the bottom of a drawer. His boss had not given him a reason for destroying the information. Ken was curious. When he glanced at the hidden file, it contained information on bribes to local inspectors. It appeared to be connected to an oil pipeline in eastern Texas.

* * *

The information Mark was gathering was painting a picture. The painting was one of corruption and bribery across the nation, with the firm in Wyoming protecting the participants involved. Mark needed more information to put the rest of the pieces in the puzzle. So far, it was missing the key people – the people that gained the most from the actions.

At the end of the day, Mark gave me a call. "Martin, how would you like to have a snack at a local pub?" I told him that I could meet him at 6:30 pm.

We met at a noisy pub in North Minneapolis. It was so loud in the place, you could hardly hear yourself talk. Mark picked a booth in the back where we could meet without drawing attention. There, he told me about the threat to Tracy. He wanted me to call her and have her contact Mark on a cell phone he had borrowed.

"What are you going to do?" I asked.

"That's the problem. We need to find the other players in this game. If we pull her out, we may never find out who they are. If we leave her there, I'm not sure we can protect her. That's my dilemma. At the same time, we have to protect her aunt. I have an idea, but I need a lot of help to pull it off without someone finding out ahead of time. I think we have a couple days to pull it off. If the information is correct, the threat is planned for Halloween. Here's my idea ..."

After listening to Mark's plans, I agreed to help as much as possible. When Mark left the pub, I used my cell to call Tracy. I left a message asking her to call me at the house phone at the pub. For twenty dollars, the owner did not mind letting me use the phone.

I told Tracy that Mark had a small break in the case. She needed to contact him immediately on a clear line. I gave her the number.

* * *

Tracy drove over the lift-bridge and stopped at one of the hotels along the channel. There she used one of their phones to call Mark Lawson. It was a long conversation. Mark told her all about the suspect who had broken into her car and apartment, and bugged both. Then, he told her what Ken Payton had told him about the event reportedly scheduled for Halloween. Tracy was shocked.

"What do you want me to do?" she asked.

"I'm worried about both you and your aunt. We don't know what they have planned or when. It would also help if we knew who it was. We need your help to find out. We need you to talk to your aunt."

Tracy listened to Mark's plan before heading back to her aunt's house. It was going to be hard to explain to her aunt what Mark had planned.

Chapter 26

The Plan

Tracy spent the next hour out on her aunt's deck in 45-degree weather, explaining Mark's plan to her aunt, Linnea Hastings. They could not take the chance that someone might have bugged her house in the past couple days. Her aunt listened intently before finally saying, "Are you sure you will be safe?"

"That's the plan. We need you to realize there is a small chance that something might happen to your place."

"I would like to do some remodeling anyway. Tell your friend if you need my support, you've got it."

"Thanks," Tracy told her. Then, they headed back inside for some hot cocoa to warm up. Later Tracy put a post on a blog. It was only two words – game on.

* * *

Mark Lawson saw the message and started the preparations needed from his end. Halloween was only a few days away. Everything had to be ready before Tuesday morning. They would probably only have one chance to catch the mysterious culprit. The problem was setting it in motion without anyone else knowing about it. There was still the issue of the insider who was giving out information. That made it much more difficult. Mark would have to call in people from other states to provide the security needed. No one local could be trusted.

* * *

The weekend went by quickly. Tracy had to work at the station on Saturday, and the work kept her mind off the danger. On Sunday, she had the whole day to think about someone watching and planning to injure her. Everyone she saw was a suspect. Her problem, she could not make it look like she was looking for someone.

Even the house was no longer a place of security. Knowing that someone had bugged her car and apartment with only an accidental spotting, gave her the chills. They could just as easily bug her aunt's house. It had been too easy for whoever it was. So far, even though she was handling the situation, she had the jitters.

That afternoon, Tracy and her aunt went for a ride into Duluth. When they crossed the lift-bridge, they pulled into the parking lot of one of the hotels and quietly transferred to another car. It was her aunt's neighbor's car. They had arranged the transfer, so that they could spend the afternoon talking and not worry about bugs. The car had been left in the lot hours earlier just for the occasion.

They drove north of town to a park along the lake. Brighton Beach was a quiet place where they could talk, while watching for anyone who might have followed them. Driving to a spot about 30-feet from the water, Tracy and her aunt watched the towering waves crashing into the rocks along the shoreline. This time of the year, the rocky beach was deserted. They were the only people in the park. It gave them a chance to talk and discuss their plans. It might be a while before they had the opportunity to see each other again.

To keep Tracy's aunt safe, Tracy was going to drop her off at the airport tomorrow morning on the way to the TV station. She would purchase a ticket, to stay with her sister in Florida until spring. The warm weather would feel much better on her old bones in the middle of winter. Linnea had already started notifying her friends that she was going to head south for the winter, and Tracy was going to stay and watch her house.

The plan was in motion. They enjoyed the afternoon together before heading back to the house for dinner, picking up her car on the way back.

It was a quiet evening. Tracy's aunt packed her two suitcases and put them in Tracy's trunk for the next morning. After watching the evening news, and hearing about the above normal temperatures scheduled for Halloween on Tuesday, they got a good night's sleep.

The next morning, Tracy dropped her Aunt Linnea at the airport, and gave her a hug goodbye, before heading off to the station. On the way to work, she made a few turns to see if anyone was following her. Monday, Tuesday, the days were too close together to let her guard down. What if someone changed the schedule?

Tracy was on pins-and-needles the whole day. You might even say she was a tad edgy. When the editor suggested a couple changes to a report, she almost lost it. Her fuse was at the very end. At the end of the day, Tracy was not sure who was the happiest that she was going home, her or the people who had to work with her today.

She shut down her computer and headed for the parking lot. Just before she left the building, she decided to make a quick stop at the restroom. If the bridge was up, it might take up to 15-minutes before she could cross over to Minnesota Point.

She put on her jacket and hat before heading out. There had been a northeast wind all day. With the 15-mph wind, the 45-degree temperature felt like 32-degrees outside. Living along Lake Superior for the past 15 years, Tracy had always kept a hat and set of gloves ready for a sudden wind change. When the wind came off the 39-degree water, even on a nice summer day when it had been 80-degrees, it could easily drop 20-degrees in a single hour. With November just a couple days away, winter might be just a wind change away.

Tracy took a close look at the parking lot before heading out. Hopefully, Mark Lawson's people would be protecting her. As she got to the car, she quickly locked the doors after getting in. Then, she headed out across the lift bridge to Minnesota Point and her aunt's tuck-under garage. So far, so good. No one was following her that she could see.

She found the small piece of paper in the top of the door leading to the house. She had left it there this morning to detect whether or not anyone had entered the door. It was still there.

The house seemed eerily quiet. The only sounds were the noises caused by the north winds. The old shingles were flapping in the strong wind gusts coming off the lake, which were sent uplifted by the sand barrier that protected the houses from the huge waves coming off Lake Superior.

Tracy checked out the house to make sure everything was locked. Then, she fixed her dinner. After eating, she took a hot shower and relaxed with a book until the news came on. At the end of the news, it was lights out. Tomorrow she would have to be alert and on-guard all day.

Mark took the rail up to Duluth earlier that evening and checked into the Hampton. He wanted to be close, just in case his men needed to talk to him.

The next morning, Tracy got up and fixed breakfast. So far, so good. She checked the street in front of the house for traffic. Just the normal bus and a few cars heading for the bridge. No one parked along the road. If someone was going to try anything, the logical time would be later in the day, when everyone was in costume.

That morning, she was scheduled to cover a meeting at the courthouse, do a special on the haunted ship in the harbor, which was specially decorated each Halloween, and finally video a message by the Coast Guard about ship safety in November. It was the fifty-year anniversary, and everyone still remembered the sinking of the Edmond Fitzgerald.

With all the items to cover, she was not expected at the station unless someone cancelled and she had a change in schedule. Her reports could be relayed to the station's editor from her locations.

Mark had security people watching as closely as possible. They needed to stay concealed, while available at a moments notice. He had one person stationed at the neighbor's house. Another had suffered the duty of watching the beach side of the house all night. Dressed like it was minus twenty degrees, he had positioned himself next to a shed, snuggled in tight all night. The word was out, catch the person. Kill only if it is at last resort.

Tracy got into her car and drove across the metal grid of the roadway on the bridge to the courthouse. The tires gave an eerie sound that howled throughout the car as she crossed the bridge. After a short meeting, she drove to the harbor and boarded the old freighter that was decorated in the slip. Even though she knew the FBI was watching every move she made, she felt like a sitting duck. If they were going to make it look like an accident, it would have to be done later, when people were not around her.

She had lunch at Grandma's Restaurant at Canal Park, used the restroom at the restaurant, and then walked the few yards over to the Coast Guard offices. The video presentation on the memory of the Edmond Fitzgerald would take a couple hours. When she was finished, she sent the reports to the station for the evening news. In another two hours, it would be getting dark. This time of year, it was dusk by 5:30 pm.

The festivities for Halloween were obvious all over the city. Ghosts were hanging outside stores, scarecrows were on the street corners along Canal Point, and black ribbons were attached to streetlights. The strong north winds were gone, but the light south breeze made the ribbons move at all the lights. It made a nerve racking drive home even worse. Watching for unusual movements was almost a tough as telling the clouds to stand still.

Bad timing, the bridge was up. As she sat in line waiting for the bridge to come back down, cautiously she kept her eyes on the mirrors. Where are you? There had to be someone out there.

Finally, she heard the loud horn on the top of the bridge that announced it was heading back down. Soon, the bridge was down and the traffic was flowing again. Another 10-minutes and she would be safe in the garage. The traffic started to stretch out as it got moving again.

Once again, she took the indirect route to the house. Driving past the house, she found a parking lot to turn around in, and then drove back slowly, watching for any suspicious cars or people. As she turned to head into the garage, she looked for other cars in both directions. So far, no one was very close or driving erratically. Maybe Mark was right, they would wait until dark. It would be easier to get off the island without someone recognizing them.

She waited until the garage door shut. Then, unlocking the car door, she got out. The paper indicator was still on top the entry door to the house. Slowly, she opened the door, peered inside and entered the house.

It looked OK. She quickly locked the doors behind her.

Soon it would be dark outside. Was the information correct? Was this the day they were supposed to try something? What if someone found out the information had been leaked? Her heart rate was rapidly beating like a drum.

Making sure the shades had been pulled in all the rooms, she made sure no one could watch her inside. Then, she fixed herself some dinner. Simple things tonight; a can of tomato soup and some crackers. Nothing that would upset her stomach any more than it currently was. In fact, she could have stayed with just the crackers. Soon, it would be trick-or-treat time.

As the evening progressed, every time the doorbell rang and someone shouted trick-or-treat; it was heart-pumping time. When someone pounded on the door, she almost jumped out of her shoes. Early in the evening, the kids were small, and many were accompanied by their parents.

By 6:45 pm, most of the tiny tots were home, counting their treats. Now, it was just the older children.

About 7:30 pm, there was a taller person in a clown outfit walking up the street. He slipped in with a couple trick-or-treat groups. As he approached Tracy's aunt's house, he skipped the neighbor's house. He was carrying a plastic pumpkin to carry his treats.

Approaching the house, he put down the pumpkin near the door and slowly walked away. Then he crossed the street. As he did, two people jumped out of the shadows and quickly tackled him. In seconds, without anyone on the street knowing what had happened, he had his arm banded with a plastic tie and was silently dragged off to the back of the house across the street.

Fortunately, none of the children on the street were watching. If they were, they might have thought someone had just abducted the clown and stole its candy.

When the FBI checked his costume, they found a transmitter in the pocket. Minutes later, when they examined the pumpkin, a small explosive device was found.

It was meant for Tracy. When the next set of kids came to the door, it was to be set off from down the street. A person in the clown suit could easily blend in with the kids running from the scene.

When Mark arrived, his men had made another discovery. The clown was a woman. It figured. If someone was looking for suspects, who would be watching for a woman with a bunch of kids? They would probably take her as one of the mothers. Without their tip, the FBI or police would have never caught their suspect.

Quickly, they took her into custody. Then, to cause some confusion, they set off the pumpkin in the middle of the yard when no one was around. Later that evening, it was reported that a large firecracker went off in a yard out on Park Point.

The suspect was taken to the Coast Guard's Boat Yard for questioning. It would keep her away from the local police. They could officially book her later. This time, they had one of the suspects for attempted murder. If someone else was going to talk, Mark had his bets on her.

Two of the agents were left watching the house, just in case someone had a backup plan. Mark did not want to be fooled by an attempt to harm Tracy, only to have someone come up later and finish the job.

At the Coast Guard building, Mark Lawson took over the interrogation. He had been hoping to catch another person, and it looked like it was his lucky night. Jenna Iken was being held in their retention cell used for holding illegal aliens who tried to jump ships, and for drunken skippers from small boats inspected on the water.

Jenna had been caught totally off guard. She had not been expecting the FBI to be watching for her. Now, she expected the worst. When caught with explosives in an attempt to injure or murder someone, even the best of lawyers would have a hard time getting her off.

Mark took it slow. He wanted her to have time to realize the situation and be willing to admit what she was doing. Meanwhile, his team was running facial scans of their suspect to see what else they needed to know about her.

After 30-minutes, Mark finally went in to see if he could get some information from her. The look of disgust on her face told Mark that she had realized the situation she was in, and that it did not have many acceptable solutions.

She figured that she might as well admit to what was done and see if she could get a lighter sentence, especially since no one had been hurt.

"You want to explain what you were doing," Mark asked.

"If I tell you, what can you do for me?"

"Tell me what you know, and I'll see," Mark told her.

Jenna explained that the plan was straightforward. She was told to set off an explosive near the door, and activate it from as far down the street as she could see the door. She was not trying to hurt any innocent kids that were going door to door. "With luck, I could set off the explosive when the kids were just far enough from the door that only the woman would be hurt."

"What was the reason for the explosive," Mark asked.

"I do not know. All I know is that I was paid to explode the device and take her out of the equation."

When asked about her employer, she refused to give an answer. Mark was waiting for his financial experts to run a search on her accounts. He was assuming that they just might find a payment from a firm in Idaho – Bent Mountain Inc. If they did, he would start that conversation again later.

Mark decided that it was late. He had to figure out what to do with Jenna Iken. He did not want to transport her to Minneapolis and confirm to someone that the FBI was on to them, and on the other hand, the Coast Guard did not want a long-term guest either. He worked out a deal to have her held as a possible illegal alien overnight. Tomorrow, he would have to move her and file charges.

Then, he put in a call to his people in Wyoming. "We just nabbed what looks like another one of S&G's people. If Neil Paulson gets word or senses that communication is not happening, he might panic. Keep a visual watch on our suspect. I don't want to hear that he flew out of the country."

Finally, he called Tracy. "Tracy, I thought you might like to know we caught the person that was supposed to harm you. It happened just like we thought. Oh, you heard about the explosive firecracker in a yard? Yes, we set it off. It was one from our stock. Actually, it was a flash grenade we had in the van. We saved the real explosive for evidence.

"Your aunt's house is fine. She may need to replace a square foot of grass though. If you call her later at her friend's house in Superior, you can tell her she can move back home anytime tomorrow. We still have someone at the house overnight to make sure they did not have a back-up plan."

"Thanks Mark. I'm glad you switched me out for a double at the restaurant. I don't think I could have calmly gone through the whole day. I was nervous enough from here. I'm sure my aunt feels the same way. I'll send you the wig back. Not my color."

"Well, it's a good thing you video'd that Coast Guard event last week after we found out about the threat. I knew the Coast Guard wouldn't say anything if you posted it as if it was live today. Are you still planning to take the next week off?"

"Yes, Martin met me at the rail last night after your person switched places with me. I'll stay down here."

"Remember, Martin might be on the list, as well. Keep low."

"OK, thanks. Please let us know if you find out anything."

Mark told her he would. He just hated to have two people who might be on their short list at the same location. On the other hand, he needed less people to watch over them when both of them were together.

Chapter 27

Confessions

Wednesday's Duluth paper did not have any articles about an attempted bombing on Minnesota Point. Neither did the news on TV. The paper did mention that someone had set off some large fireworks that scared some trick-or-treaters.

Agent Mark Lawson's people were busy checking the history of Jenna Iken. They were hoping to make a link between her and S&G Security in Wyoming. If they did, their case would become a lot more solid for the DA. He got an update before meeting with her at the Coast Guard detention area.

Once again, they were able to find a couple of fund transfers from the same Idaho firm - Bent Mountain Inc., to her accounts. It was the link they needed. Now, it was not a random employee, the tracks were there that proved involvement.

Mark's meeting with Jenna Iken was interesting. She demanded to know why she was being held at the Coast Guard building and not in the city jail. Mark explained that she was going to be booked under Federal charges. The Coast Guard detention cell is part of the Federal Government's holding area. When asked about a lawyer, Mark replied, "Right now, you are being held on terrorism charges, possession of explosives, and attempted murder charges. Under these charges, we have a couple days to determine if you are part of a terrorism plot, and need to be transferred to a Federal Prison for detainment, or if you should be turned over to the Federal DA for charges.

"If I were you, I would consider talking real fast. I would not want to be held in a Federal Prison waiting for a court date to have a Federal attorney assigned to you. You might want to think about how we happened to be in the bushes waiting for you."

Jenna's expression dropped. What had she gotten into this time? In all of her other cases, she had been well prepared with proper escape routes planned. This one looked easy. All she had to do was to set it off from a distance. Now, they were hinting that she had been set up. Who? Why? She did not want to go down without a fight.

"Are you saying that someone told you I would be there?" she asked.

"You figure it out. The person you were hired to hurt was not even at the house. Our agents were all around it. On top of that, don't you think it might look bad if you have to explain to a judge why you were trying to kill an investigative reporter?"

She just sat there staring at Mark.

"And, if I tell you what I know?"

"No promises. You talk, I'll listen. If you can convince me that you have information we don't have already, you have my promise that I'll work to have things lightened up."

"If I don't?"

"Well, I'll put you on a plane to Leavenworth, Kansas this afternoon. When you get a chance to change your mind, you can send a message. Hopefully, it will get to me."

Jenna sat there looking forlorn. If someone had ratted on her, there was little she could do to get out of this one. She took three deep breaths, then turned to Mark, "OK! However, you have to promise out loud, so the video camera can hear it. I want you to say that you agreed to work with the DA."

The interrogation took about four more hours. Jenna Iken detailed how she was paid from a company in Idaho. She had been working for a man in Wyoming, Neil Paulson, for about four years, who ran a protection company. So far, she had been given only six assignments. However, the pay was generous, and up-front.

That confirmed the wire-transfer of funds Mark's team had discovered. Now, they had one more positive link to the Wyoming firm.

Just like Ken Payton, Jenna Iken had not been told why she was to perform her assignments. She was simply given a task and told when it needed to be accomplished.

One plus, Mark now had a list of five other assignments that she had done for the firm. He sent a note to his team to investigate the occurrences and see if there was any overlap involving the other cases they were investigating.

Jenna was probably going to get some time for the attempted bombing. However, with the information she was giving Mark, he would make sure that the DA reduced these charges. As to the other cases she told them about, he would have to look at each of those separately to see what was involved. Those cases, along with the cases Ken Payton had been involved in, might shine a light as to who was actually behind the whole thing.

Now, the question in Mark's mind was what to do with her. He could not keep her here, and if he sent her to Minneapolis, the word would be out in minutes. After thinking about the situation, he decided to cash in a couple of favors, and contacted the Sheriff's Department in Washington County. The jail was close for talking to Jenna Iken, only 30-miles from the Federal Building in Minneapolis. Yet, it was quiet enough that investigators in the Cities might not know they were holding someone for the FBI, especially if the Sheriff could keep her isolated. It would probably buy Mark at least a week – maybe two. A phone call and fifteen minutes later, the deal was done. She would be booked under an assumed name to keep her safe.

Jenna was told the same story Ken Payton had heard about Luke Carpenter, and how he was disposed of in Wyoming. It did not take her long to agree to being held under an assumed name to protect her.

She was transported by car to the Washington County Sheriff's jail later that afternoon.

* * *

Thursday morning, Mark met with his team of investigators in Minneapolis. It was time to look into the cases that Jenna Iken and Ken Payton were involved with, to see if they could tie up more loose ends in the case.

The second item on his agenda was trying to figure out how to detect the source of the information leaks. It would be much easier to work the case if the FBI could depend on the other people they normally worked with. Having to hide suspects and information, along with not working with the local police forces, was making things much more difficult. Was the leak in the police department, the television station or someone else?

The third item: Keeping Martin and Tracy safe.

When the teams looked at the suspects and the cases they knew that Ken and Jenna had been involved with, they realized it was Ken Payton who supplied them with the most information.

He had been involved with the bugging of Tracy's car and apartment, the drugging of a Pipeline worker, a break-in in Texas to remove pipeline information, the stealing of information from a candidate that was running for office in Montana, and the bugging of an office in North Dakota that was receiving bids on a construction project. Mark pointed out that these were the cases that Ken Payton had supplied to them. There may be more that he is not willing to let the authorities know about. Ten years was a long time to work for a firm, and the FBI only knew about six cases.

Jenna Iken told them she worked for the firm for only four years. She was caught with the attempted bombing of Tracy. When pushed for more information, she reluctantly told them about a couple other cases

216

she worked on. She was involved in the removal of the missing files at the DNR. She bribed a worker to purge the file, which covered the radiation data near the deep well at the power plant in western Minnesota. Mark's crew would have to deal with the DNR worker later. The other case involved a break-in at an engineering firm in Colorado. The interesting fact was that it was the same firm that Neil Paulson, the manager of the Wyoming Security Firm S&G Security, had made the phone call to, right after one of his people tried to break into the Senior Center. That one puzzled Agent Mark Lawson and his crew. Why did they break into a firm they were already working with?

It took a few minutes, but Agent Butch Thomas came up with an idea. If someone broke into the firm, they would be blamed for leaking information on bids. That would leave their man at the Colorado firm, Peter Skiff, free from looking like a suspect. He could gather all kinds of information and no one would be the wiser.

It still left Luke Carpenter. The man from Wyoming that followed Tracy and was killed by his firm, presumably. What he did in his ten years of working for the firm was still a mystery.

One of Mark's investigators mentioned something to Mark. "Didn't Ken Payton say that they had a secret internet site where they shared information?" Somehow, that had slipped into the cracks of information. Now they needed to pursue it with Payton. Perhaps it would fill in the blanks on Luke Carpenter's career. There was also the issue of what they did when they left the country after their cases were completed.

The list was long. However, as they were crossing off their leads, they were getting to the end of them too quickly. They still needed more information. The person who had followed Martin and Tracy was still in the field. They had not picked him up, hoping that he would lead them to the two other members of the firm for whom they did not have names or locations. Every step he took was being monitored.

Mark assigned two of his people to work the rest of the day with Ken Payton to decipher his email account and find out what other cases the firm had been involved with.

They had enough information to indict Neil Paulson of S&G Security. However, Mark wanted to nail down the leak first. He had a plan that just might lead them to the person responsible. As long as his people kept Neil Paulson under surveillance, he would not run terribly far. Mark wanted to take down the entire organization, including whoever was behind all the cases. Neil Paulson was just the intermediary. There had to be someone else.

Mark laid out his plan to his co-workers. He was going to let out some information, bit by bit, and see where it led. With the information Ken Payton had given them, Mark's idea was to let several people know that they had apprehended a suspect, who was talking to get a reduced sentence. The catch, each person he told would be given slightly different information. If the wiretaps on Neil Paulson picked up one of the trick pieces of information, they would have a fair idea where the leak was coming from. Perhaps they would get a voiceprint from someone calling to warn Neil Paulson.

The trap was set. Information would be released to LT, the news room, Lieutenant O'Riley of the police department, and to the press group at the Capitol in St. Paul. Then, Mark and his group sat back to wait. If they were on the right track, it would not take long. In addition, if Mark was right, Neil Paulson would be in a hurry to try to leave the country.

Mark waited until 4:00 pm to slowly release his information. It would restrict the people aware of it. If Neil Paulson did not get a phone call until morning, he knew the leak was someone deeper in the organizations. Each of his phone calls was ended with the message, "Keep this information quiet until we can arrest a few of the other suspects." If that didn't kindle the fires, nothing would. One thing for sure, if everyone started heading for cover, it would take the pressure off Tracy and Martin. No one was going to worry about them finding information if the FBI was announcing they were about to arrest multiple suspects.

Chapter 28

Closing the Net

It was about 45-minutes before Neil Paulson's cell phone rang. The caller was brief, and used very few words to convey the information.

"Yes?" Paulson answered.

"They have Payton, and he is talking about a drugging," was the message the caller gave to Paulson.

"Understand. Shut it down," was Paulson's answer.

Before Neil Paulson had a chance to delete his computer's hard drive, the FBI was entering his office with an arrest warrant. He had been caught flat-footed with no chance to escape. Mark's plan worked. Now, they needed to quickly trace the call, and find the person that was on the other end of the conversation.

The message given to Paulson, about the drugging, was the lead given to the police – Lieutenant O'Riley. Mark found it hard to believe that O'Riley would be the leak. He had worked with O'Riley many times in the past, and found him to be extremely dependable.

When Mark listened to the message, it was not O'Riley's voice. Mark was relieved. Now, they had to determine who it was.

The phone trace came from a desk phone at the police station. The caller had been smart enough not to use a personal cell phone. Mark called O'Riley and told him about the trap.

"Why didn't you tell me earlier?" O'Riley asked. "We could have locked down the station, until we nailed his hide to the wall."

"Sorry, O'Riley. I had to make sure it wasn't you. No offense, but you know, protocol."

O'Riley wrote down the phone number, and quickly found the desk from which the phone call had been made. Then, he put an evidence sign next to it. As rapidly as possible, he began questioning people who were still there, about who might have used the phone between 4:45 and 5:00 pm.

Most of the officers and desk people had either left for the day, or left for their supper break. The two people still in the area could not remember seeing anyone using the phone.

O'Riley got the phone replaced, and sent the old one to the lab for a forensic search. He hoped there was a fingerprint, some DNA, or any other type of evidence still on the phone.

Mark got to the station about 6:30 pm. He had a copy of the voiceprint. He figured that someone had to recognize the voice on the other end of the conversation.

When the evening crew got back from their dinner break, O'Riley and the desk sergeant called everyone in the area into the break room. As O'Riley explained what had happened and that they had a voiceprint of the phone call, Mark looked into the eyes of everyone in the room. He was hoping that someone was squirming or intentionally looking too casual. So far, no one in the room saw anyone using the phone at that specific time of day. When they played the voiceprint, no one recognized the voice.

"Wrong department," Mark told O'Riley. They used the phone up here to get us off the track.

"Anyone see anyone from another department on the floor around that time?" Mark asked.

That got a couple responses. Two people had been seen in the area shortly before 5:00. It took a while, but Mark and O'Riley pieced the descriptions of the individuals to people from the call center, and from the mailroom. Everyone knew what the individuals looked like when they were described, but it took almost 10-minutes to put a name to the people in their memory.

When O'Riley checked, both had left for the day. He got their home addresses, and sent detectives out to bring them in.

The mailroom clerk had just gotten home after stopping off for some fast food on the way home. He was just about to take a bite of his double-layer cheeseburger, when he heard a knock on the door. *"This better be good,"* he thought to himself as he went to open the door.

As he opened the door, four police officers barged into his house. "Hey, what's going on?" he asked.

"We have orders to bring you in for questioning," the officer told him, as he started to read him his rights. Within minutes, he was swept away, his cheeseburger left uneaten and going cold on the table.

When they arrived at the station, a couple of officers ID'd him as the person they saw up on the floor just before 5:00 pm. When they asked him if he had indeed been on the floor, he told them, "Yes, I dropped off a package on a desk just before leaving for the day. Why?"

O'Riley checked the desk where the clerk reported leaving a package. There was indeed an envelope that was addressed to one of the officers on the desk.

Mark Lawson had been listening to the clerk ever since they brought him in. His voice was similar, but his diction was slightly different. He turned to O'Riley, "I don't think we have our man. Why don't you see if he saw anyone else up there, before he left."

When, O'Riley questioned the mailroom clerk, he mentioned that he saw one of the call-center officers when he was delivering the package. He was on the phone, and he just waved at him as he passed by.

O'Riley's eyes opened. "Do you remember which desk he was at?"

As they walked onto the floor, he pointed to the desk where O'Riley had already confiscated the phone.

After signing a statement, O'Riley apologized to him for interrupting his supper, and told him that when this thing is over, I'll treat you to a dinner.

"Thanks, O'Riley. Actually, I have always wondered what it would be like to be on the wrong side of you guys. I think I'll stick to the mail and not rob any banks." They had an officer give him a ride home, via a shop to pick up a hamburger.

Their prime suspect was now long overdue at his house. Perhaps, he had the same plan that Neil Paulson had in place – get out of town quick. They put out a BOLO alert on the individual that included his photograph.

* * *

Agents in Wyoming tried to get Neil Paulson to talk about his firm's activities. So far, he had been unwilling to talk, and was insisting on an attorney. The agents were looking through his computer and office records, looking for additional information. Once he got his attorney, the hope of getting information directly from Mr. Paulson was slight.

Mark decided not to pick up Scott Lenard. He was hoping that they had good enough surveillance on him that if there was a chance he might contact any others in their group, it was worth the chance.

* * *

About 10:00 pm, I took a call on my cell – it was Mark Lawson. He told me about the evening's activities. "Martin, I figured I better tell you before LT asked you all about it," he told me. We talked for about 20-minutes before hanging up. Then, I tried to explain to Tracy what happened.

"They could have told us ahead of time," Tracy huffed. "What if they came after us?"

223

"I think that is why they did it. They wanted to protect us. With the information on the street and people in jail, there is no need to follow or harass us. Mark had it under control."

It did not make for an easy night's sleep for either of us.

The next morning, I noticed a news article on my netbook that the FBI had arrested several suspects and was concluding an investigation that had been ongoing for years regarding the death of a pipeline engineer in North Dakota. It claimed that they were close to concluding several other cases in the area. I was sure that Mark Lawson's interpretation of the news article would be – they still can't get the facts straight, even when we spoon-feed them the information.

LT met me at the door when I arrived at the station. "Sorry LT, I did not know what Mark had planned either. He wanted to find the leak and protect us. I guess he probably blew some chances to find the leader of the group, but figured that our safety had to come first."

"Did he really think I was leaking information?" LT asked.

"No, but he needed to pass the information down our channels just in case there was someone in our organization. I'm glad there wasn't."

"So, can you write a news clip on it?"

"Probably not. The article on the internet was just part of one of the plants Mark sent out. Someone printed it without checking out the facts, not that we might not do the same. No, we will have to wait until Mark lets us know the real facts. I'm not sure if he has any leads on the organizer of the case or not. I'll stay in contact."

"OK, just make sure we get the facts first next time," LT said as he turned toward his office, mumbling something about *"You can't even trust the FBI to give you the real facts."*

* * *

Agent Mark Lawson's team gathered again in the late morning to review the evening's activities and determine their next plan of action. Their suspect from the police department was still on the run. They were following leads based on relatives, known travel records, etc. to see if they could find him.

Neil Paulson was not going anywhere. In spite of having his attorney, they had him listed in the involvement of murdering two people, breaking and entry, illegal surveillance bugging, and a number of other minor charges. They listed him as a high flight risk. No judge was going to put him out on bail. So far, his files were not showing anything. However, that was to be expected. They needed to look for hidden locations and coded entries.

That led them to Ken Payton's internet account. With a court order, they had all the old messages restored. It was going to take Mark's team a while to sort through all the messages that Luke Carpenter and Ken Payton had left for each other. If Ken Payton continued to cooperate, it would make this job a lot easier. Mark told them to get to it as fast as they could.

"What about our other man?" Mark asked, wondering if he had contacted anyone or showed any attempts to travel.

"Scott Lenard is still in his apartment," Mark's agent Butch Thomas told him. "Maybe he hasn't read the news?"

"Keep on him. If he knows something, he'll lead us to it, as long as he doesn't know we are on to him. I hope, Ken Payton's files will give us a connection to him, and we can tie him in with the others in the case. So far, all we have on him is a misdemeanor," Mark told them.

"Are there any signs of a flinch by our Senator?" Mark asked.

"None that we can see. Think he is still involved?" Agent Butch Thomas asked.

"Don't know. Just not throwing anyone off the list at this point," he told them. "I'm flying out to Wyoming. Maybe, with a little extra convincing, I can get Neil Paulson to talk. If not, maybe a change of locations for Mr. Paulson might improve his memory."

***

Martin's mind was uneasy all day. The whole set of events just sat strangely in his thoughts. He could not put his finger on it, but something seemed strange. One good thing, at least Tracy was staying at his place. He wasn't sure he would see her again for a long time. Then again, now that everyone was in jail, was she going to head back up to Duluth? Nothing seemed to calm his mind today. It was just one of those days.

***

Mark's computer experts spent the entire day with Ken Payton looking over his files. Ken was surprised that all the old files that he and his friend Luke Carpenter had deleted years ago, were already restored onto the computers at the FBI office.

It was something that a few years ago would have taken them a month, even after the FBI had a warrant for the information. After losing a few cases in the courts about blocking investigations, the industry finally saw the light. When a judge signed an order for the information, it meant expediently or face some time for interfering with an investigation. When a few managers found themselves with up to a year in jail time, and an appeals court upheld the contempt citation, word got out.

Now, Ken Payton and the FBI had close to five or six years of messages to look at. They weren't exactly pen pals. However, a couple encrypted messages a month was still a treasure for the FBI.

They spent several hours looking at the messages, deciphering the links between the file dates, days mentioned in the message and whatever location they could pick up. It was not an easy job. The cases Ken personally worked on, he could supply the missing information that they were looking for easily. The cases Luke Carpenter worked on were much more challenging.

Just like the other cases S&G Security was involved in and the FBI had in their files, there was very little information given to the perpetrators as to why their missions were conducted, only the tales as to what S&G had instructed them to do.

When the FBI looked at their list of dates collected from Howard Long's files, they had a few possible matches.

The death of the pipeline engineer out in the Dakotas had files from both Ken Payton and Luke Carpenter. They showed coded

226

conversations between Ken and Luke about the drugging of the engineer and the accident it caused. From the messages, it was obvious that the intention was to cause an accident that would take the engineer off the job for a few weeks, not necessarily kill him. They wanted him off the job, so someone new would finish the work. To the FBI's surprise, it was Luke Carpenter who took over from Ken Payton. Like Scott Lenard, Ken Payton was also sent to Mexico for a few weeks to prevent links to the drugging.

Luke's messages told about the new engineer overseeing the replacement pipe. It talked about keeping the cause of the corrosion secret, and making sure any communication within the pipeline company did not have any messages that would point to a problem. Obviously, between Ken Payton and Luke Carpenter, they had bugged the pipeline company's communication equipment and had searched the files.

Luke's final message told Ken that he was heading for Williston. An earthquake had caused a release of hydrogen sulfide, and he needed to keep the information silent.

Mark's agents looked at each other. So, there was a link between Howard Long's files. It would have been a lot easier if Howard had just left a summary. Now, with a little more enthusiasm, they dug deeper into the computer messages trying to find another link.

On their break, they called Mark Lawson and filled him in on the information gathered so far.

"Always knew there was a link," Mark told them. "Keep up the good work. Any sign of other names?"

"Sorry, Mark. That's as far as we have gotten. We'll keep looking. Let you know if we find anything."

* * *

227

Chapter 29

Coded Messages

I was wondering what Tracy's plans included. It felt good that she had taken refuge at my place when threatened in Duluth. But, now that the threat seemed to be gone, it was time to talk to her and see what she was going to do. The weekend was coming, and so far, Tracy had not indicated any strong plans for returning to Duluth. She had told her boss that she would be gone for a week. I assumed that it meant that she would be back on the job Monday morning.

When I got off work, Tracy offered to take me to a restaurant for dinner. They had a special deal for Friday nights – all the fish you could eat for $15 each. I wondered where the fish came from. I knew it was not walleye from Minnesota.

As we sat at the restaurant, we talked about the events of the week. It seemed as though it was a month, not just a week.

Tracy told me that even though she liked living in Duluth, she missed being able to see me after work. She wished that LT had an opening. I figured that she was looking for a reaction from me. There were two parts to the equation. One was the need for the job opening. The other was staying with me. I reached out and held her hand. "Thanks, I was worried that you wouldn't miss me."

We finished eating and headed back to my apartment. We held hands all the way back in the car. This was new grounds for me. I was not sure what to say. I realized the next step was probably up to me.

* * *

Agent Mark Lawson's team spent hours combing through the coded messages between Ken Payton and Luke Carpenter. It was like crossing a pond to save the effort of walking all the way around. As you get into the muck, every step takes so much longer than it should. By the time you get to the other side, the energy required feels like you have traveled a hundred miles.

What started on Thursday afternoon dragged into Friday, with no end in sight. Every new line brought the question, "What did Carpenter mean by that?" One thing, Mark's agents were thorough.

Mark met with Neil Paulson from S&G Security. Between him and his attorney, they were staying silent. Mark decided to have him transported to Minneapolis since one of the deaths occurred there.

Before Mark headed back to Minneapolis, he figured it was time to make a surprise visit to the consulting firm in Colorado, specifically to Peter Skiff. Even though they did not have any direct evidence leading to him, there was always a chance that a mild bluff might get him to disclose something interesting.

The flight to Denver was a short one. Well, it would have been if the commuter plane flew directly. Mark wished he could have gotten some frequent flyer points for the actual distance traveled. To him, it was like riding on a roller coaster. With every cloud they went through, the small plane went up and down, up and down, until finally they touched down in Denver. One of his agents picked him up at the airport and drove him into town. He was glad that it took over an hour to drive to the consulting firm. It took that long just to settle his stomach.

At the consulting firm – O3 Engineering – Mark found his target, Peter Skiff, hard at work at his desk. When the suspect looked up, the firm's secretary had already escorted Agent Mark Lawson to his desk.

"Hi, my name is Agent Mark Lawson of the FBI. Do you have a conference room around here where we can talk?"

It caught Peter by complete surprise. He showed Mark to the conference room and looked totally unaware of a problem.

Mark began by asking Peter Skiff what his relationship was with S&G Security. He could see by the expression on his face that the individual was unquestionably blindsided by the question.

"Look, we can have the conversation here, or at the local FBI office, or if you prefer, at the jail where a few of the S&G employees are eating free meals."

That resulted in a deeper expression in his eyes.

"Do I need a lawyer?" he asked.

"You tell me. We can do this the easy way or the hard way. I'm sure your co-workers are wondering what is going on."

"I didn't do anything," he responded defiantly.

"OK, so tell me about it."

For the next hour, Peter Skiff told Mark how he was hired by S&G to observe what the firm in Denver was working on. His instructions were to watch for discussions or projects related to deep well operations in five states.

They asked him to monitor the operations in Montana, North and South Dakota, Wyoming and Minnesota. For doing this, they paid him a monthly fee.

"Do you know what they were going to do with the information?"

"I assumed they were going to use it for competitive bids," he told Mark. They wanted information on pipe materials used, operating conditions, and people involved. They said they had a few other engineers in other firms doing the same thing."

Mark responded without cracking a smile, "I hate to tell you, but I assume your employers aren't going to be paying you in the near future. I think we need to go downtown and get you to fill out some paperwork.

You are probably in a lot of trouble with your current employer. I'd suggest cooperating all you can."

Mark took him to the FBI office in Denver, where agents read him his rights and recorded information from him for the next six hours. Later, Mark took the last flight back to Minneapolis.

While almost asleep on the flight back, he kept wondering, *"Why did Neil Paulson call the suspect he had just left in Denver."* They were trailing Martin and Tracy, and when the tail was almost caught in the act, he called Paulson who called Peter Skiff in Denver. What was in that conversation that would cause Paulson to call Denver? He put a note in his file – check wiretap from Wyoming to Denver in the morning. With all the cooperation Peter Skiff was giving them this evening, he never indicated why Paulson had called.

First thing Saturday morning, Agent Mark Lawson checked the file on the wiretap in Wyoming. The message, which was given to Paulson by the tail, was that he was spotted and had not had time to bug the apartment. The message sent to Skiff in Denver was essentially the same. Was Paulson letting Skiff know that the bug was not planted because Denver was leading the parade? Mark called his agents in Denver and suggested that they spend a few more hours with their guest.

* * *

LT had given me the day off. He said I had earned it for covering all the days without Jake Schwartz's crew. Actually, it "was" my day off. I almost forgot about it until I checked the schedule. It was my scheduled weekend off. And I thought LT was doing me a favor.

I wondered, *"When was the last time I had the weekend off? Surely, it had been long before Jake's helicopter accident. How many extra days had I put in without any extra pay to account for it?"*

Tracy, however, slept in late. I was awake from 6:00 am on. I kept thinking about what to do, and what to say to Tracy. It's astonishing how you can wish for a situation, yet when it arrives, you don't know what to do.

About 8:30 am, I rolled over and gently rubbed the small of her back, until she woke up.

"You don't have to quit," she told me. "Feels good."

She rolled over and gave me a kiss.

"You want breakfast in bed, or do you want to get up?" Tracy asked.

"Depends on what you are serving."

We stayed in bed holding each other for another half hour. I'm not sure if either one of us wanted to get up. It felt too good, rolled up tight to each other and staying in each other's arms.

Finally, the phone rang. It was my father. He was calling to brag about how much money he had won from his gang last night at cards. After talking to him for a few minutes, I hung up. Somehow, the call had broken the mood. It was time to get up and face the new day.

Tracy decided to see if her boss would grant her two additional weeks away from the job. Even though it was Saturday, she gave him a call at home to discuss the possibility of extending her leave a couple more weeks.

Her boss was sympathetic to her request. Tracy kept him tuned-in to the events of the past few weeks by both the FBI and LT, and after the quick relocation for her safety earlier in the week, he figured that her head was still spinning. As a result, he told her to take her time. Just call every few days to keep in touch, to make sure the station was handling everything OK.

Tracy was relieved. Since I had the weekend off, I asked her if she would like to go back to pick up her car, or if I should take her to Duluth to pick up more clothes. The weather would be changing very quickly, and with the rush to get out of town, she grabbed only what she needed. We decided to take the rail up to Duluth and drive Tracy's car back. That way, she had mobility during the week. I reminded her that Mark might need to scan the car to remove any bugs. Her apartment should probably be included. It was another reason Tracy did not want to head back home and stay in Duluth.

Mark Lawson had found three bugs in my apartment, and had them disabled after picking up Neil Paulson in Wyoming. There had been another under the seat of my car. I called Mark and told him that Tracy was going to stay at my place for a couple weeks. We were going to bring her car down today. He told us he would have someone meet us in Duluth at the Link station, and they could remove any bugs left in Tracy's car or apartment. It would save us a cab ride.

Saturday service on the Link from the Cities to Duluth was light, mostly tourists and shoppers. It only took an hour and a half to get there. Mark's agent was waiting on the platform for us. He had our pictures, which Mark had attached to his text mail, so he could recognize us.

The view of the lake was spectacular as we headed up the hill from town. This late in the season, it seemed as though the blue sky was bluer, and the water had an even darker blue color. The only thing missing was the leaves on the trees. The fall winds had removed them for yet another season.

It did not take long to scan the apartment and Tracy's car. The FBI agent located the bugs and removed them from both locations. We thanked him and he left us to pack up a few things before we headed back to the Twin Cities.

When we were about to leave, Tracy's neighbor stopped us in the hall.

"Tracy, where have you been the past week? I was looking for you, and when I did not see you, I was worried that maybe you were sick or in the hospital," she said quite emphatically.

"Oh, hi Mrs. Albush. No, I'm fine. Just took a few days off and spent them in the Cities. In fact, I'm heading back down there today. Got some more shopping to do before winter comes. I need a new coat and boots."

"I'm glad to see you are OK. You know, you had several of us neighbors worried. You must know how we all look after everyone here. And, who's your friend?"

"I'm sorry; I didn't introduce you to him. This is Martin Berman. He works for one of our sister stations in the Cities."

"It is nice to meet you," Mrs. Albush told him, checking him out to see what kind of guy Tracy was hanging out with.

"I almost forgot; you know that mail person we keep griping about? Well, she did it again. She stuffed some of the mail into the magazines. I was trying to catch up on my reading this week, and I noticed that I had one of your letters stuffed into my National Geographic.

"I hate when she sticks things inside the magazines. Unless you make an effort to look, you can miss some bill or something valuable. What if it gets stuck into some advertisement that you throw in the garbage? It is terribly pathetic when other people's mail gets stuffed into your mail. I wish they would fire that mailperson. You know, several other people have had the same problem with their mail. I don't know why we put up with it."

Tracy looked surprised. "Yes, it has happened before. I'm glad you spotted it."

Tracy wondered what it was that had slipped into Mrs. Albush's magazine. Was this the missing letter from Howard Long? If it was, and had it been delivered to the correct address, Tracy might never have gotten it. Whoever was watching her place would have taken it. When she looked at the letter, it was postmarked from Minneapolis, with no return address.

She thanked Mrs. Albush, and quickly stuffed it in her purse. She did not want to open it in front of anyone else.

We got down to her car, and drove a couple blocks to a park before Tracy stopped the car and opened the envelope. She did this after making sure no one was following us or watching our car. This time of year, the park was deserted. All the tourists were long gone to warmer locations downtown.

As she opened the envelope, both of us were cramming our eyes to see whom it was from, and what it contained. It was a bill. The bill was for a cleaning service in Minneapolis. It was just a laundry service.

We both sat there looking at each other. "Have you used this laundry service?" I asked her.

"No, never heard of it. Think it is Howard Long sending us another cryptic message?"

"Has to be. What's the date on the bill?"

Tracy checked. The invoice was generated on October 5th. Something had been brought in for cleaning prior to that and was ready for pickup and payment.

"You think it is still there?" she asked.

I looked at the bill. There was an address and phone number of the cleaning service on top. "Let's find out."

I called the number and spoke to a clerk. After giving her the invoice number, she said, "Yes, the item is still here. You know, we only agree to keep things for 30 days. You better pick it up soon."

I checked the time that the shop was open. It closed in 15 minutes, at 2:30 on Saturdays. The shop would be closed long before the time we got back, and they were not open on Sundays. That meant we would have to wait until Monday to see what they were holding in their shop for Howard Long. That would drive both of us crazy until Monday morning.

We headed out of town and gave Mark Lawson a call on the way back to the Cities. After thanking him for the ride to the apartment and for debugging the place, I told him about the letter. Unfortunately, the shop was closed by this time; it was 2:45 pm and he would not be able to pick it up either. We would all have to wait until Monday morning.

It made for an interesting conversation on the way back to the Cities. What could Howard Long have left at the cleaning service? Was it even readable after going through the cleaning?

235

* * *

Mark Lawson got a call in the late afternoon from his agents who were working with Ken Payton and his internet files. It seemed that they had matched up another set of dates with an event in Howard Long's files.

"When we were looking at Luke Carpenter's notes, we found one that indicated that Carpenter had turned down a job to modify a gas tank. Luke Carpenter had cryptically told Ken Payton that he was asked to rig a fuel sender. Carpenter told Paulson that he was not comfortable working on it, and they assigned it to another person."

"Is there any chance that the other person's name was in there?" Mark asked.

"Just a last name – Young. Ring a bell?" he asked.

"No, but it is a starting point. I assume that the date corresponds with the crash of the DNR guy," Mark stated.

"I guess that's why they made you the boss, you hit the jackpot again," his agent told him.

"OK, let's see if we can trace a money transfer at the same time. If we do, Mr. Paulson is going to be lucky if he ever sees the outside of a prison again. Also, if there is a money transfer, maybe the account will give us a first name."

Mark hung up the phone with a smile on his face. The case was slowly closing in. Now, if there was anything at the cleaners he could use, maybe by Monday afternoon they could start to figure out who was behind this whole thing.

* * *

Chapter 30

The Wait

We spent Saturday night talking about the case again. Amazing how one little item can change the atmosphere and the line of discussion. In a way, I felt like I was off the hook. On the other hand, I was still trying to find the right things to say to Tracy, and this was not helping me out.

We did not have all the facts that the FBI had put together the past week. As a result, all we could do was conjecture. It was almost 9:00 pm before I remembered that I had not called my father back to listen to the rest of the results of his card game.

"What's the matter? That girl friend of yours taking too much of your time to call your father?"

Ouch! He hit the nail on the head, again, the first time. "Sorry Dad, I took Tracy up to Duluth to pick up her car today."

"And, you didn't invite me?"

I figured at that point that he was kidding, and trying to give me a hard time. It was working. After talking for 10-minutes, he let me go. "Say hi to Tracy. Tell her the place just isn't the same without her."

"Thanks Dad, I will."

When I got off the phone, I told Tracy that my father told me to say hi to her, he missed having her at the place.

We watched the news and then headed off to bed. When we got to bed, Tracy thanked me for going with her to Duluth to pick up her car and extra clothes. I told her I was glad she decided to stay for a couple extra weeks.

I stayed awake the next hour trying to decide what to say next. My elegant statement that I was glad she decided to stay for a couple extra weeks would not make a cut in a movie like "Gone with the Wind." Maybe I had lived a bachelor's life a little too extreme lately. Had I lost the touch on how to let a woman know I genuinely cared?

We woke up early Sunday morning. As we were getting up, Tracy turned to me and asked if we could go to church this morning. I had to stop a moment and realize it was Sunday, and with work, I had gotten so out of the habit that I forgot people do go to church on Sunday morning. I did not even know which church she belonged to.

"What church do you want to go to?" I asked.

"Which church do you attend?"

"Well, I used to go to Mount Olivet Lutheran Church in South Minneapolis," I told her.

"I usually go to the First United Methodist Church in Duluth," she told me. "How about going to your church this Sunday and a Methodist church next week?"

"Sounds like a fair trade," I answered. We had plenty of time before the late service.

I used to go to church with my parents every week when I was growing up. Then, when I went to college and started working long hours, I guess my attendance started to slip. As I was thinking about it, I mentioned to Tracy, "OK if I invite my father? He has been going to a service at the Castle, but would probably love to see the old church."

"I think he would love to join us," she said.

When I called my father, he was just getting ready to join his gang downstairs. "You want me to drop my gang for going out with a good looking girl? What's my gang going to say?"

"I think they are going to say you're getting smarter in your old age," I told him. He said he would love to join us.

We picked him up on the way to church.

It was nice to spend a Sunday at church with Tracy and my father. I was feeling real good until I looked at the topic of the sermon – "Making a Commitment." Was someone upstairs aiming that one at me?

Tracy was impressed with the size of the church. She said, "You could fit my whole congregation into one wing of this church."

"We have a large congregation. Ten years ago, it was even larger. It seems that people's lives have gotten too complicated. I'll bet half the members only make it to church on Christmas and Easter. I guess I have fallen into that category myself lately."

After church, my father thanked us for including him, and offered to take us out for lunch. He said it was like the old days. We would always go to church as a family and then to a restaurant so my mother would not have to cook a meal right after church.

I could tell that my father really liked Tracy, and she seemed to be intrigued by his sharp sense of humor. After eating, we took him back to the Castle and headed back to my place. So far, we had not even mentioned Howard Long and his files all morning.

It was almost 3:00 pm before we got back to the apartment. Our weather people at the station kept hedging their bets on cold weather moving in, as it had been a balmy 40-degrees and sunny all day. Unfortunately, it was just cool enough that a long walk along one of the parks in Minneapolis might feel cold. If I felt uncomfortable before, now I was squirming in my shoes. I wished that we could open up the cleaning service early and break the quagmire in my mind. I felt like a little kid that just could not decide if I should step onto the newly frozen lake or not. Talk about a lack of confidence.

On top of that, I was remembering that I had to work next weekend. I hated to let Tracy know that I had to break our date for church so quickly.

I decided to take her to a movie that night. I'm not sure if it was to escape from reality or to help with the situation. We picked out a romance movie and went to the 7:00 pm showing. Tracy liked it a lot. I thought the plot was a little too feminine for me.

The best part was Tracy holding my hands throughout the movie and seeing the emotions build in her eyes. It was an emotional side of her that I had not experienced. Much different from the stoic reporter, or the scared silly victim. There was obviously a softer side to her personality, and I enjoyed seeing it.

When the movie was over, she walked tight to my side back to the car. Once again, I missed the chance to let her know that I would really like to keep her around – permanently. The situation was right; I just couldn't find the words to tell her.

Monday morning, we were both ready to stand in line waiting for the cleaning service to open up. Or, should I say the three of us? Agent Mark Lawson was ready to join us as well. All of us wanted to know what was hidden in the cleaning. Was it the missing clues, or was it something that just got washed away in the laundry?

There were three people standing in line when the owner opened the door that morning. "Hold your horses," she told us, "it will just take me a second to get opened up."

We gave her a couple minutes, then, Mark showed her his badge, and the invoice I had given him. "Could you please look into your racks and find the item listed on this invoice?" Mark asked.

It took her almost five minutes to find it. When she came back, she had a grey lightweight jacket with her. "You're lucky I still have this one. Another day or two and it would have been in the pile for the Goodwill. You know, I tell everyone that I only hold cleaning for 30-days. Which one of you is Howard Long?" she asked.

Mark informed her that Howard had been killed a few weeks ago. We were there to pick up his belongings.

"Well then, who is going to pay for this?" she asked very indignantly.

I finally offered to pay for the cleaning, just to get the jacket, and start us on the quest to find what was so important about it that Howard Long had sent the invoice to Tracy. There had to be a reason for sending it to her.

As we were walking out of the shop, Mark checked the pockets – nothing. Then, he turned and asked the shop owner "Was there anything else that he left with you, or anything in the pockets?"

"No, we check all pockets before we accept jackets. People leave things in there. If we don't, I would have a treasure chest filled with coins, cell phones and car keys if I didn't check."

It was not what Mark was hoping to hear.

Mark joined us in our car to look at the jacket. There had to be a clue or something else in there. We hunted to see if there were any interesting markings.

Howard Long had worn a 44 regular jacket. It was a grey, polar fleece, Washington Peaks jacket, with a hidden hood, which was rolled up behind the collar.

Tracy took a close look at the jacket. There has to be something hidden here. She checked the inside of the jacket. There was a model number, but no hidden names or numbers when she turned it totally inside out.

"OK, there has to be a key to the clue," Tracy stated. "Let's see, Washington Peaks. That could be Mount Rainier or Mount Baker. There must be a few others, I just can't remember," she said.

"Are you thinking he hid a clue in a file that the name will lead you to?" I asked.

"Just grasping for straws," Tracy answered. "Any other ideas?"

Unfortunately, we didn't. It looked like we had all bit on the treasure map, only to find it was a false lead.

"Mark, doesn't the laundry put a mark on all garments to keep from losing the owner?" Tracy asked.

Mark grabbed the jacket and went back into the shop.

"You have a black light in here?" he asked the owner.

"Sure, want to use it?"

"Please. I want to see if someone put a mark on the jacket."

Mark beamed the black light onto the inside of the jacket.

Chapter 31

The Mark

When Mark put the black light on the jacket, a number showed up on the manufacturer's tag. "That's my ID mark," the shop owner stated. "I put it on all coats and jackets so customers can't claim their coat was a more expensive coat. It is invisible ink. If they bring it in again, I have an eraser pen that can remove the mark, and I can put a new mark on the same spot."

As Mark moved the light around the rest of the inside of the jacket, a small area near the sleeve lit up. He looked at it closely. It was a phone number.

Mark thanked the merchant and headed back to the car.

As he was climbing back into the car, Tracy asked, "Did you find something?"

"Well, I think your man Howard Long was a much more practical person than we have all given him credit for. Either that or the two of you have been watching too many crime scene shows and Mission Impossible movies.

"I don't think he went out and purchased a jacket with a brand name that would lead us to a mountaintop experience. If I'm right, he dropped off his old jacket, had the bill sent to you, and probably bought another jacket in the shop next door. If someone was watching him or tailing him, they probably didn't even recognize the difference when he walked out wearing the same jacket."

"So, what was the clue?" Tracy demanded.

"The owner marks all jackets on the tag to keep people honest when they claim their old jackets. It looks like Howard Long borrowed the pen and wrote a phone number in the jacket for us to call. Unless you knew about it, no one would ever know. Now, all we need to do is find out who is on the other end of the phone number, and what they know."

I told Mark that I needed to get to work. Since we did not see the Holy Grail at the cleaning service, LT would want me back on the street. I hated to miss the next episode, but Mark would have to give me a call with an update.

Tracy asked if she could tag along with Mark, and see if they could find out why Howard Long had left them the phone number. Mark thought that would be OK, as long as Tracy let his men do the actual work. If it involved more investigation, she had to let the FBI take the lead from now on. He did not want to put the two of us back into jeopardy.

* * *

Mark and Tracy headed back for the FBI offices in Minneapolis. On the way, Mark called his office and had one of his people do a run-down on the phone number.

By the time they got to the office, he had his answer. His agent informed him, "The phone number is for an Arnold Marble in Thief River Falls, Minnesota, which is in northwestern Minnesota."

"Any link to our Howard Long?" Mark asked.

"Don't know. He's not a long lost brother if that's what you mean," his agent answered. He gave Mark a short description of the individual that he had gathered from the public records: Age 67, widowed twelve years ago, retired farmer.

"OK, I'll give our new "best friend" a call, and see why Howard Long left us his phone number. It's a long drive up there. Let's make sure there is something here before we drive up north. Tracy, you can listen in on my speaker phone as long as you let me do the talking."

Mark looked at his watch. 9:50 am. Hopefully, Arnold Marble was home. He dialed the number.

The phone rang for the next couple of minutes. Just as Mark was expecting an answering machine to pick up, a person answered. "Yeah, what do you want?" It was a rather gruff greeting for a phone call.

Mark replied, "Hello, is Arnold Marble there?"

"Yeah, why?"

"Is this Arnold?" Mark asked.

"Yeah, that's what I told you. Why? What do you want?"

Obviously, Mr. Marble was not in the mood for salespeople calling and bothering him at home.

"Mr. Marble, this is Agent Mark Lawson from the FBI."

"Oh yeah, and I'm the 'Wizard of Oz'. Prove it."

Mark chuckled. This old coot was not about to give up easy. "Well Mr. Marble, I can do that the easy way or the hard way. You can hang up and look up the FBI phone number in Minneapolis, and then call me, or if you would like, I can tell you to the penny how much the Federal Government put in your savings account last week on Friday, along with the current balance."

That got Arnold's attention. "You can do that?"

"Yes sir. On the other hand, we can make it a lot easier, and the two of us can have a regular discussion. A friend of ours gave me your phone number, and I wanted to ask you a couple of questions."

Arnold Marble was slightly shocked to realize it was the FBI and not someone playing a joke on him. As for Mark, he really did not have the numbers he told Arnold he had. He knew that the Social Security checks were direct deposited last week, and he figured if Arnold called his bluff, he could get the information within an hour from his agents.

245

"OK, what do you want to know?"

"Mr. Marble, do you know Howard Long?"

"Yeah, why?"

"Did you know that he died a few weeks ago?"

"Yeah, I was at the funeral."

Mark just shook his head. We look all over for clues, and the man was probably standing right next to us.

"Well, Mr. Marble, we are investigating his murder. Howard had some information that he sent us, and left us your phone number. Now, I'm trying to figure out why. He must have had a reason for us to call you. How did you know Howard Long?"

"He was my sister's husband," Arnold told Mark.

Mark just shook his head again. How did they miss this guy?

"Did you know him well?" Mark asked.

"Sort of. Used to see him when I saw my sister. Haven't seen him much since. Too bad someone killed him. You getting close to finding out who? Can't imagine anyone mad at him. He was a technical marshmallow. Smarter than all heck, but never got into an argument. I used to bait him into getting him to argue politics. He would never bite, no matter which side I argued."

"When was the last time you saw him alive?"

"Oh, he stopped by about two years ago. He was consulting out west."

"And you haven't seen him since?" Mark asked.

"Like I said, it was about two years ago."

"Do you have any idea why Mr. Long would leave us your phone number?" Mark asked.

"Well, he didn't have any family that I knew of. Probably wanted to let me know he was gone."

The conversation was not going the way Mark had hoped. Tracy leaned over and asked Mark to see if Howard left anything with him.

"Arnold, did Howard ever leave anything with you for safe keeping, or for you to work on?"

"No, when I moved off the farm, I moved to a small apartment. Ain't got a lot of room. He had the big place on the lake."

"What did you do when you weren't farming?" Mark asked.

"I had a job in town at the hardware store for 20-years, why?"

"Just wondering. With your name, I was waiting for you to say you ran a marble factory," Mark joked.

"Yeah, I hear that one a lot. That and are you missing any of your marbles? Doesn't help that they mine marble in the area. Anything else I can do for the FBI?"

"Probably not at this time. We were hoping Howard had left some information with you that would solve his murder. He sent us some files, but so far, not enough information to figure out a killer."

"Did you check all his files?" he asked.

"That's what we are looking for," Mark replied.

"How about the internet account in my name? When he was here two years ago, he asked me to set up an account in my name. He said he would pay for it. He's been sending me $50 around Christmas to pay the bill."

That got Tracy and Mark's attention. "Can you tell me about it?" Mark asked.

"I don't remember the password or anything. But, the bill has an identification on it. The company sends it electronically every year and I just pay it."

"Do you have a copy of it?" Mark asked.

"No, I deleted it after a while."

"Would it be OK, if we asked your provider to restore your deleted files so you could send it to us?" Mark asked.

"You can do that? Get the old deleted files back?"

"Yes sir. All you need to do is give me the name of the provider and stay on the line while I connect us to them."

"Well, OK, on one condition."

"And what is that?" Mark asked.

"About a year ago an old girl friend of mine tried to contact me. Before I realized it, I hit delete all, instead of deleting junk mail. Can they restore her message as well?"

"I'm sure we can arrange it. Can you give me your internet provider's name and your email account name?"

It took Mark about 30-minutes to get all the information, send an official fax to the provider's number, and get them to agree to restore Arnold Marble's files within 24-hours. Mark told Arnold that he would call him tomorrow and get permission to retrieve the file Howard Long had set up once they have the ID.

Tracy sat there with a big smile on her face. "You did it," she told Mark.

"Don't count your chickens before they hatch. We still don't know if there is anything there or not. It might be an empty file. At least we know that there might be another hidden file out there. I'll let you tell Martin.

"That reminds me. I was going to ask, but you can tell me to butt out if you want. Things getting warmed up between the two of you?"

"Sometimes. Why?"

"Well, I've known Martin for a long time. I didn't tell you this, but sometimes he has a keen ability to pick out an exceptional girl. The problem is he never seems to know how to catch them. That's how I found my wife. She got tired of waiting for Martin, and I came along. I think Martin was mad at me for years after that."

"I guess that explains a few things," Tracy answered. "I wondered why he went around the obvious by asking his father to talk to your father if you were old friends."

"Well, let me know if you need some help. I still feel like I owe him something, just don't tell him I said that."

"Thanks Mark. If I decide I need your handcuffs, I'll give you a call."

"No problem. Would you like a ride home?"

Mark and Tracy talked all the way to my apartment. It seemed that now she had both Mark and my father trying to get Tracy and me together. So far, she was not resisting their efforts.

* * *

When she got back to the apartment, Tracy put in a call to me. I called her back about 10-minutes later. "Did you find the information?" I asked.

"Another delay. We found a brother-in-law who set up an account for Howard Long. Now, it is going to take a couple days before Mark can get into the account. Legal stuff."

"Well we waited this long, what's another day or two? You back at the apartment?"

Yes, Mark brought me back. I think I will do some shopping this afternoon. See you when you get back."

* * *

Mark finished doing a full review on Arnold Marbles. He didn't want any surprises showing up later. So far, he could not find anything in his past that would indicate anything unusual. When they did a financial review, he was able to spot the electronic payment for $49.95 to a cloud database company. Now, even if they had delays with their other requests, he had a payment record that would provide the FBI with the correct account.

He told his people to prepare an official request for access to the account, and send it immediately. If Arnold Marbles had lied and not told him the full truth about access to the account, he could have a copy of the files by morning even if someone tried to delete them. He did not want to take any chances. Even with the files, he would still go through the motions with Arnold, just in case there was something else Arnold might think about, while working with the FBI.

* * *

Tracy spent most of the afternoon shopping for clothes. After the discussion with Mark, she figured that she needed some clothes that would do a better job of grabbing Martin's attention. With everyone in jail, she could finally pick up some bright clothes that would make her stand out in a crowd. The trick was to get Martin's attention.

On the other side of the thought, she needed some clothes anyway. The variety available in Duluth was much more restricted than in the Cities. She spent almost four hours wandering around the Mall of America looking for clothes.

* * *

Tracy got back to the apartment just before I did. She spent the next hour trying on and showing me every piece of clothing she had purchased. I had to admit, some of them made her look extremely good. She even picked up a sweater for me that was on sale. I was surprised that she knew what size I wore.

During supper, Tracy told me everything that happened in the phone call with Arnold Marbles. So far, it looked extremely promising. She left out the conversation she had with Mark.

She spent a lot of time that evening asking me questions about my past. She would mingle the questions into the middle of other discussions, so that I did not feel like she was digging into my ancient history files.

Somehow, even though both of us knew how to get questions answered that someone did not want to talk about, it took me awhile to realize she was using the techniques we both were trained to use, checking out my past. The thought occurred to me about the same time I realized that I did not know very much about her past.

By the time the evening was over, both of us knew a lot more about each other than we had before the conversations.

Tracy told me about her parents, and where she went to school. She had been on the high school's volleyball team. Because of that, some friends at Duluth, who were a year ahead of her, talked her into going to the University of Duluth to play on the same team they were on. Unfortunately, she was not tall enough to keep a spot on the University's team. She spent most of the time on the bench. However, it did give her good exposure to life other than academics.

I was tempted to ask her about any of the boys she dated in high school or college. Then, I thought better of it. She would probably be offended if I did. No, if she wanted me to know, she would let it slip out. Whatever the reason someone had not picked her up and swept her away, I was not going to ask. Maybe she was like me. Too busy to let anyone get too close.

We also talked about the plane crash her parents were in. Tracy was working for the station at the time, and her parents took a long awaited trip with some friends from her home church to Africa. Near the end of the trip, someone asked them if they wanted to see some wildlife from the air. A missionary over there had a plane and needed to take some food to a remote mission. Apparently, something went wrong. The plane crashed, killing everyone onboard. It took Tracy a while to get over it.

She told me that her aunt helped her get back on track after that. She would call her regularly, and they would get together for a meal every week or two. Tracy said that she was depressed and sort of fell into a shell for a couple years after the accident.

By the time the news came on, I felt as though I was starting to know the other side of the beautiful woman I liked to hold tight. So far, if she had any daggers hidden in the woodwork, I had not found any of them. I wondered if she still felt the same about me.

The evening news had a short story about the awarding of contracts for the upcoming pipeline from Lake Superior to the Twin Cities. The report made the project look like it was the most progressive project in the last ten years, guaranteeing adequate drinking water for the whole state for years to come.

Tracy commented about the news. "Do you really think the project is that important?"

"No, not from what I could see when we were up in Grand Marais. I think my father has the right answer on this one. Someone is using the excuse of poor water to spend taxpayer dollars. They need to spend half that amount on cleaning up the waters.

I had just finished saying it when the cell rang. It was my father. He had watched the same story and wanted to remind me how the news networks always made things look considerably more prominent than they actually were. In his words, "What ever happened to investigative reporting? Don't you guys ever end a story with your impression of the report – Phooey?"

I thanked him for his viewer's opinion rating and told him I would mention it to the news anchor. Then, I added, I would talk to him in the morning.

When I hung up, Tracy laughed. "Your father really does not like anything the state is doing with water, does he?"

"Can you blame him? They don't have an exceptionally solid record of accomplishment. They are always blaming someone or something for an event that they could have solved long before it became a monumental problem.

Once again, a phone call had broken my train of thought. It took a few minutes of snuggling in bed to bring my thoughts back to where they had been before the news.

I wondered what Tracy was thinking.

* * *

The next morning, Mark Lawson got the files listed under Arnold Marbles, which he had requested. This time, it looked like the treasure chest he was looking for. Howard Long had hidden the mother load of information under Arnold Marbles' name. When he and his team opened the first file, there was a detailed summary of what Howard Long thought he had found on the subjects. And, that was only one of the twelve folders they looked at.

Mark told his team to go through it with a fine-tooth-comb, and give him a periodic update on what they found. He wanted a meeting tomorrow afternoon to review the case. By then, Wednesday afternoon, they should have an idea if the files finally pointed to someone or some company that was behind the whole operation. He had an appointment with his superiors the next morning, and wanted to show them that all the effort was finally paying off. If he could put the finger on the person behind the murder of a DNR Commissioner, it would be icing on the cake.

* * *

I went off to work, leaving Tracy home to relax and finish her shopping if she wished. I figured that there was nothing we could do about the case until Mark called. I told Tracy I would call her in the afternoon.

* * *

Later, in the day, Mark Lawson called Arnold Marbles and went through the motions to get permission to see his files. As he did, he slowly gathered additional information about Howard Long, which came out in the conversation they were having. Even though Mr. Marbles claimed he was not close to Howard, it appeared that over the years, he and his sister had discussed Howard and how he was constantly investigating the projects he had been working on. So far, Mark was slowly getting a better picture of who Howard Long was, and how he ticked.

About 3:30 pm, Mark met with his team to go over the results of their search of the files and see if they could put together the real story of what he expected was murder and possibly bid rigging.

Chapter 32

Collected Facts

The Wednesday afternoon review was full of information. Mark's team had deciphered most of the new files that Mark had given them and had a long list of reoccurring facts and dates between the files. This one was seriously starting to sound like a "who dun it." It had all the intrigue, and the only thing missing was Sherlock Holmes to walk in and solve it. I guess that was Mark Lawson's job.

"OK, what do we know?" Mark asked. "Lay out the facts for me."

Agent Butch Thomas and the rest of his team showed them the summary that Howard Long had prepared for each of his twelve folders. "And there are supporting details for each of these?" Mark asked.

"Enough for your man in Wyoming to forget seeing freedom for the next century," Butch told him.

They laid out the facts and connected the dots for Mark.

Apparently, Howard Long picked up on their scheme while working in North Dakota. He ran into problems with surface water and started investigating it on the side. It didn't take him long to figure out why hydrocarbons were showing up in the surface waters. All the fracturing of the rocks deep under the water table, combined with earthquakes, had allowed the hydrogen sulfide laden CO_2 to escape to the surface. The bubbles in the ponds, lack of birds flying around them, and the sick farmer, were all clues for Howard Long. He just couldn't give up on a good investigation.

The engineering firm that was used to design the piping at the power plant, Deep-Pipe Engineering, had made some design flaws. The valves used to divert the stream to the proper locations used the wrong internal gaskets. As a result, they leaked. Actually, they read closed when they were still partially open. The operators at the plants had no idea they were contaminating the environment.

To protect them, Deep-Pipe Engineering hired Neil Paulson's Wyoming security firm – S&G Security to keep it a secret until they could fix the valves and replace the corroded piping.

Unfortunately, at that point, things were getting out of the control of the original engineering firm. They asked a couple of the engineers from the firm to go work with engineers from competing firms to contain the situation. That way they could keep it from getting out of hand, and once inside those firms, they could monitor the jobs and get a competitive jump on bids to replace the pipes.

Howard figured that out when he did some consulting work for the oil field after he had retired. He found some of the same engineers he had seen at Deep-Pipe working for their competitors. It didn't take long for him to put two and two together.

"Is all that documented?" Mark asked.

"Everything but their confessions," his agent answered. "He could have joined the FBI with his ability to sort out the facts. He even had part numbers listed for the valves."

"OK, where else does this go?" Mark asked.

Butch Thomas explained the next folder on the list. "Howard was concerned when he heard about CO2 injection in the western Minnesota area. He knew there was low-grade uranium in the ground and with his experiences in North Dakota; he investigated the deep wells used. This time, Deep-Pipe had the valves and pipes correct. They learned their lessons.

"The strong earthquake in 2014, however, was much stronger and closer to the surface than was anticipated. The resulting tremors cracked the underlying rock structure allowing the CO2 to get up into the upper layers of rock, which were the layers that contained the uranium. Deep-Pipe once again called on S&G to secure the situation and keep the public from being concerned about radioactive drinking water. This time, the radiation was extremely low, and the EPA and DNR were not terribly concerned. However, to keep it out of the hands of aggressive reporters, they deleted the records recorded by the DNR.

"The public would never know if the fish they were eating or the water they were drinking contained low levels of radiation or not. That's where the suspect Jenna Iken came in. She bribed an employee to delete the file."

"Did Howard Long know about that?" Mark asked.

"No, he knew there should have been a report, and one was missing at the appropriate date. However, he did not know who did it. We've combined our suspect's statements along with the two sets of files and everything we have found appears to complete the broken lines."

"OK, I can't wait to hear where this leads. Go on."

They brought up the next file. "Apparently, the only one that knew about the file was the person who wrote it, and the DNR Commissioner. The firm was bidding a job in northern Minnesota to provide water and CO2 injection into the ground for mining copper. It was close to the same time the whole carp problem hit the fan. It took a lot of work, but we followed the money and leads.

"It looks like a suspect named Cal Young tampered with the fuel gauge on the DNR's plane. They did not know they were low on fuel until they ran out. Then it was too late. The field worker for the DNR died of a car crash about the same time. It took a while for us to connect that line. We followed a guess that one of their employees went missing or retired at the same time. After checking out four employees, we ran across him and talked to his family. They said he had worked in western Minnesota and did water monitoring. We put two and two together."

"How did Howard Long know about that one?" Mark asked.

"He didn't. He just knew about the missing report, and the plane going down. We had to put the rest together."

"Like I said, you guys are the best. Anything else? Does our Senator fit into this somewhere?"

"As far as we can see, he is an innocent partner in the problems," he told Mark. "We followed the river poison as far as we could. Other than the public demanding action and Bill Epstein being in the legislature at the time, we cannot find any correspondence, money trails, or anything else that can connect him to anything other than poor judgment. He tried to save the state money. It cost them a fortune."

"So why did Howard Long put a file in there?" Mark asked.

"We thought he was laying the case for future problems. Howard questioned the need for water from Lake Superior. When the key bids were coming from Deep-Pipe, we think he smelled a rat. There is nothing in the report saying that pipes were wrong or pumps were incorrect. Deep-Pipe beat out other firms, probably because they knew what their bids were going to be. However, Howard was on to something else. He was questioning the need. Why did they need water all the way from Lake Superior? Why did the Canadian government allow it so easily? I think Howard had his nose to the grindstone again.

"Howard was putting two and two together. That was his specialty. The only reason they needed Lake Superior water was if they suspected the other sources were contaminated. Or, it might be contaminated in the future. Mark, you think you can draw the line?"

"Oh, I think you left a dotted line all the way across the state," Mark replied. "Let me guess, fish poisoned water in most of the rivers, radiation in the water leading into the Minnesota River or Red River headed toward Canada, and then there is the CO2 leaching of heavy minerals in northern Minnesota getting into the Mississippi."

"Bingo!" Mark's field agent Butch Thomas shouted. "Give the man a prize."

"And the other folders?" Mark asked.

"Minor in comparison," he answered.

"You missed something. Who is in charge?" Mark asked.

"That's what we need to prove. We have some ideas, but we are lacking evidence."

They laid out their theories to Mark. So far, all they could do was conjecture. So far, all the lines are pointing to Deep-Pipe.

"OK, it's time to put pressure on Deep-Pipe. We need to monitor all their projects, contacts, bids, and get some wiretaps in place. Someone is going to be going on a long one-way trip. I only hope we have not scared them into hiding under a rock. I'm sure they have a feeling that we may have run into their name in our investigation. Especially now that S&G is shut down. Let's put the same manpower on them that we had used on S&G. All we need is a crack in their armor."

Mark was right. Now the question was how many of Deep-Pipe's people were involved and was there anyone else. It would be a shame if all their convictions had to stop with S&G. Mark wanted someone at Deep-Pipe, and he wanted it soon.

As they were exiting the meeting, Mark got a message from his secretary. "Looks like we lost a suspect," he told the group. "Art Singer, our police dispatcher, was just found shot to death. That means that S&G is still operational, or someone at Deep-Pipe is directing traffic. Let's get busy and find out. Keep monitoring Scott Lenard. See if we can get him to fill in any blanks. Maybe he will call someone, or they will call him. I'm sure they are trying to find the other three S&G people we have in custody along with their president."

The FBI put blanket coverage on all three Deep-Pipe locations. They had offices in Montana, Oklahoma, and Louisiana. The main office was in Tulsa, Oklahoma. Mark had obtained court permissions to wiretap their offices and had a search warrant he could use in connection with the murders. So far, they had almost nothing that would hold up in court that tied Deep-Pipe to the murders. Howard Long's files told them the story, now they needed to prove it.

Mark got some information, which he assumed he would be hearing on Peter Skiff, the engineer from Denver. He was out on bail. Charges of corporate espionage and bid rigging were not enough to keep him in jail for more than a few hours. Even though the FBI was monitoring him, it would be hard to get information from him once he was on the street.

Mark turned to working with his two cooperating suspects already in custody, in an effort to put more pieces into the puzzle. Someone had to know something.

* * *

The next two days were extremely busy in reporting the news. It must have been an attempt by every agency to get their airtime in to claim their fair share of next year's financial budget. Each day I came back wiped-out from all the time spent trying to put the best light on the reports. No one wanted to watch a lackluster report on television. Sometimes, it took a little creative editing to make things look interesting.

Friday morning, when I walked into the station, LT met me in the hall and reminded me that he was paying for dinner. It was our regular get together for the crews at a dinner. LT told me that I could invite Tracy to join us. She would probably enjoy being part of the gang again. I called Tracy and reminded her about the social get-together.

By 5:30 pm, I was glad to be done. I cleaned up a little at home before Tracy and I met the group at a sports bar in Golden Valley. Tracy enjoyed seeing everyone, and you could see by her energy level that she missed working with them. Keeping low and spending time shopping was OK, but she truly needed the interaction with people. When the food came, the conversations slowed as everyone dug into the food.

LT was giving me a hard time about inventing nice things to say, when Jake Schwartz gave me a wave and said he had to go to the restroom. The beer was getting to him.

Tracy gave me a strange look. "Jake wasn't drinking beer; does he have to work tonight?"

"Just keep talking," I told her. "That's Jake's way of telling us that he wants to check something out."

I watched as Jake went down the hall and past the restrooms. He went out the rear exit to the restaurant. About three minutes later, he came back.

"You see that person at the far table? Jake said. "He came in after we did, just before you arrived. He's been watching us the whole time. I just checked out the cars in the parking lot. I took a few pictures with my cell phone of some licenses. Also, I got one of him when I walked back to the table. I wanted to make sure he was on his own, and did not have a partner outside."

"Maybe he is just waiting for someone," I told Jake.

"Doubt it. He ate a small sandwich, very slowly. He is in no hurry to leave. I noticed that he paid particular attention to the two of you when you walked in."

"OK, let's keep an eye on him. Photo, you think you can wander off and set up outside so we can see where he goes?"

"Like I said, that's my specialty." Photo slowly got up and said, "I have to go and meet someone." Then, he slipped out the front door and watched from his car for our visitor to move.

It was hard for all of us to sit and talk without looking at the stranger in the corner. Was it a false alarm, or was someone watching for Tracy again?

Tracy was nervous and squeezed my hand. After about five minutes, I wasn't sure I had any feelings left in my fingers. She had squeezed so hard it was cutting off the circulation.

When we were finished eating, LT suggested we let a couple people get to their cars before we left. If the stranger tried to follow us, they would be close behind. If not, they could at least see where he went.

Photo was out front, Jake Schwartz and Tim Baker needed to start their shift. That left Shawn and LT to track the person. They would head out just before we left and watch from their cars.

When we were finished eating, the stranger was still in the corner, trying to look like he was finishing his meal. Shawn and LT headed out to their cars. As they did, the stranger asked for his bill.

Tracy turned to me and asked, "If he tries to follow us, what are you going to do?"

"I'll lead him to my apartment. If he is following us, I'll give O'Riley a call, and he can meet us there."

When we walked out to the car, the man waited, and then went to his car, which was parked in the lot. He was so busy trying to figure out which way we were heading that he missed the others that were watching him.

As we drove down the street, I got a call while sitting at a stop sign. It was LT. "Grey Buick sedan about two cars behind you. I picked up Photo. We're a few cars behind him."

"Can you ask O'Riley to meet us at my apartment? I think I'll lead him there."

"Good! Stay safe," LT said with a little excitement in his voice.

Shawn was a couple cars behind LT, just in case they needed to switch leads. I was going to have Tracy send a text message to Mark Lawson as we drove. However, with the new laws, it was disabled. We had to wait until we stopped again. This was one time I wished the new law had not been enforced.

It was still five miles to my apartment. Unfortunately, we had to travel on some roads that did not have a lot of traffic. About four blocks from my apartment, he turned off on a side street. LT followed me, letting Shawn attempt to follow the stranger from a distance.

When we arrived at the apartment, we stayed in the car watching for people in the parking lot or in the shadows. So far, we could not see anyone. LT and Photo drove in and parked. I watched as LT went in to check out the hallway. No one was in sight.

After a couple minutes, I got a call. It was Shawn. "Sorry, I lost him. The car was about two miles north of your apartment when he cut through a shopping center, and I got cut off by someone backing out. I'll join you in a few minutes."

With no one around, LT, Tracy and I went into my apartment. "I guess you still have a secret admirer," LT told us. "Any idea why?"

Neither Tracy nor I gave him a satisfactory answer. I waved at the ceiling and walls, and pretended to swat a mosquito. LT got the hint quickly. We needed to watch what we said. Someone might have been working inside my apartment again.

A couple minutes later, I spotted O'Riley swing into the lot. He had his red lights on and switched them off just before he got to the apartment parking lot. We joined him outside where we felt it might be safer to talk.

"Martin, you know I don't work the late shift," he greeted us.

LT told him how Jake had spotted a man at the restaurant and how he followed us almost to the apartment before getting spooked and heading north. We had his picture and a license number of his Buick.

"Someone thinks you are a real threat to them," O'Riley responded. "You better go back into hiding until we figure this out. These people tend to make people disappear. I would hate to have you two join the rest of them. They may have been following you trying to figure out where Tracy was staying."

"We talked in the parking lot for about a half an hour before figuring that whoever it was, was probably not coming back. Then, I called my father. "Dad, you got a safe place available over there?"

"Martin, why don't you get a hotel room?" he asked.

"Need a safe place tonight."

"OK, Hank has two bedrooms in his place. You and Tracy can stay here. I'll tell Hank he has company for the night."

"Thanks!"

We went up and packed for the next couple of days. Then, we drove over to the Castle. I hated to kick my father out of his apartment, but for the night, he and Hank could trade stories. Besides, Hank's unit was just a couple doors down the hall.

When we got to my father's apartment, he met us at the door. "Sorry Dad, was Hank upset?"

"It would have been better if Tracy had called and asked," he replied. "You can tell me about it in the morning."

Our hearts were still pounding so hard from the evening that I was not sure if we would get some sleep or not. We helped ourselves to my father's beer in the refrigerator. It took the edge off the excitement. Why were they still following us? It did not make any sense.

Just as we were about to try to get some sleep, the cell rang. It was Mark Lawson. "I think I need to put a GPS on the two of you. My, you do like moving. You OK there?"

I answered, "Thanks for the concern. I thought you had everyone in jail. Who's following us now?"

"I got the photo from LT. We're scanning it now. I know this is not what you want to hear, but this might be the guy we're looking for. We knew that S&G had one more operative, this might be him."

"Great, just tell me we are safe," I told him.

"Keep your locks on. Good news, LT agreed to give you the weekend off while we find this guy. I don't think you are in danger. I think he was trying to find out where Tracy was staying. I just had my boys do a quick scan of your apartment. You were right, it was bugged.

"On the other hand, now that he knows we are on to him, you might be in danger. He might want to end it. So, stay low."

That was a reassuring thought just before going to bed. I thanked Mark for the information, hoping that my cell wasn't cloned, and someone was listening in.

It took a couple hours to get to sleep. The evening's events put all kinds of questions in our minds. The leading one of which was "Why?"

* * *

Chapter 33

Visitors

The lights were lit late at the offices of the FBI that night. When Mark Lawson called in for messages at 7:00 am Saturday morning, he had a message on his call center – "Identified your picture from last night. We put the file on your desk." It was exactly what Mark was hoping to hear. By 8:00 am, he was back in his office trying to get to know everything about his newest suspect.

* * *

Eddie Starr had been busy last night. He trailed Jake Schwartz to the restaurant. Figuring it was going to be our regular burger get together of the news crews, he was hoping I would invite Tracy to the meeting. What he didn't realize was that Tracy had been staying at my place. He had someone place a bug in my apartment, while we were at the restaurant and he knew I was out for some time. He was right. His only mistake was that he was not expecting Jake to be alert to anyone following him. Eddie had figured it would be safer to follow Jake than me to our group meeting.

When he had followed us to just a few blocks from my apartment, he spotted a car behind him that turned when he turned. Since we were close to my apartment and appeared to be heading that way, he decided to break the tail, and lose the car that might be following him. Now, the question was; "Was someone on to him?"

When the bugs in my apartment went dead a couple hours later, Eddie knew that someone had spotted the tail. The good thing was that someone had removed the bugs. Now, he could go back in and put new ones in their place without anyone knowing it. If Tracy came back, he would know about it. A simple pick of the lock, and he was back in.

Since Tracy was at the restaurant with me, Eddie figured that she was still in town. The question was where? Last time, she stayed at the senior center. Did we head back to the same place? He decided to get some sleep in the morning, before resuming his hunt.

* * *

Mark Lawson looked over his file on his desk. Eddie Starr's file looked like a mirror image of Luke Carpenter's file. College student that joins the military before his senior year. Left the military to work for a private security firm – S&G, then the trail gets blurry.

Mark cursed, if he had access to all the IRS files, he could have found this person weeks ago. They could have run a scan for past and present employees of S&G. Even though S&G had switched to paying their people through an internet company in Idaho, Bent Mountain Inc, the IRS would have had him on their lists.

Mark called O'Riley and let him put out an arrest warrant for Starr. He figured he owed O'Riley a few favors.

* * *

I had my father check on the guest room at the Castle. I figured he would prefer his own place back. Unfortunately, someone was actually going to use it on Sunday, and they did not want to have to re-clean the apartment on a weekend. My father told me that Hank was OK with him staying there for a couple days if necessary. He came over and spent the day talking to us about the events of last night. For my father and his gang, this was as good as it gets – a real action event.

For supper, I had some food ordered in. I figured that I needed to do something for Hank. Since he was putting up with my father, we'd invite both of them for dinner. We had a marvelous time chatting at the table. Tracy had Hank telling tales about my father when he was

266

younger. It sounded like the two of them got into enough trouble to keep half the town looking for them.

Her favorite story was when Hank and my father figured out how to beat a hockey team that was much better than they were. Hank and my father snuck into the equipment room and flattened the sharpening stone on the grinder used to sharpen skates. When the other team arrived and sharpened the edges of their skates, they ended up with a figure skate shaped blade rather than a hockey skate. You see, the concave shape of the blade allows it to catch the edges better. The figure skate's design is meant for spinning.

As a result, they beat the favorite team and won their division.

We were about to have dessert when he heard a knock on the door. My father looked through the peephole. It was one of his gang. We had not invited the whole gang to supper.

He opened the door slowly, telling his friend that we were just finishing supper, when his friend barged in and closed the door.

"I just saw someone get into the guest room," he told us.

"Yeah, they have it rented for tomorrow. Probably cleaning it for them," my father told him.

"Not with a lock pick."

Hank jumped up and said, "Call 911. I'll be right back." As we looked down the hall, the door was closed. Two of my father's gang were in the hall between the apartment and the exit. If someone came out, they had to either go through them, or down the hall past us.

Tracy turned to me and said, "Martin, someone is going to get hurt. We don't know if they are armed or not."

When I looked around, Hank was back. He had his hand in his pants pocket. "Maybe Tracy should step back into the apartment until this is over," he said.

I looked at Tracy and told her to step back into the apartment. Then, we walked over to the guest apartment and waited, just out of sight of the peephole. If someone came out before the police arrived, my father's gang and I would stop them.

It felt like an eternity waiting by the guest room door. You could hear everyone breathing heavily. With their older age, their heavy breaths were louder than I would have liked. After a couple minutes, I heard the faint sound of a police car. I knew, if there was an intruder, and if the police car pulled into the parking area, they would come flying out of the room looking for a safe place to hide, not knowing if the police were there for them or someone else.

The siren stopped right in front of the main door. Seconds later, the door to the guest room opened, and a man came out in a hurry. He didn't even see the people in the hall waiting for him until he had shut the door behind him.

Then, he spotted two men in the hall. When he turned, he saw the three of us in the other direction – the direction of the exit and elevator. He was about to bolt and run through us, when Hank pulled his hand out of his pocket and said, "That's far enough. On the floor, now!"

Hank had his Saturday night special pointed at the intruder. Even though the intruder was not worried about some old men trying to stop him, the gun changed the odds. He had one also, but it was not in his hands. Hank looked like just the kind of guy that might shoot first and ask questions later. On top of that, Hank did not look like a weak 70-year old, he was in good shape.

Reluctantly, the intruder dropped to the floor. As he did, I walked over and removed the gun he had behind him.

I'm sure it was only minutes, but it seemed like an eternity before the police came up the stairs. Tracy had run down and directed them up to our area. In another couple of minutes, they had whisked him away, out of danger from the gang that brought him down.

O'Riley met the police outside, and talked to the man before they took him downtown and booked him. Then, he came back up and met with us.

"Everyone OK?" O'Riley asked.

"Yes, I think so," Tracy answered. "Any idea who he is? One of John Berman's friends spotted him picking the lock and sounded the warning."

"We'll find out by morning. So far, he's not talking. Hank, I understand you held him at guard with a rolling pin," O'Riley stated.

Hank looked surprised. "I did what?"

"You threatened him with a rolling pin to get him to lie on the carpet until we arrived," O'Riley repeated himself.

Then Hank wised up, "Oh, if you say so."

"Let's just leave it that way between all of us. Wouldn't want anyone kicked out of the building for breaking the rules you know. I'll have our lab sweep the room. I'm not sure if he was bugging the room or waiting for you to return. Either way, if anyone is counting, they are losing the war. We have most of their crew in jail. I hope we are nearing the end of this case."

"Did you call Mark Lawson," Tracy asked.

"Yes, he is going to meet me downtown and see if our friend is enjoying the weather. My guess is that he would rather be in Mexico or some other location outside of the US."

O'Riley told us he would give us a call if he found something. So far, even though I was right in the middle of the action, I couldn't even get credit for reporting on it.

My father broke into his stock of beer he had stashed away and offered a bottle in celebration to everyone in the gang that had foiled the bad guys. "Here's to the gang that fought the battle and won," he stated.

I was concerned; the outcome could have been entirely different. I was hoping that no one outside of the gang knew that Hank had a gun in his apartment. If he was forced out of his apartment, it would be a bittersweet celebration.

About 10:30 pm, I got a call from Mark Lawson. After seeing how quickly the FBI was in on the case, the man decided to cooperate. Apparently, he was hired to bug the room. He had assumed that we were staying there.

He did not know the name of the man that hired him, but he did pick a picture from their files. It was Eddie Starr. Eddie had paid him to bug Martin's apartment last night as well – that was twice. That got my attention.

Mark wanted to let us know that it was bugged again, just in case we went back.

"What are they after?" I asked.

"Darn if I know. Someone thinks Tracy still has something. The only way they will know for sure what we have is by bugging your conversations. We'll pick up Eddie Starr as soon as we can find him. I think they are running out of players. Get some sleep. I'll call you tomorrow," Mark told them.

We watched a late show, letting our nerves settle down. After about a half an hour, Tracy turned to me and said, "You still have Sunday off? Are you going to take me to church in the morning?"

How could I argue? It was obvious someone was looking after us. "Sure, just look up the time so we aren't late."

In the morning, we attended the big Methodist Church in downtown Minneapolis, Hennepin Avenue United Methodist Church. Similar to the church I attended, the church was a massive building built in the days when stone and spires marked the location of the churches. Being an intercity church, its worshipers represented a wide variety of backgrounds. Because of this, since Tracy's and my best clothes were at my apartment, we didn't think we would stand out as badly as if we attended a church in the Edina or Richfield suburbs. We were dressed in casual clothes rather than dress clothes we usually wore for attending the service.

When I looked at the bulletin, the sermon title caught my eye. It was, "Recognizing all that is given to you." I think I was starting to get the point.

Tracy thanked me for taking her to church this morning. It has been a crucial part of her life, and she enjoyed sharing it with me.

When we got back to the center, my father was waiting for us. With all the activity the evening before, the building managers were worried that we were putting people in danger. He tried explaining to them that they had caught someone breaking into the guest room and that we were not staying there.

It caught the morning manager by surprise. She did not have a response for the fact that my father's gang had caught someone breaking into someone else's room. Somehow, my father had bluffed his way through the conversation long enough that the manager thanked him and headed back to her office. Then, my father quickly told the rest of his gang what to say about the intruder, if asked.

"Any word from Mark Lawson?" he asked.

"Yes, he called late last night. The person he arrested was paid to bug my apartment and the guest apartment. I guess we shouldn't tell the management downstairs."

"So, someone is still looking for you?" he asked.

"That, or at least wants to listen in on our conversations."

"You can stay here for a couple days if you need to. Hank wanted me to let you know. The gang can keep an eye on the floor."

I told him to thank Hank. I truly hoped Mark could bring this thing to a quick end once he found his suspect.

* * *

Chapter 34

Smoke Trail

Mark Lawson and Lieutenant O'Riley were searching the Cities for Eddie Starr. If he was the sixth agent of S&G Security, they wanted him in the fold along with the other guests in their jail. Mark knew that Starr had to be taking orders directly from someone other than the S&G group. They were all either in jail or had tight surveillance.

About 2:00 pm, Photo was covering a protest on the steps of the capitol when he noticed a person near the back of the crowd. When he zoomed in with his camera, he recognized him as the person he was watching the night before – Eddie Starr. Without hesitation, he called O'Riley and told him where he was.

In less than a minute, Capitol Police were standing on each side of their suspect. What had been an attempt to spot Martin at the protest had turned into an arrest. By 3:00 pm, O'Riley and Mark Lawson had their man where they wanted him – in interrogation.

Mark's crew had linked Eddie with Bent Mountain Inc. through their financial records, so Mark figured he had his missing man. The only one on the loose was Scott Lenard, and they had been monitoring him hoping he would call or receive a message from someone.

Mark and O'Riley sat down with Eddie Starr. "You understand, this is not a case of illegal bugging of an apartment," Mark told him. "We have your boss and four others in jail right now. The fifth member is about to be picked up as we speak. I know about how you were paid through Bent Mountain, and many of the jobs your group had completed in the past ten years. Yes, people are talking.

"I'm going to give you one chance to cooperate and put an end to this investigation, or you can plan on playing cards with your other members for a very long, long time in an extremely cold damp place.

"I don't know what you are talking about," he adamantly informed them.

Mark laid down some pictures. "I know you all work independently, but you look like you are a smart man, and I'm sure you recognize a few of your fellow cohorts."

Eddie Starr looked at photographs of his boss – Neil Paulson, and the six other pictures. Mark could see from his expression that he recognized a couple of the photographs.

"What's it going to be Eddie? Are you going to help us finish the case, or let one of them do it and you go along with them in the charges? You know, murder or conspiracy to commit murder, they both carry a long sentence," Mark told him.

"Eddie, they have enough to throw the book at your whole group. Take the offer," O'Riley suggested.

Eddie Starr sat there a couple of minutes looking at the pictures. From what he knew, if any of them had talked, the FBI would tie them all together on a number of cases. At best, he might get out of jail by the time he was in his 80s. Eddie agreed to talk.

It turned out that Eddie Starr had put together a security file the past four years. If something went wrong and Neil Paulson tried to eliminate him, as he had done with two earlier people, Eddie had a file that would implicate the group. He only told Paulson about it once, but it was enough for him to realize that eliminating Eddie would not be in his best interest.

To Mark and O'Riley, it sounded like a gold mine. One thing for certain, Eddie Starr was going to get protection until all the information was in their hands. No one was going to slip in and silence their man.

Eddie told them where the information was located. It was hidden in a metal box in a friend's basement. O'Riley sent a detective over to pick it up. Meanwhile, Eddie told them everything he knew, from the time he first met Neil Paulson, to projects S&G asked him to complete. When he was finished, it was obvious that someone else in the group was often called upon to finish a job that another person had started. That way, if anyone had an idea of what was happening, they were long gone by the time any police figured out who was involved. However, by putting together the stories of a few members of the group, the extent of their projects were becoming evident.

Like the others, he did not know very much about the organization. However, there was one exception. He fingered Peter Skiff from Denver as someone who worked for S&G in Wyoming. "I remember seeing him there when I was first hired," he told Mark. I figured he was a relative of someone because they treated him differently."

A relative, Mark thought. That might explain things. If they put him in places to get information, they would want someone trustworthy. Mark sent a request to his agent to follow up on the lead.

Even though it was Sunday, there was a skeleton crew working back in his office. A few minutes later, he got a text message back. They had Peter Skiff's family tree listed. It showed that his father had died when he was 14-years old. His mother remarried a few years later. According to the information, his stepfather worked for an investment agency. They specialized in land speculation. The firm was called RG Holdings.

Mark was pleased with the revelation. If they could link the whole affair to land speculation, it might be the thing that ties all the files together. Still, it did not explain any of the murders or break-ins. Or did it?

If they knew where the projects were going, a land speculation team could buy up land at a cheap value and turn it for a profit. If it was oil, they might get royalties for the next 50-years if they kept the mineral rights. Maybe the same thing was happening in each of those locations. Mark asked his team to pull up land title records for each of the areas in the files to see if there are any common buyers or sellers.

Mark was about to leave the police station when he received another message from his researchers. There was one more note that followed the original message. Peter Skiff's stepfather has a brother who owns Deep-Pipe Engineering.

Now, things were starting to make sense. If Deep-Pipe got the bids, they would know the extent of the operations. They would know where pipes needed to be laid, and where minerals were to be mined. As long as they kept getting the bids and had the drawings, their land speculators could go in with a high degree of certainty and buy up the undervalued land where operations were planned years later. They would be competing with the buyers from the oil and mining people, but as long as they knew the real value of the operation, they could easily bid up a significant share of the profits. They would know about operational delays, delays in permitting, and perhaps have a finger in the permits. In fact, they had an edge on the mining people.

Mark sent a note to his team. *"Meeting 8:00 am, in my office tomorrow morning."* Now, it was time to tighten the noose, and see whose neck might get caught in it. It would be a good way to start the week.

* * *

Tracy and I had spent most of the afternoon with my father. The stories she had heard about his youth had made the stories about my life a little less stressful. By late afternoon, we had about worn ourselves out talking about our family's history. When the time for supper came around, my father told us that he would like to excuse himself. He wanted to eat with his gang downstairs. He felt we needed a little time to ourselves. Besides, he wanted to hear all the stories about how they stood up to the evil ones.

He was hoping they could have a table in the private area, which was enclosed, so the other residents did not hear what they were talking about.

Before he left for dinner with the gang, I asked him to stay with Tracy, while I slipped out to pick up some takeout. I did not want her roaming around any more than she had to. The trip to church this morning was probably a risk. Until we heard from Mark, I wanted Tracy to stay put.

I made a quick trip out, picked up some fried chicken and came straight back, with the exception of a few turns to make sure no one was following me.

When I got back to the room, my father smelled the chicken and said, "Maybe I should stay with you and make sure the chicken isn't poisoned."

I told him, he would do a better job helping us downstairs, keeping his gang in control, and not blabbing to everyone in the Castle. Reluctantly, he agreed, but only after we promised that if there was any chicken left, we would keep it for him.

We ate our chicken in front of the television, watching a romance movie Tracy had picked. It was one of those chick-flicks where the girl meets a guy, only to have to move away for several years because of her job. Then, after four years, they meet each other at a restaurant and immediately fall in love.

Does it really happen that way, or is it just in the movies? Here I am sitting with my arm around a beautiful woman, and can't even figure out how to address the issue.

When the movie was over, I asked her, "You think it really happens that way?"

"People get separated all the time and somehow still love each other when they see each other," she said.

"No, I meant, do you really think that two people can instantly fall in love like they do in the movies?"

"Depends on the people," she answered. "Do you feel different when you meet someone you know?"

"I feel different when I am around you."

She smiled. "How so?"

"Well, when I see a smile on your face, or a glimmer in your eyes, I melt immediately."

"Really, I thought it was only when I give you a long kiss, like this." Tracy leaned over and planted a kiss on my lips. What started as a light peck turned into a long kiss. She was right, I could feel the blood flowing from my lips to my toe nails.

When we stopped, she asked, "That melt any ice?"

I gave her another long kiss. Then, I answered her, "Well, it is kind of like chocolate. Sometimes you have to try a second piece to make sure you like it."

"And?"

"I decided I like this brand." I gave her another kiss.

"How about you?" I asked.

"You think I would be here in your father's place with you if I didn't like the brand?"

"Just checking. Can't be too sure you know."

"And are you sure now?" she asked.

If there was a point to get nervous, now was the point. Tracy had helped me open the door, and I stood there. As my father would often tell me when I was learning how to dive at the pool, "Just do it. What do you have to lose?"

I kissed her again. "I'm sure. I really don't want you to go back to your job in Duluth with me here in the Cities. I want you to stay here permanently, with me."

Well, it would not make the movies, but I said it.

Tracy looked me in the eye, and answered softly, "Let me think about it for a while." She could see by my expression that my heart had just skipped a few beats. After all that, how could she give me that answer?

Two minutes later, she turned toward me and said, "That's long enough. Are you asking me to stay with you, permanently? You better ask again."

I realized what she was asking. Somehow, I needed to get my tongue unstapled from the roof of my mouth.

I looked her in the eye. "I really meant, would you marry me and stay with me forever?"

"You would ask me that sitting on your father's sofa?" she asked.

"I think he would approve."

"In that case, I would love to."

The next kiss felt like an eternity.

I'm not sure what happened the rest of the evening. I know we missed the evening news. Tracy and I decided to keep our news quiet, at least for a few days, until all this surveillance stuff was over.

***

Monday morning, Mark Lawson's investigative team sifted through the data with a fine-toothed comb. Once they had an idea what to look for, minor bits of data that they might have missed before stood out like a spotlight.

They started with the death in North Dakota of the pipeline engineer. If Deep-Pipe had designed the pipeline and contracted the engineering firm to maintain it, and if any news that they had improperly designed the pipes and valves leaked out, then they would have probably lost their position as the leading consulting firm in the area and reduced their ability to bid on new projects. By eliminating the engineer, and silently fixing the problems, they remained the leading firm for piping bids. That included the CO2 deep wells in western Minnesota.

Once again, they had to hide a report to keep the project on course.

The trail's next stop led to the proposed in-situ leach mining of copper in Minnesota. If Deep-Pipe Engineering was in on the bidding, they would know the locations of the copper ore, and where pipelines needed to be drilled. They would drill down and flood the ore with water. Then, they would pump it back up to the surface and remove any of the copper that had leached into the solution.

The project had been held up by the DNR for a few years, but now it had a limited go ahead. Had the DNR Commissioner been eliminated to get the project started?

If that project got a reasonable start, then they could do the same thing to pull the weak uranium ore out of western Minnesota. The hold up to both projects was the worry that they might contaminate the ground water.

If they had a back-up supply to the ground water, and it was already considered contaminated, then the permits would not be as hard to obtain.

Mark leaned back in his chair. "OK. This looks like a road map to financial security for someone. Let's find out who has their fingers in the water." He gave his investigators their marching orders. Follow the money.

* * *

I called Tracy on my break between assignments.

"Hi, just wanted to call and see if you changed your mind after last night."

"Did the offer come with a 24-hour option?" she asked.

279

I laughed. I guess I earned that one. "Sorry, no guarantees, or warranties on this one. What you see is what you get."

"Well, until a better offer comes along, I guess I'll take this one," she jested. "When are we going to tell your father?"

"Think you can keep it from him for a few days? I think he is still working on his match making."

"Maybe he is finding me a better deal. You ever think of that?" Tracy asked.

"Then, he would lose you. No, I think I know his motives."

"OK," she told me. "However, I'll bet he figures it out before you tell him."

"You're on. Talk to you later."

I don't know why, but I was still nervous talking to her about the subject. It would be hard to keep it from my co-workers.

When I got back to my father's apartment later in the day, he and Tracy were sitting on the sofa talking.

"Martin, I have some good news for you," my father stated. "The guest room is available and Hank talked to them about letting you stay there for another week if you needed to."

I looked at Tracy. She gave me a smile and a wink.

"Thanks Dad. I talked to Mark Lawson today. He thought he was making progress, and hoped that I would be safe by the end of the week."

We had some dinner together, after which, when my father was out of the room, Tracy turned to me and asked, "Mark hoped that you would be safe? Where's that 24-hour option?"

I knew the comment caught a nerve when I said it.

"Sorry, I'm not losing the bet," I told her. Then, I gave her a kiss.

When my father came back into the room, he said, "So, can I give you a hand moving down the hall? I think Hank would like to have me and my snoring out of his place as soon as he can, not that I blame him. Do you think I snore?"

I just nodded.

We cleaned up my father's place and moved down the hall. Somehow, it felt better kissing Tracy in the guest room rather than in my father's apartment.

* * *

Chapter 35

What Lies Below

The next morning, O'Riley called Mark Lawson. His men had picked up Scott Lenard. Mark and O'Riley grilled him over for the next couple of hours, trying to establish a link to Deep-Pipe Engineering or the land firm, RG Holdings.

Unfortunately, S&G had done an admirable job of insulating both companies' names from the projects they had people work on. It appeared that only Eddie Starr had any communications with someone after Mark had pulled the plug on Neil Paulson and the S&G Security firm.

Mark needed to prove the connection between Eddie Starr and someone in those firms to keep the investigation moving. He had the five contract employees in custody – Ken Payton, Jenna Iken, Cal Young, Eddie Starr, and now Scott Lenard. The sixth, Luke Carpenter had been eliminated by their boss – Neil Paulson at S&G, who was also enjoying the inside of a jail cell. Art Singer, the police dispatcher was dead. That left only Peter Skiff from Denver, out on bail. They needed Peter to make a mistake and give them the solid link to Deep-Pipe or RG Holdings.

Although they had him under surveillance, they decided to increase the level. They needed to monitor all of his cell phone calls. If necessary, they would even bug his car and home. So far, he was staying in the Denver area and did not appear to be trying to fly the coop. Mark made sure he would have a problem leaving the country. He put Peter Skiff on the do not fly list. If Peter made a reservation, the FBI would be notified immediately. The problem was, he could still fly under an alias or be picked up in a private plane. Mark's agents would have to monitor him closely.

* * *

While I was out reporting on a break-in at a liquor store, where the crooks, with an obviously sophisticated palate, only stole Jack Daniels Whiskey, Tracy got a call from Mark Lawson.

"Tracy, we were going through some notes. Do you recognize the names Deep-Pipe Engineering or RG Holdings from any of your reporting?"

"Sure, I did a report on RG Holdings a few months ago. Why?"

"Do you still have your notes on the report?" Mark asked.

"Maybe. Is it important?" she asked. "It is probably on my data drive in Duluth."

"Can you access it from here?"

"Yes. You think it is linked to the case?" she asked.

"Can you send it to me, or give us access?"

"You're not going to tell me why are you?"

"Not yet," Mark told her. "I want to see if it leads to something."

Tracy gave Mark her links to get to the drive and password that protected it. "Just stay out of my list of guys I dated," she told him.

"Thanks. Your secrets are safe, I won't tell Martin. Call you later."

Tracy waited about twenty minutes and then pulled up the file herself. She wanted to see what was in there that Mark was looking for. The report was on the planned expansion of the copper mining just north of Grand Rapids, Minnesota. Several companies were buying up mineral rights in the area, which included RG Holdings. Benjamin Cahill was listed as the President of RG Holdings. There did not appear to be anything unusual about the report. The project had been on hold for years, and then allowed to proceed on a limited basis about 30-miles north of where the mineral rights were being purchased. Land speculation was common in the area. The gist of the story was that miners were hoping to find alternate work in northern Minnesota, after all the iron mines closed down. She had a list of properties that had filed new contracts for mineral rights with the county.

Later, when I got back, Tracy told me about the call and showed me the information she had in the file.

* * *

Mark Lawson had checked on land and mineral acquisitions in western Minnesota, northeastern Minnesota, and western North Dakota. He was not surprised to find RG Holdings had made the majority of the acquisitions in the past five years. It was less than 50% of the contracts. However, it was a very high amount for a single company that was not directly involved with the mining or exploration. More important, it required an extremely substantial amount of money to acquire the contracts. This was definitely not an operation where a few farmers simply threw a few hundred dollars in a pot and bought out a neighbor's field.

If there was one thing the FBI did well, it was following the money. Ever since the early days of Al Capone in Chicago, the FBI knew the importance of accountants in tracing money. They had specialists that did nothing more than trace money trails. In the days of the Chicago mobsters, this was how the FBI finally sent them to jail.

Mark assigned a couple specialists to look into RG Holdings. "Find out where their money is coming from," he told them. "Also, see if you can see any link between them and Deep-Pipe Engineering. There might be a money link there as well."

Mark expanded his "do not fly" list to include the managers of Deep-Pipe Engineering and RG Holdings, although both firms listed owning their own aircraft. At least this way, he might have an idea if one of them was traveling somewhere. Several airport towers were alerted that the FBI wanted to know if their corporate planes were about to leave.

It would probably take a few days for his accounting specialists to come up with the leads he needed. It would be a lot easier if they could subpoena the corporate records. If they found evidence of crimes, that would come later. For now, things had to be done the old-fashioned way, one transaction at a time.

The investigators started with the list of directors and managers of each firm. They were looking for any transfers of money to or from one to the other. RG Holdings was a little more complicated. The agents needed to find the investors. Typically, that was not public information. With a court order, they could attempt to look at bank records. Someone trying to hide their identity in money transfers to a location like the Bahamas, and then to RG Holding would make it hard to follow. He knew the team had their work cut out for them.

Mark jokingly called the team his squirrels. They would hunt and dig until they finally found a hidden treasure. It was a job that he would not want. It would drive him nuts looking for a single entry in someone's financial records. For Mark to understand what was going on, he needed to see the bigger picture.

Mark's fears were substantiated when his accounting specialists called him the next day. After pulling some bank records of RG Holdings, they found a number of contributions and payments made to a number of offshore bank accounts. These would be difficult to track down. It did indicate that they had a number of investors that did not want to be identified.

There were a few legitimate investors, enough to probably throw off any novice investigator. However, the money required for the contracts far exceeded those amounts. The legitimate investors appeared to come from mutual funds that had invested money into the company. They had a small share in several land acquisitions. Even these would be difficult to track back to individual investors.

Later in the afternoon, they had a small breakthrough. They had spotted a transfer of funds from RG Holdings to an account in the Cayman Islands, and a transfer of funds from the same account number to the bank account of the President of Deep-Pipe Engineering. The transfers were not on the same day, nor were they made out for the same amounts. However, it was the first sign of the leak of funds from one company to the other. It also gave them the incentive to look for additional transmissions of funds. As they scoured the files, they were able to find other transfers. All of which were small enough not to be flagged by IRS bank transfer filters.

It was encouraging to Mark. It was not the vast movement of funds they were looking for, but it did provide the link that the courts would look at later if the FBI requested access to corporate records.

On Thursday morning, one of Mark's investigators came in with another surprise.

"Mark, you remember how you wanted us to put a number of those company executives on the do not fly list?"

"You bet, did we get lucky and spot one of them trying to flee?

"No. However, it gave me an idea. These guys are doing a superb job of hiding their conversations. I remembered you mentioned the fact that both companies had corporate planes. These things have to have flight records. So, I pulled the FAA records on both planes."

"And I thought you guys had no imagination," Mark told him. "Did you find anything interesting?"

"Well, I saw a lot of flights by the officers of Deep-Pipe Engineering. When I compared it to the flights for RG Holdings, about once a quarter, they flew to the same city, at the same time."

"Good work," Mark told him.

"That's not all. They met right after Howard Long's death, and then almost every week since. I know that was not what you were looking for, but I thought it would get you a little excited."

"You get the gold star on the forehead award for the week for this one. Maybe we should talk to the pilots and find out where and with whom they were meeting," Mark suggested.

"Well, I think I have one better. I found four visits to Canada by RG Holdings' plane. One was just before the pipeline conference in Grand Marais; the other three were a month or two apart before the meetings. When we looked into older books, we found trips to the same location leading back several years."

"So, they liked fishing in Canada," Mark told them.

"Flight records only show one passenger on the flights. He must like fishing by himself."

"OK, just tell me! Who was on the plane?" Mark barked.

"Just the President of RG Holdings – Benjamin Cahill. I called his pilot. He told me he had a meeting with some Canadian official on his last trip. Did you find any Canadian investments when you reviewed their holdings?"

Mark sat back in his seat. A Canadian official? What was a Canadian official doing with the President of RG Holdings? Were they discussing future investments in Canada?

"You don't suppose someone up there was a major investor in their projects do you?" Marks agent queried.

"Did you say they met just before the pipeline conference? An old friend, Martin Berman, told me that he thought it went too smooth. Canada rarely agrees on water issues with the US without getting something in return. Can we put the finger on who he met with?" Mark asked.

"I think you need to talk to some of your Canadian Mounties' contacts up there," Mark's agent suggested, "I personally do not have the type contacts we need up there in Canada."

Mark agreed. He would talk to his contacts in Canada, while his agents looked for additional information on the flight plans from the company planes.

287

Over the years, Mark had developed a number of contacts in the Canadian Ministries. Now, the big questions in his mind; if it was a Canadian official that was involved, who could he trust to check it out without tipping everyone off? The flights had all been to airports in the Ontario Province. He decided to call an old friend who had retired a few years ago, Captain George Morrissey.

Morrissey had been in charge of the Royal Canadian Mounted Police in Ontario prior to his retirement. Even though the Mounties in Canada operated slightly different from the police in the US, Mark knew that if he could talk George Morrissey into helping, he would know who could be trusted and how to get the information he was requesting.

Mark gave him a call. After giving each other the initial greetings, Mark got down to business and told Morrissey what he was looking for.

"So you think someone in the Ministries is double dipping, eh?

"I think so. However, all I have is some flight records and information from the pilot. You think you could talk to a few people and see if there might be some fire under all this smoke?"

"You forget, I'm retired," he reminded Mark.

"That's why I called you. I figured you had been retired long enough to be itching to get your feet wet again. Think you can make a few calls?"

"Well, for a bank robber, I'd probably make you call the Ministry. But, since you think it is someone in office, I'll do some checking. It might take a few days, eh."

"Beats watching the television doesn't it?" Mark asked.

"Eh. Talk to you soon."

Mark knew that George Morrissey would not quit until he found the person who was betraying the government trust. If there was one thing the Mounties were famous for, it was maintaining their loyalty to the Government. It didn't matter if George was retired or still on the payroll, loyalty was loyalty.

Now that he had George Morrissey on the job, Mark could spend more effort looking at the flight plans and see if he could connect someone else to the money.

* * *

Chapter 36

Contacts

It did not take George Morrissey long to make a number of phone calls and collect a few favors from the Mounties who had worked for him. By afternoon, they were consulting with ground workers at the two airports where the RG Holdings plane had landed.

Customs would have had to inspect the plane before allowing the occupants to leave the area. Fuel trucks would have been there to refuel the airplane. Finally, there were the workers on the tarmac. If anyone on the RG Holdings plane met another plane, the workers would know about it. If they met someone that arrived by car, there was still a fair chance they saw them. However, if the people from RG Holdings met someone away from the airport, unless they listed the location with Customs, no one would have known who or where.

After checking with the airports, it appeared that the constables were drawing a blank. The flight listings did not reveal a common flight at the locations and times of the RG Holdings' departures.

However, the Customs official who checked in the flight just before the pipeline conference told the constable, "I remember the man. He said something about attending a meeting at the Windermere Manor, you know the hotel and conference centre, by the University, eh."

It was the lead the constable was hunting for. He followed up on the possibility by going to the Windermere. There, after looking through the room records, one of the reservations stood out. He was able to spot a room reserved for two days by the Minister of Natural Resources, Francis LaCrea.

Francis LaCrea's title made him the steward of Ontario's provincial parks, forests, fisheries, wildlife, mineral aggregates, and the Crown lands and waters, which make up 87 percent of the province of Ontario. The constable copied the reservation records and sent a copy back to his old friend George Morrissey.

Morrissey gave Agent Mark Lawson a call. "Mark, Morrissey here, I'm afraid you might be right. I had my friends do some checking. A Customs official remembered your man going to the Windermere for a meeting. When we checked the books, we found the Minister of Natural Resources stayed there for a conference. That doesn't prove that he was involved with your man or one of his associates, but it might give you the link you are looking for."

"I knew you couldn't retire," Mark teased him. "You are still as fast and thorough as you always were. Was he the only person from his department there?"

"Yes, I believe so, Mark. His office only reserved one room, for one person."

"I need one more favor. Can you pull his financial records and see if there might be one or more transfers to a Cayman Island account, number 01422..., which he might have made in the past three years? If I can link him to the account, I think we may have grounds for an official investigation."

"That's a lot of favors. You have to remember, we don't move particularly fast up here. Let me see what I can do," he answered.

If Mark could link Francis LaCrea to the RG Holdings account in the Cayman Islands, it would not prove involvement. However, it would give the Mounties a lot of ammunition for investigating everything LaCrea had been doing, and why he met with Benjamin Cahill of RG Holdings. Consequently, if they could prove that he gained by supplying favors to the group, he would not be in that position terribly long. Mark wondered in his spare time the rest of the day what connections the FBI would find between RG Holdings and LaCrea.

* * *

Thursday evening, Tracy was starting to get worried about having to move out of the senior center. Hank had arranged for them to stay up to a week, but that was Monday. When I came back after work, she asked me, "Martin, what are we going to do if Mark doesn't wrap things up and we have to move out of here again?"

"Don't worry; we still have a few days. Mark told me he is getting closer. He said he could not tell me more. That must mean he is chasing something. Let's just trust him."

It didn't give Tracy a lot of encouragement. Martin seemed to let things go until they needed action. She was wishing that this was one of those times that he had a back-up plan in place.

At dinner, she suggested that we have an alternate plan.

I just shrugged it off again. "Don't worry; I'll come up with something." I realized that Tracy was getting concerned. However, until Mark told me that he was stuck, I did not feel that we were in danger. Besides, if we needed to, LT could find us a temporary place to stay.

I could feel the tension between us most of the evening.

* * *

It was at the first light of day, on Friday, when George Morrissey gave Agent Mark Lawson a call. "Mark, Morrissey here, I was wondering if you would like to join me for an evening at the casino? You seem to be running on a lucky streak."

Mark was pleased to hear his comment. "You got good news I suspect."

"Not for Mr. Francis LaCrea I'm afraid. Our finance people located five transfers to that account you gave me. Each for $50,000 US. That's a substantial investment I'd say."

"He must have been promised a good return on his dollars wouldn't you agree?" Mark asked.

"I'd say! I think we should start to use some official channels on this one. If you don't mind, my replacement is uncommonly talented. I can place a call to him, and I am sure he would like to see what Francis LaCrea was planning to retire on. You don't suppose he was just hiding interest from taxes, eh? I don't suppose so. You can expect a call from the Ministry."

"Thanks George. If we break this one, I'll personally come up and buy you a dinner."

"Good! I'll pick the best restaurant in town."

Mark was pleased. He still couldn't figure out how Morrissey was getting the work done so quickly, but he was not about to complain. Now, if they could find the other RG Holdings investors, it might show a pattern. All it would take would be to have one of the investors tell the real story behind the transactions.

It only took another hour before he had a phone call from Canada.

George Morrissey's replacement was eager to get on the trail. After a discussion that lasted an hour, he told Mark Lawson that he would discretely investigate from his end. When he found something, the FBI and the Mounties could coordinate the next series of responses.

George Morrissey's replacement did not tippy-toe through the tulips; his approach was more like a lawn mower. When he found out that Francis LaCrea had a conference in Montreal, which started yesterday and he would be attending for two days, he quickly sent two people to LaCrea's office to investigate his records. He was playing a hunch. Based on what FBI Agent Mark Lawson had told him, if LaCrea had a partnership with RG Holdings, then he wanted to see what paperwork was generated the days following the meetings that Mark Lawson had supplied him. If there was a pattern, LaCrea would pay for it.

It took his people only four hours to find the pattern with the assistance of LaCrea's secretary. She pulled the reports generated after those dates, and the investigators put together the pattern.

After each meeting, LaCrea had supplied his people with information on projects in the US involving water. A few were on the Lake Superior pipeline. Others were on water quality coming from northeastern and northwestern Minnesota. Both of these areas had water that flowed from Minnesota northward to Canada. In each case, the reports indicated that he was telling his department they should be working positively to assist the US in the monitoring of water quality and allowing water flows into Canada, which would lessen the flood potentials in the US.

On the surface, they looked extremely positive with the emphasis on cooperation. With a different view, it was a change from normal scrutiny, allowing new US policy changes to be allowed without question. The Mounties instructed LaCrea's secretary to keep the investigation secret. Her pension would depend on her discretion.

* * *

Later that day, Mark Lawson received a call from Canada. It was good news. It looked like he would owe Morrissey a dinner. From what they found, it sounded like RG Holdings was convincing LaCrea to allow water from Minnesota into Canada. That would remove all the normal delays that approvals would take, sometimes up to a year, allowing the copper mining companies to get their approvals for ground water seepage, and probably setting the way for an approval in a few years for uranium mining.

The last thing in RG's way was the back up plan – the pipeline from Lake Superior with uncontaminated water. Getting that approval without any delays was an absolute feather in their hat.

The next question in Mark's mind; was the new DNR Commissioner in their pocket as well? He replaced the Commissioner who died in the plane crash, who was opposed to waterflood projects in the rocky regions of northern Minnesota.

Mark sent a note to his investigators as to the current progress they had made and the need to investigate the DNR.

* * *

When Francis LaCrea returned to his office, very late in the day on Friday, he had a couple visitors waiting in his office to meet with him. They had three files of paper on his desk linking his memos with meetings he had made with RG Holdings. The Minister of the Royal Mounted Police was also in the office. It definitely was not what he was expecting as he returned from his conference.

They laid out their findings in front of him. The argument was quite convincing and they gave him a number of suggestions. First on the list was to sign a letter of resignation along with a full confession of his involvement. Second, officially, he would take a two-month leave of absence, sighting medical reasons. During this time, he would work with Canadian and US officials as they directed.

Finally, at the end of the investigation, if he cooperated and did not pre-inform those under investigation, he would be allowed to officially resign and receive his pension. If any of the terms were violated, they would push for jail time and revocation of his pension.

Francis LaCrea sat there quietly. It was not how he expected to end his career. He had been a faithful servant of the public resources. Now, if RG Holdings fell apart, all of his savings and the money he planned to get when the projects were approved would go up in smoke. If he was lucky, all he would have would be his pension. It was going to be hard to explain to his wife. The retirement home they were planning along the St. Lawrence River would never get built.

LaCrea signed the agreement. Now, he would be taking orders from the Royal Mounted Police as to what they wanted him to do next.

* * *

Mark Lawson, while working late in the evening, almost fell out of his chair when he got the message from the Royal Mounted Police that they had confronted LaCrea. Somehow, they had gotten him to agree to assist the investigation of RG Holdings. So much for the slow approach.

Now, Mark's investigation would have to take on an increased speed. Otherwise, it would risk RG Holdings finding out one of their conspirators had been made.

His agents had spent considerable time looking into the finances of the current DNR Commissioner and his family. To their surprise, they could not find any financial dealings with RG Holdings, direct or through someone else. In fact, the Commissioner appeared to live on a modest income from the State of Minnesota. He owned a cabin in northern Minnesota, and between making payments on the cabin and his house, he did not have much of a reserve to invest with. Unless he had received some promises made for future payments from RG Holdings, they could not connect him to any of the cases. His only fortunate opportunity was in being almost as conservative as the previous Commissioner, such that when the previous Commissioner was killed in the plane crash, he inherited the job.

Likewise, their investigations into Senator Bill Epstein came up blank. His dealings with the "carp kill" did not appear to be linked to anyone else.

Mark's investigators were shocked. They thought for sure that one of those two was tied to the case.

Mark decided now was the time to get court orders and raid the offices of S&G Securities, RG Holdings and Deep-Pipe Engineering. What they needed to find had to come from these companies along with the evidence the Canadians were gathering.

He suspected that most of the evidence was already destroyed. However, if there were financial links, they would be able to find them.

The next morning, all three companies were essentially shut down as FBI agents removed box after box of files and computers. If they hadn't figured out by now, the managers realized the game was over. Someone had given the FBI enough information on them that they were able to get court warrants to raid their offices. Now, it was just a matter of time to see how many of them would be indicted.

Everyone was accounted for except Peter Skiff from Denver, and his stepfather's brother, Victor Mann, President of Deep-Pipe Engineering. Both of them were not to be found.

It was obvious that Peter had jumped bail and saw the handwriting on the wall that the FBI would be looking for Victor Mann in the near future. Somehow, the two of them had gone missing. The question of the hour was where.

The company plane was still in the hangar. No one had reported them from the do-not-fly list. Mark put out a warrant on both of them to be arrested.

As soon as Benjamin Cahill from RG Holdings was informed that Francis LaCrea of Canada was cooperating in the investigation, Cahill had seen the writing on the wall and figured that cooperation was the only way he could reduce any sentence he might get for the dealings his firm had made. His dealings were all financial; he wanted to separate himself from the talk of murder cases.

It wasn't long before Mark Lawson was able to put most of the puzzle pieces into place.

Mark found that Benjamin Cahill and Victor Mann became partners in the land development scheme after Victor Mann had convinced Cahill that he had inside information on oil and mining development. With Victor's advanced knowledge and Benjamin's ability to raise capital for investments, they had a sure win.

It was working so well in North Dakota that they decided to expand into Minnesota, where projects were still strangled by red tape. Unfortunately, Victor got a little greedy. He found, if he knew about competitive bids, he could undercut them and make more money. He funneled the money into more and more land speculation.

When the projects finally got approval, and mining companies started buying up the land, his fortune would be immense. The catch was state approvals.

Victor Mann worked with his old friend Neil Paulson, of S&G Security, to get information on competitive bids. He had to make sure the states did not find information that would cause delays in projects any longer than Victor wanted them delayed. Occasionally, a small delay would drop the price of the land in question. However, once they had their objectives, they wanted the projects to go through as quickly as possible.

When Benjamin Cahill found out that Victor was using S&G to burglarize and eliminate evidence, he was terrified. The problem was, he was into the projects so deeply that no one would believe he was not running the operation. His dealings with Francis LaCrea of Canada was an offer of a fee for an insurance policy. They needed a backup just in case one of the Minnesota projects contaminated the water. They did not want either or both projects stopped, leaving them with a huge investment in land.

As a result, LaCrea was offered $500,000 to let the water agreements through without any red tape. He would be paid from an offshore account as soon as the agreements went into effect.

LaCrea saw the potential of the projects and wanted a slice of the pie. As a result, he insisted on investing $250,000 in the project, expecting it to return one to two million dollars. If all went as planned, he would get at least that much money and perhaps a lot more.

Cahill told Mark's investigators that it was his stepson, Peter Skiff, who oversaw the espionage into the bidding on projects for Victor Mann at Deep-Pipe Engineering.

Peter Skiff had gone to work for Deep-Pipe Engineering out of college. Later, it was his intuitive knowledge that put together the marriage of Deep-Pipe Engineering and RG Holdings, when he figured out the huge potential in land development. Peter worked directly with

Neil Paulson at S&G to plan the protection on some of the projects. He also worked as a hidden partner at Deep-Pipe Engineering. Actually, it was Peter that did the bidding. If there was an exceptionally ambitious project and it was extremely necessary, he would occasionally take a temporary job with a competitor to make sure that both RG Holdings and Deep-Pipe Engineering had the full inside information for the pricing and potential of the project.

That information explained to the FBI why Paulson at S&G Security had contacted Skiff when the surveillance of Tracy went bad. Skiff had been directing the entire operation.

When Cahill finally turned over his list of contributors, and explained the codes used on some of them, the FBI had a dozen individuals that were on the list. The majority were simply investors or funds that were investing in the operations. Assets invested exceeded six billion dollars. It would probably take a team of lawyers to figure out how they would get their money back. One thing for sure, the lawyers would get rich over it.

Now, all the FBI had to do was to find Peter Skiff and Victor Mann.

* * *

Mark Lawson gave me a call.

"Martin, thought you might like to know, I think you are pretty safe. We have a number of people in custody and those that aren't, have warrants out for them. I think we will have them in a day or so.

"Can you tell me about it?"

"Sorry, all I can tell you is that it involved an engineering firm and a land holding company. You will have to wait until the District Attorney lets us give out any more information."

"Are you sure we are safe?" I asked.

"Yes, I think the two of you can breathe easier. I have a couple people in jail that have confessed. I think the pressure is off."

"Thanks Mark. We appreciate the help."

"Couldn't have done it without you Martin, couldn't have done it without you. Say hi to your father for me."

When Mark hung up, I informed Tracy about his call. I could feel the easing of the hairs on the back of her neck.

"Does that mean we can move back to your place tomorrow?" she asked.

"Only if you tell my father," I told her. I knew she still wanted to win the bet. However, if it meant that my father would know that I asked her to marry me; she was willing to lose the first bet.

Chapter 37

Missing

The next day Tracy and I moved back to my apartment.

I won the bet. It did not take my father more than a couple sentences into the discussion about the two of us moving back to my apartment before he started to pry into, "When are you going to figure out you like each other and ought to get married?" We finally decided to tell him to get him off the subject. It was either that or face both my father and his gang every time we talked to them.

Both of us wondered what Mark Lawson had found about the case now that he finally had a number of people in jail. They had to be filling in the blanks. Was there something in the files we gave them, or did they find information somewhere else? Either way, he was not going to let it leak out and ruin the FBI's case before everyone was in jail. The best we could do was to call him occasionally and see if he would throw us a bone to keep us from calling for a few more days. It felt as though we were pulling teeth just trying to find out what was happening. Even Lieutenant O'Riley was tight lipped.

Slowly, Mark filled us in on the case, provided that we kept it out of the press until it was over. As he did, we kept updating our report, which we hoped to be able to file when the case was closed. For now, all we could do was wait and see.

* * *

One thing about pipeline engineers, they are used to climbing around in rugged places and packing light. They are always ready for the next location.

When Victor Mann first heard that Peter Skiff was arrested by the FBI in Colorado and later released on bail, he knew it was just a matter of time before the whole operation started to unravel.

Howard Long had made the mistake of asking too many questions of too many people. By the time Peter Skiff had heard about Howard, Howard had already put together the links between the piping problems, the death of the pipeline engineer and the land company investments. So far, the FBI thought Peter Skiff was simply a plant to get information on bids.

However, if the FBI had enough time, they would find the links that would lead all the way to Deep-Pipe Engineering. Victor Mann had secretly started to shift most of the company's extra cash flow into an offshore account in the past couple weeks. Now, he and Peter needed to disappear long enough that the FBI would give up on them, and then they could slip across the border into Mexico. From there, they would find a nice warm southern location to retire. It would be much more comfortable than a jail cell.

Victor rented a cabin in the high hill country of western Texas for the winter. He found it on the internet. The two of them could sit out the winter looking like any other tourist until it was time to slip quietly into Mexico.

They would pay cash, monthly, for the cabin. No one would care who they were up in the hills. Their emptied bank accounts would get them through the winter. It was remarkable how the bankers didn't think twice about their withdrawing $5,000 here and $6,000 there. It did not take long for them to empty their bank accounts. Even the FBI had missed it in their early investigations.

Peter used some of the connections available that S&G Security had used, to obtain fake driver's licenses. He knew who the connections were that S&G had used, and it only took a few days before Peter and Victor had a new drivers license with their photo and someone else's information on it. The names on the licenses were real people. That way, if someone checked the ID, it would come up as a valid license. With all the clandestine activities S&G had done over the past ten years, it was often necessary to have a fake ID on one of their operatives to gain entrance or at least confuse the authorities as to who they were dealing with.

The plan was in motion. They paid cash for an old car, a 2011 Ford Focus on which they conveniently forgot to register the title, and drove down to Texas. Once in Texas, the car was scrapped and another used car with Texas plates was purchased from an individual.

As for getting into Mexico, Victor figured no one was looking for people heading into Mexico, they were watching for people going the other way.

* * *

The FBI scoured their financial records, hoping to find a trail that would lead them to where the two were hiding. So far, the pair had been exceptionally adept at masking their existence. To Mark's team, it looked like the pair had crawled into a hole and simply disappeared. That was the way Victor had planned it. Even the cabin Victor reserved had been rented using a friend's cell phone. The friend had no idea that Victor had used it to reserve their hideaway.

A few weeks after the FBI shut down the operations of Deep-Pipe Engineering, the State of Minnesota announced that they were rebidding the pipeline project. They cited an irregularity in the bidding procedure. The state announced that it might cause a delay in the spring construction that was already planned.

At the same time, it was quietly disclosed that permits for uranium mining in western Minnesota were put on a long-term hold. No reasons were given. The state was also reviewing pollution concerns from copper mining. So far, there had not been any problems. However, the state wanted to recheck their monitoring procedures.

* * *

The next two months, Peter Skiff and Victor Mann spent their quiet time in a cabin close to Alpine, Texas. It was about 25-miles as a crow flies, from Mexico. No one knew who they were, and even their closest friends had no idea what happened to them. Once they were convinced that no one had figured out their route of escape, they started to move about by checking out the neighboring border towns. They were looking to see which one would be the easiest to use to cross into Mexico. The border patrol had too many patrols watching for people crossing in the desert area. They did not want to risk being picked up on their motion detectors. Worse yet, someone on the Mexican side might mistake them for hidden Border Patrol scouts and shoot first as they approached the desert border.

The only thing they had to worry about was accidentally speeding on the back roads. Unless someone pulled them over on the road, no one was going to bother them. Since they were purchasing their food using cash, no one would question their identity. The biggest problem they had was that they were starting to run out of books to read while waiting for their opportunity. Staying put in the cabin up in the hills was starting to drive them stir crazy.

Finally, to break the boredom one day, they were brave enough to drive up to Roswell, New Mexico.

On the short trip, they drove around the town famous for a reported crash of a flying saucer on the 4th of July, in 1947. While they did see a number of strange looking signs and pictures, unfortunately, they did not see any alien spacecraft on the trip that could simply beam them to Mexico.

As they drove back to the cabin, they had a surprise. There were lights flashing on the highway ahead of them. Victor was driving. The look of enjoyment on his face after getting out of the cabin for a day was replaced with a look of concern. "What do you think?" he asked Peter. "Accident or police looking for someone?"

Peter studied the situation. It was too late to make a quick u-turn. If they did, someone would figure that they were hiding something. "Don't panic. What ever it is, just stay calm and cool. Unless they suspect something, we should be OK."

There were three cars and a van ahead of them. The Border Patrol was pulling over vehicles, making a routine stop to look for illegal aliens. As they approached the congestion, they saw the Border Patrol officers inspecting the van up ahead. They were checking to make sure any illegals were not hiding inside. The cars had to open their trunks to show that no one was hiding in them.

"Relax," Peter told Victor. "Just smile and let them inspect the car."

As the patrol motioned the car up, Victor took a deep breath and slowly let the air out.

"License please," the officer asked. "and open your trunk."

Victor pushed the button on the dash opening the trunk door.

As one officer was inspecting Victor's license, the other went around and looked into the empty trunk.

"Busy day?" Victor asked.

"So far it has been a quiet one," the officer replied. "The two of you here on business or pleasure?"

"Pleasure," Peter replied, knowing that the officer was looking for foreign accents. "We were just up in Roswell looking for space crafts. So far, the only bright lights we've seen are on your vehicles."

After getting the OK sign from his partner, the officer told Victor they could go. Another car was approaching the inspection station.

Neither Victor or Peter looked back as they drove off. About a mile down the road, Peter looked at Victor, "You can breathe now." It took another ten miles for both of them to get their heart rates back to normal.

Since neither of them spoke with any kind of foreign accent, they had been sent on their way. The patrol had not even checked their Texas license. For Peter Skiff and Victor Mann, they had gone from high concern to a sense of celebration. The encounter had given them a sense of false confidence that they could easily bluff their way past the Border Patrol if they were stopped anytime in the future.

By the middle of February, Victor and Peter were going nuts locked up in the cabin. It was the heart of the tourist season. If there was a reasonable chance to slip into Mexico without notice, slipping in with a bunch of tourists was their best chance. Of the crossings they had evaluated, the crossing from El Paso into Juarez was where they would cross. They would leave everything at the cabin just in case they had to return. Even the car would be left on the US side of the border, and they would simply slip in line to walk across with the other tourists. If asked, they would tell the Border Patrol they were on a shopping trip for gifts.

On a busy Friday, mid-morning, Victor Mann and Peter Skiff got in line to walk across the US – Mexico Border Bridge. The pair had acquired forged US Passports that matched their driver licenses to get into Mexico. They knew that Mexico did not check visitors very closely.

Victor and Peter dressed just like all the other tourists in line.

Security was tight, as it always is at the crossing. The Patrol was using dogs to check vehicles arriving from Mexico, and the line of cars and trucks trying to cross from Mexico into the US was long.

In the other direction, there were a few cars, though mainly trucks, returning to Mexico as well as a line of tourists walking through the turnstiles on the bridge crossing the river looking for bargains just across the border.

Parking their car about two blocks from the border crossing, they could almost smell freedom. As Victor and Peter walked past the start of the crossing, what they did not spot was the security cameras mounted high on a post monitoring both sides of the crossing.

Unknown to most tourists, the US Border Patrol had been using facial recognition software for a number of years on the country's borders. They use it to watch for stolen vehicles, known enemies and fugitive foreigners trying to enter the US. It also scans for fugitives in the US, trying to leave the country.

The crossing was about a block long. So far, it looked good. About half way across, they noticed an officer come out of a building. It appeared he was counting the people crossing into Mexico. When Victor and Peter reached the turnstile, which marked the crossing to Mexican territory, the Border Patrol Agent stepped out and politely asked them to step inside. He gently told them that they had the lucky number and had been selected for a random drug check.

Neither Peter Skiff nor Victor Mann realized that this was going to be a one-way trip. Since they had no drugs on them, they smiled and casually walked inside for a pat down and perhaps an inspection by one of the Border Patrol's dogs.

To their surprise, once inside and away from ordinary tourists, the pair was met with armed agents. Their pictures were on the monitor in front of them along with a digitized wanted poster with their names on it. They didn't even get a chance to say a word. In seconds, their freedom had come to a sudden end. Their great escape was foiled by a simple facial recognition program. Both individuals were put in cuffs and quickly escorted to a holding cell.

Agent Mark Lawson got a phone call. "Agent Lawson, this is Border Patrol Agent Shriver. We just picked up two of your suspects this afternoon trying to cross into Mexico. You want to have your people pick them up?"

When Mark heard the details, he leaned back in his chair. "You bet. I have been looking for this pair for a couple months. I'll send a van to pick them up."

Within hours, the FBI took control of their suspects and arranged transportation back to Minnesota to stand charges that included murder.

In the midst of a light snowstorm, Agent Mark Lawson met the plane that transported them back to Minnesota. If you looked closely, you could see a small smile on his face as he welcomed them back.

* * *

Mark Lawson gave Martin and Tracy a call to let them know that Peter Skiff and Victor Mann were finally in custody. He had waited to make sure they were safely in jail in Minnesota.

"Martin, I just wanted to make sure that you were the first to hear we have Victor Mann and Peter Skiff in custody and make sure you have the scoop on the other stations, now that the case is finally coming to a close." Mark filled me in on how the pair had been apprehended crossing into Mexico.

"Thanks Mark. It is a relief to hear that it's over. Tracy will be happy to hear it as well. I'll let LT know."

When Mark filled me in on where they had been hiding and how they had been captured, I was amazed at how easily the case had ended. The pair had told his officers on the flight back how they had been living in the hills of Texas for the past few months.

To Tracy and me, it put a final nail in the case. Now, we could finish our final report on the case, as we knew it. Unfortunately, it was not what the networks needed or wanted. It ended up in a thirty-second sound bite, stating that the FBI had arrested Peter Skiff and Victor Mann crossing the border into Mexico. They were brought back to Minnesota to stand trial for the murder of St. Cloud resident Howard Long.

In a way, it was a bittersweet end to the case. No one really wanted to know the real story. The information and involvement of a Canadian official was never disclosed. Like my father said, no one really covers the facts.

* * *

Mark eventually did figure out why Peter Skiff and Victor Mann were worried about Tracy Saunders finding too much information.

Apparently, on one of the evening newscasts from Duluth just after Tracy left to start her temporary assignment in the Twin Cities, the local news anchor was doing a report on the proposed copper mining in the area. He inadvertently mentioned that "maybe we should check into the proposed mining area to see who's cleaning up on the land." Since Tracy had done a report on a copper land acquisition by RG Holdings a month earlier, word of the anchor's comments reached Peter Skiff. Since Howard Long had tried to contact Tracy, Peter was worried that Tracy had picked up additional information and was going to investigate all the land purchases. If she did, a report would cause all kinds of investigations. It set the whole their operation into chaos. Was there a smoking gun out there? If they found it, all their investments into land acquisitions might be lost.

Mark was also convinced that there were other serious crimes that Peter Skiff and Victor Mann were linked to, which they were worried that Howard or Tracy would discover. He wondered if Tracy would have spotted the missing clues to their operation without the confessions by the S&G operatives. Peter and Victor were so worried about her finding the links that they accidentally shed light on their whole operation. In addition, had they simply disappeared and not tried to cross the Mexican border at the crossing, and left Tracy and Martin alone, Mark doubted that anyone would have ever caught them. They could have retired in style.

* * *

For the gang at the senior center, life returned to normal these past months. The card games in the evening, once again, were the excitement of the day. That is with the exception of when Tracy and I come for a visit. Then, the discussion always seems to get back to the security gang at the Castle.

Oh! There was a little excitement when they were invited to our wedding. Hank even offered to provide security for the bride and groom. He figured the gang could cover things from the second row.

Tracy insisted that he leave his Saturday night special at home.

There was a small gathering at the church in South Minneapolis for the wedding in April. Tracy's aunt and a few of her friends came down from Duluth for the festive event. Many of my co-workers and friends were there also along with my father and his gang.

Just 15 minutes before the start of the wedding, word reached the group – the bride had been stolen. Quickly, I looked to see if Jake Schwartz was sitting in the church or if he was missing. It would be just like him to pull something like that. To my alarm, he was sitting in the fourth row.

After a quick look around, I was almost ready to call O'Riley for assistance. Fortunately, Hank had spotted Mark Lawson kidnapping the bride and figured that he'd have to return her, or face the wrath of my father.

Ten minutes later, he returned Tracy to the custody of Hank's gang. He told Hank he just couldn't resist one more attempt to steal my girl.

* * *

The investors in RG Holdings battled in the courts for several years. The value of the land had indeed increased markedly. However, there were so many lawsuits over the land and the ownership, that investors had not seen a dime of return. The outcome is still in question.

About the Author

David Fabio is the author of two youth adventure novels –
The Hidden Passage and The Second Summer.
He has also written a historical fiction novel centered on life on the
Mississippi River – Tales from a River's Bend.

Now, his four mystery novels – Search and Seizure, Secret of the
Apostle Islands, Bayfield's Secret Notebook, and Water Pressure
challenge the reader's imagination.

He is an educator, photographer, and an outdoor enthusiast. His
love for nature and learning about the outdoors is evident in many
of his writings.

Suggested other mysteries by the author:

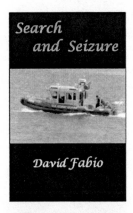

Search and Seizure – a suspense mystery about scientific research, espionage, and murder.

When a researcher is killed and another shanghaied, attempts to uncover the killer and solve the mystery by FBI Agent Lawson leads to unexpected places.

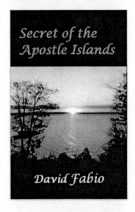

Secret of the Apostle Islands – the mystery of a lost sailboat, last seen in the Apostle Islands.

When a woman's husband goes missing, the story leads to adventure, romance, and intrigue in solving the case.

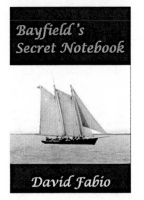

Bayfield's Secret Notebook – a historical fiction.

A long hidden notebook is discovered that tells about its writer's involvement in the Confederacy's attempt to return gold to England at the end of the war.
The story leads from Kentucky to the Mississippi River, leading to Stillwater, Minnesota and eventually Bayfield, Wisconsin.

CPSIA information can be obtained at www.ICGtesting.com
Printed in the USA
BVOW082104301112

306851BV00003B/8/P